Pitching Up at Heather Glen

Margaret Amatt

LEANNAN PRESS
INDEPENDENT PUBLISHER

Leannan Press

The Glenbriar Series

A Quick Note

This is book three in *The Glenbriar Series*. It can be read as a standalone but you may enjoy it more if you read the other books in the series first. *The Glenbriar Series* is linked with the *Scottish Island Escapes* series which is set before this series.

There are some crossover characters throughout both series and hopefully you'll enjoy catching up with some familiar faces as well as meeting some new friends.

Happy reading!

First Published by Leannan Press 2023

Book Cover designed by Margaret Amatt

eBook ISBN: 978-1-914575-75-4

Paperback ISBN: 978-1-914575-74-7

Chapter One

Logan

Early June

Logan Ramsay bounded up the slope to the top field over the ridge to where he could see the whole campsite, a few colourful tents flapping in the breeze, the trees swaying to the right and the babbling brook beyond. Two kids ran ahead towards a dark green tent.

They'd leapt into the shop a few seconds ago screaming about a burst pipe. Just what he needed on top of everything else.

He poked his head around the tent. 'Where—'

Water slapped his face. He jumped back as the cold jet blasted him. 'What the—'

The kids and an older teenager doubled up laughing.

'Gotcha.' The teenager raised a giant water gun.

'Seriously, you guys. Is this the leak?' Logan shook his head, rubbing his face.

'Haha, fooled you!' The kids picked up water guns and took aim.

'Tell your parents that's an extra twenty on the bill for the cheek and it's coming out of your pocket money.'

The kids laughed.

'I'll get you later!' Logan covered his head as the kids pulled the triggers and he bombed away from them. 'Better watch out when I get the Super Soaker going.'

How awesome would it be to stay and play water fights all day? But an outdated booking system, a storm-damaged water sports centre and a campsite that had seen better days clamoured for his attention. The situation was getting desperate. Running Heather Glen Campsite and Water Sports Centre had been a dream of his for years, but setback after setback had plagued his first months in the job.

When he got to the dilapidated building that was the shop and reception area, a rotund man in a bright orange high-vis jacket was outside, scrolling through a phone. Who was he? Logan wasn't great at remembering names, but faces stuck, and something about this guy struck a memory chord. He definitely hadn't checked in, so maybe he was after a maintenance job? If so, Logan had exactly the position for him.

'Can I help you?' Logan asked, unlocking the door.

The man lazily dragged his face from his phone and contorted his features into what was presumably meant to be a grin but was more like a sneer. He was a lot shorter than Logan and looked him up and down before pocketing his phone. 'I heard there was a planning application for a new building,' he said. 'I came to see if the work had started yet.'

Was he a builder? 'Do you mean the new boat shed and water sports centre?'

'Aye, maybe that. And there's a house, I believe?'

Logan shook his head. 'No. Why? Are you after a job?'

'No, no. You obviously don't know who I am.' The man's lip curled into a smirk.

Got that right. Am I supposed to recognise you?

'I'm just a curious party. Take care.' The man turned and sauntered towards the visitors' parking area near the main gate. Logan watched him with a frown as a burgundy car pulled in. Who was he? And what was that about? Unease niggled its way into his stomach. Something about the man's expression and his words didn't sit right.

The car drew into the parking space close to the shop door, and Logan headed inside. He'd barely settled behind the desk when the rickety shop door burst open, clattering into a nearby shelf. *Another thing needing to be fixed.*

'Oh, crikey. I'm so sorry. I didn't mean to push it so hard,' a woman's voice said.

'It's not a problem.' Logan stood up and glanced over. *Oh...* He blinked and did a double take that was probably cringingly obvious. No water guns in the face this time, but a young woman with blonde hair, sharp eyes and elfin features. He rearranged his expression and his hand jumped to straighten his t-shirt, wishing he could as easily steady his heartbeat. Christ almighty, she was beautiful, and here he was with wilderness-style stubble and damp clothes, standing in a shop that hadn't been upgraded in over twenty years. 'Can I help you?'

'Um, yes, please. I have a booking for a tent for two people for seven nights with electric hook-up. On the pitch near the oak tree by the stream.'

'Yes. Of course.' He ran his hand over his t-shirt, flapping out the wet patch. Did he have to look such a fright? 'What's your name, please?'

'Eleanor Kendrick.'

He smiled. Even her name had a pleasant sound. Their eyes met and he couldn't look away. She was the most stunning woman he'd ever seen. Fact. He swallowed back an odd sensation, like longing or desperation. Something was pulling him closer. His throat was so dry all of a sudden. *Oh god.* He'd never had a moment as cheesy as this in his thirty-one years. What the actual...? They hadn't met before, had they? And yet there was something so familiar about her. He cleared his throat. 'And what about the other guest?'

'Andy Kendrick.'

Ah, dang it. A husband. Well, what did he expect? And it wasn't like he could chase after the campers anyway. 'Perfect.' He glanced up and met her gaze. Yes, she *was* perfect. Astonishingly beautiful, but her pale blue eyes were glassy, almost sad. 'That's you booked in. If you can stick this in your car window.' He handed her a ticket. 'Then you can come and go as you please.'

'Thank you.' Her fingertips briefly touched his as she took it and he swallowed back a tremor. This was not normal.

'This is a map of the site.' He lifted one from a pile and pushed it across to her. 'And we ask you to keep the noise down after nine, as this is a child-friendly campsite. Please, no music on speakers but you're welcome to play instruments.'

'We won't be doing that.'

'Well... Enjoy your stay.'

'Thank you.'

He watched her leave with a sigh. She glanced back from the door, fixing her blonde hair into a claw clip, and gave him a brief smile. One day, he might meet someone when he was in a position to ask them out. Right now, he had other things to do.

It didn't stop him from wandering by the streamside pitch later for a second look. A twisted curiosity had him wondering what her lucky husband looked like. But he only caught a brief glimpse of her as he chatted with some other campers and he didn't see a man with her.

The following day, thoughts of her prompted him to pay unusual attention to how he dressed. He picked his flattest t-shirt (because seriously, who owned an iron these days except his mum?), his least worn-through jeans, and he even semi-shaved, so at least if he ran into her, he might look almost respectable. Not that it really mattered. But it might help him get through the work faster if he was smartly dressed. He'd started an application for a grant to upgrade the so-called water sports centre. In reality, it had never been more than a ramshackle old boat shed with a few kayaks, paddleboards and some pretty useless wetsuits. Not anywhere near enough to pull in enthusiasts or even to satisfy the campers.

Come mid-morning, he'd got no further forward. 'This makes no sense,' he muttered into his phone.

The woman on the other end laughed. 'Yes, it does. It's your answer that doesn't.'

'My answer makes perfect sense. The questions are just so repetitive.'

'I don't make the questions,' she said. 'I just process the applications. You still need more up-to-date information to satisfy the criteria.'

'That's the problem. I don't know where to find it. I wonder, hang on.' His fingers scrabbled for a box file on a high shelf. He was tall, but the shelves lining the tiny office were taller – installed over the years to accommodate the endless paperwork and records.

The shop door in the adjacent room clattered open.

He tugged at the box, clamping his phone to his ear with his other hand.

'Excuse me,' snapped a loud voice from behind him.

As he wheeled around to look into the shop area, the box file slid off the shelf, bashed him on the shoulder and landed on the floor. The contents spilled across the space between his desk and the doorway that linked to the shop and reception area.

Half closing his eyes, he took a breath. 'Listen, can I call you back, please? This is going to take a while.'

'Excuse me,' the man repeated, narrowing his eyes. A green-hued serpent tattoo snaked down his sunburned arm from under a white wrestler vest.

'Remember, the sooner we have the information, the better it'll be for processing your application,' the woman on the phone said.

'I'll get on it as soon as I can.' He dropped his phone onto the counter and smiled.

The man placed his hands on his hips and exchanged a glance with a woman next to him. Her fists were balled as if welcoming a fight.

Not happy campers then... For a campsite, that did not bode well.

The man muscled forward. 'The electric hook-up isn't working.'

'That's pitch eleven, isn't it?'

'Aye.'

'Ok, I'll check it out when I do my rounds.' Logan glanced at the clock. 'That'll be in the next twenty minutes. If you need power in the meantime, you can unplug your cable and use the socket beside.'

'But that's someone else's,' the woman said. 'And we've paid for it.'

'Not all the sockets are in use. Just find the nearest free one and use it until I get there. It's not a problem.'

The couple left, rolling their eyes and muttering. Hopefully, it was just a faulty cable, but he'd check out the sockets anyway. He dropped to the floor behind the desk and sifted through a couple of documents. How old were they? Ten years... Christ, this one was dated fifteen years ago. Was there nothing more up to date? He needed *recent* evidence of improvements. A groan escaped him and his shoulders slumped. This was pointless. Nothing had been done to upgrade the facilities in years. Objectively, he knew it, but it left a bitter taste. He only wanted to see this place as the exciting and happy site it'd been when he was a teenager, not the weary shadow it was now.

The front door burst open again, clattering against the shelf full of protein bars and chickpea crisps. *Really must fix that.*

'Excuse me,' a woman said.

He sprang to his feet at the sound of the voice. It was Eleanor, the woman he'd spied yesterday.

'Can you help me, please?' she panted, holding her chest. Her blue eyes were wide and glistening, her skin pale, almost ghostly except for rosy cheeks. Had she been running perhaps?

'Sure, what's up? What do you need help with?' He pushed through the ridiculously small gap between the desk and the shop area, gazing intently at her.

Her chest rose and fell rapidly, like she was trying to catch her breath. 'It's my dad. He's had a fall on the hiking track.' Her eyes misted up. Should he comfort her? Not his place. Too forward? Creepy? Or just human? What a frigging fine line. But she needed a hug from someone, and if not him, then who? His fingertips burned with the urge to reach out and make contact with her.

'Your dad?' Not her husband then. Judging from her stricken expression, the slightest touch might break her and yet he was convinced she'd welcome a shoulder to lean on – he wasn't forward enough to test the hypothesis though. 'Where is he?'

'Not too far from here, and I don't think it's serious enough for the mountain rescue, but he's too heavy for me to get him all the way back. I really need some help.'

'No problem.' He squeezed back behind the desk and opened a cupboard. 'Let me get the first aid kit.' All ideas of finding documents and fixing sockets evaporated. He pulled out a rucksack. 'I'll come right away.'

Rucksack on, he opened the door. 'After you.' He let her out, then flipped the sign around so it read *Back Shortly – Call this number if there's an emergency.*

Let's hope there isn't. One at a time, please.

'So, where exactly is your dad?' Logan moved in step with her.

'Near a hairpin bend on the Bealach Pass.' Her accent was English and well spoken. She pronounced the final 'ch' in Bealach as 'ck' and it reminded him irresistibly of the times he'd corrected English people's pronunciation of loch. *It's not a lock, that's what you have on your door.* But he said nothing and used the moment to drink her in. Her face was magnetic. As she led the way through the site towards the gate onto the path, his eyes were on their own trip, following every swish of her narrow hips in what looked like brand-new hiking gear: a pink North Face top, grey three-quarter walking trousers and thick-soled trainers in charcoal with a pink trim. He ran his hand around his jaw and took a deep breath. He was acting like a total perv. She turned to him. 'Can we run? I hate leaving him.'

'Sure, let's go.'

She broke into a jog and he fell in step with her. It would have been quite companionable if the circumstances were different. Together they ran towards the lower slopes of Ben Vrack along a path lined with ancient Caledonian pines. Hopefully her dad wasn't badly hurt. The Bealach Pass was steep in places – its name meant mountain road and it was notorious in winter and bad weather. Logan glanced at Eleanor, and she blinked, then looked away. They didn't talk, but something about her presence felt right. Exactly right. Like she was meant to be there beside him. He tried to shake off an almost out-of-body sensation and concentrate on the job in hand. Find the injured man and get the hell back to running the campsite. But whoever this woman was, it seemed clear they were destined to meet. He just had to hope the reason was a good one.

Chapter Two

Eleanor

Dad, Dad, Dad. Must get back to Dad. That one thought should have been the only thing on Eleanor's mind, and it was definitely right up there. She pushed herself to keep going up the path. *I'm so not a runner.* Walking was fine, give her a distance or a slope and she'd do it but running – no thank you. Her chest was ready to split open and her legs ached.

Not only was the pace torturous, but her mind wouldn't focus either. *Just get back to Dad.* But what about the man jogging beside her? Who *was* he? She knew he worked at the campsite, possibly owned it. He emitted a calm, steady aura like a protective shadow in the wilderness. If bears or wolves still roamed in Scotland and chose this moment to come hunting for human prey, Eleanor imagined this guy stepping in front of her with his arms wide, ready to protect her at all costs.

The pain in her lungs got to crisis point. She stopped, bending over and panting. 'I can't run anymore. It's too far.' Dad's image appeared in her mind. *Oh god. Must keep going*. Her feet might obey, but her chest protested.

'It's ok. We'll just walk for a bit.' The man waited. 'One casualty is enough.'

'Ok.' She inhaled slowly, trying to catch enough air as they walked on.

'Was your dad in pain when you left?'

'When he tried to stand, he was struggling. I don't think he's broken anything, but he's probably sprained his ankle.' She glanced sideways at the man. He was quite a bit taller than her, slim and broad-shouldered. Yesterday, when she'd arrived and chatted with him in the shop, something about him had caught her eye. Maybe his rugged good looks. How could she not notice someone like that? Especially when they smiled as much as him. His laugh had rung around the site last evening as he talked to campers, his mellow Scottish accent blending with the wood smoke from campfires and carrying on the gentle breeze as she'd pitched the tent.

He was ruddy cheeked from the run, but not as out of breath as her. She had a stitch, and her lungs were still gasping for air, but she couldn't seem to get any in. Taking things slower with yoga or Pilates was more her style, nothing as energetic as this. This man, however, was clearly built for working out in the fresh air. His clothes were outdoorsy and his legs and arms were muscular... Hell, were they. Eleanor sucked on her lower lip, ogling him from behind as he powered on ahead.

'I've got bandages in the first aid box.' He turned to face her, almost skipping backwards up the gritty track. 'I can try and strap him up and see if he's able to stand. If he can walk at all, I'll help him back.'

Crikey, he was handsome... More handsome even than she'd thought yesterday. Heat stung her cheeks and she swallowed back the notion. He was exactly the kind of man she wished she would meet one day, as long as he had a good heart too, but not on holiday. That was asking for trouble. But thank god he was here. If she was on her own, she'd just want to sit down and cry. A feeling she'd got to know only too well over the last year. *Must not succumb.* Definitely not in public. *Must be strong*. If not for herself, for everyone else.

'If he's in really bad shape, we should call the mountain rescue.' The man stopped and waited for her to catch up.

'It's not like we're actually up a mountain.'

'Honestly, it's ok. If your dad needs help, they'll come, but let's see what we can do first.'

'Maybe I shouldn't have left him, but there's no signal up there.' She couldn't afford to lose anyone else. Her feet quickened, though the soles burned in her new hiking shoes.

'We'll be there soon. Is that the bend there?' The man pointed into the distance, through the trees.

'I think so.'

He ran his hand across his thick, well-cut hair. Lighter, almost blond, strands flecked through it, mingling with the predominantly deep chestnut shade. Were they natural from the sun or dyed that way? 'Is it just you and you and your dad on holiday?' He cast her a smile and her heart flipped in a ridiculous fashion.

'Yes.' She fidgeted with the cuff of her lightweight pink walking hoody. 'We lost my mum last year.'

A crease formed across his forehead. 'Oh no. I'm so sorry to hear that.'

'It was a big shock.' She glanced away to the view of green and purple hills. A river snaked through the glen, meeting fields and woodland for miles and miles. If scenery could cure a broken heart, she was in the perfect place. 'She was diagnosed with cancer and didn't last six months after. None of us could have prepared ourselves for the shock and my dad's been so lost ever since.'

'I bet. That's so sad.' The man tilted his head and shook it slightly. 'It's such a horrific disease. Steals too many good people.'

'Yup.'

'Adjusting must be so hard. Impossible, I guess. Do you help him out?'

'I moved back to live with him.' It wasn't a choice. He was so helpless, and she was the only one who could. Her brothers were both married with families of their own.

'Wow. That's really great of you. That must be a task in itself. I love my parents, but it would be...' He pulled a face '...challenging, moving back. I guess after something like that though, you do what you can. It's just gutting that it had to happen at all.'

Yup. Exactly that. 'Dad's never lived on his own and it was too much on top of what he'd already been through to expect him to try.'

The man flicked her a smile that could melt a glacier and it penetrated her soul.

'We came here to relive some happy times. I didn't expect something like this to happen on our first day.'

'Have you been here before?'

'We used to come here when I was younger. It was such a drive, back then. It still is, but when you're a child, it seems like forever.'

'I can imagine. Where are you from?'

'We live in Chapel Brampton in Northamptonshire.'

'Sounds pretty.'

'It is very pretty. Dad's lived around there all his life, and so have I.'

'Hopefully, he'll be ok. This is a long way to come only for you to have to go home. And that's a lot of motorways to navigate. I lived in Cambridge for a while. I remember the motorways around there being a nightmare.'

'Oh. You lived in Cambridge?' What had he done there? 'That's about an hour from us.'

'Only for a few years.' His cheeks reddened slightly. *Best not ask him any more.* His body language indicated it wasn't a favourite subject.

'The motorways can be annoying. Dad's not fond of them; he likes a scenic route, so it took us even longer to get here yesterday.'

She stole another prolonged look at the man. His smile was still there. Not condescending or fake, just present, assuring and understanding. Heat attacked her face and neck, but she didn't turn away. Neither did he. A wobbly sensation trembled around her heart. Her limbs went squidgy and light. She blinked, retraining her focus on the path. This was like crushing on guys at High School – guys who were too cool to notice sensible little Eleanor. Thank god those days were long gone. The trees swayed in the gentle breeze and she screwed up her nose in their direction, so the man didn't see. *Not like I can have a holiday fling, is it?* Even if she wanted to – not that she would. Opportunities would be non-existent with Dad nearby. She almost giggled through the jumble of worries. Why was she even thinking stuff like this? Her best friend, Hattie, would laugh herself silly. Goody two-shoes Eleanor have a holiday fling! Even saying the words in relation to herself sounded like she'd lost her mind. And if Hattie saw the man... Well, she'd give Eleanor a poke, tell her to dream on and remind her that guys this good looking were always in relationships.

'I think it's here.' She swept away the nonsense from her brain, readjusted her sensible head, and put on a burst of speed. She jogged to the corner where Dad had slipped on the scree and toppled awkwardly about forty minutes ago. Her heart hammered a tattoo in her chest. Where was he? Thick bushes grew at the side of the path, but beyond was a drop into a gorge of tangled trees. She placed her hand on her forehead and squinted around. 'Where is he?' She couldn't hide the desperation in her voice. Not down there. Air jammed in her lungs. She put her foot on the mossy edge and peered down. Had he gone over? No one could fall there unless they were running and tripped. The bushes would bar the way. But what if he threw himself off? Had things got too much? *Oh god.* She pressed her fingertips to her lips.

'Hey.' The man moved closer, bringing with him a masculine scent of wood and spices that blended perfectly with the rugged surroundings. The desire to crumple into his broad chest was overwhelming, but no. *Must not yield. Stay strong.* She stood still, her trembling hand the only part of her that felt alive.

'He couldn't have gone down there.' His voice was reassuring and confident, but he didn't know what her family had been through that year. The overwhelming pain swelled so strongly at times that the desire to end it all swooped in before rationality had a chance to kick in. Had Dad succumbed?

'But... What if...' Her ribcage was caving under a crushing pain, like it had when she'd heard Mum's prognosis. Utter helplessness. Life would never be the same again. Dad couldn't be gone too.

'Hey. It'll be ok.' The man tilted his head slightly, making strong eye contact. He put out a hand and gently touched her shoulder. 'Stand back from the edge a bit. Come on. We'll find him.'

She swallowed and let him gently guide her back to the path with his palm resting lightly on her lower back.

'He can't have gone far. What's his name again?' he asked.

'Andy Kendrick.'

'Oh yeah. I remember now. I thought he was your husband.'

'Did you? Oh?' Heat flared in her neck.

'I'm going to shout his name in case he's around somewhere. Just warning you so you don't get a shock.' He patted her back softly, then let go.

'Ok.' Life and hope crept slowly back into her body, starting where his palm had touched her.

He cupped his hands around his mouth. 'Andy! Mr Kendrick.' He strode to the other side of the path. 'It's Logan from the campsite! I'm with your daughter. Can you hear me?' His deep, clear voice echoed around. Eleanor clenched her fingers at her side, holding her breath, watching and listening; her ears peeled for even the slightest rustle.

'Up here,' came a weak voice. Eleanor's hand leapt to her mouth and she exhaled with a whimper.

Logan was already jogging up the slope and around the corner. Just above the hairpin bend was a secondary bend, and there was her dad.

'Oh my god, Dad.' She dashed after Logan as he bent at her dad's side. 'There you are. I thought you were gone.' She rushed to him. He'd moved from the ground to a rock and had his leg outstretched. She threw her arms around him.

'No, I'm not gone. Where could I go to?' He wrapped her in a gentle hug.

'I'm sorry. I was at the wrong bend.' She glanced at Logan.

'No worries,' he said, kneeling beside them on one knee, smiling and checking through his rucksack. His tan hiking shorts pulled taut over his shapely legs. 'All's well.'

'I'm so sorry to be a bother,' Dad said. 'I didn't want Eleanor to have to get help but I really am struggling. She's always so sensible. I knew she'd work out what to do.'

'It's not a bother at all. Can I have a look at your ankle?'

'Yes, but perhaps you have something for my hand first. I cut it on the rocks and it's stinging.'

'Sure, let's have a look. I've had first aid training, so we'll see if I can put it to good use.' He checked over her dad's palm and she winced at the bloody mess. 'Let's give it a wipe and then I'll wrap it up.'

She edged back, watching as Logan carefully cleaned the wound and bound it with a gauze dressing.

'Now, let's see your ankle.'

Her father stuck out his leg and Logan rolled down his sock.

'It's swollen and red.' He turned the ankle in his palms. 'I can't feel anything broken but sometimes it's hard to tell. My mum broke her ankle years ago; she chipped the bone. It seemed like a sprain, but she couldn't load-bear for weeks. Do you feel like you can stand, Mr Kendrick, or is that not possible?'

He shuffled forward on the boulder and pushed himself up. Eleanor kept hold of him and helped him to his feet. 'I can stand, though I'm not sure how far I can walk.'

'Ok, well, if I strap it up, then we can take it slowly.' Logan swung his arm under her dad's, helping him back onto the boulder. 'Let's get your shoe and sock off and I'll see what I've got in here.' The rucksack was full of supplies made for this moment and he made no comments as he wound a bandage tightly around Dad's ankle. Eleanor sunk her teeth further into her lower lip. What beautifully strong and capable fingers. She ran her hand along her collarbone. What might they feel like on her skin? *Get that thought away. He's bound to be married.* The good ones always were.

'There. I think that'll feel better.' Logan sprang to his feet and cast her a smile. She returned it before swallowing and looking at her father. He put his arm around her dad's back. 'Use me as a crutch. We can stop and sit down any time.'

Dad nodded, and Logan pulled him up. Eleanor took the other side, and they started the descent, slowly and steadily, letting her dad set the pace.

'I think you should go to the community hospital in Glenbriar,' Logan said. 'As soon as we get back. Your ankle should be checked out properly, especially after walking on it all this way.'

'I agree.' Eleanor adjusted her position under her dad's shoulder. 'I think it's a good idea.' Except she loathed hospitals. Visions of her mum's suffering wound their way into her psyche: her frail, lifeless body. The nausea surrounding visits, the dread of bad news, clouds of pain and tears as they left, wishing things could go back to how they were before. She never wanted to set foot in one again.

'Yes. That's fine.' her father panted a little as he hobbled between them. 'Though I'm managing better than I thought. You're a very good crutch.'

'Thanks.' Logan grinned his kilowatt smile, delivering a shock to her nervous system.

'What did you say your name was again?' Dad asked.

'Logan.'

'Well, thank you, Logan, for speeding to my rescue. I wondered who Eleanor might get. I didn't think there would be many people around during the day.'

'I was working in the office.' He'd looped his arm under her father's and anchored it at his back. Eleanor was the same on the other side, just some inches smaller. Their hands grazed against each other, and she trembled. Actually trembled. *What is this all about?* His touch, even minuscule, had powers.

'Sorry.' The word was out before she could stop it. She couldn't have him thinking she was some flirty woman, making any excuse to touch him. She wasn't. Really. No. Not her style at all.

'For what?'

'For... Er...'

'I hope we haven't kept you from urgent business.' Dad saved the day. Probably not on purpose, but phew.

'Not at all. There's nothing more urgent than this.' Logan's pinkie brushed against hers and her stomach swooped. That was on purpose, surely? She didn't pull away. His touch was so warm. He rubbed his little finger along hers. A spark shot through her, waking her insides and setting rusty wheels into action. Then he returned his finger to her dad's back.

That did just happen, didn't it? It had been an age since she'd experienced anything close to this. Romance and relationships had gone out the window with Mum's diagnosis. Everything had changed and her love life was one of the first things to suffer.

But what the hell was she thinking? This was insane. She hadn't behaved like this since… Oh no… A truly cringy memory burst out like a Jack-in-the-box and punched her in the face. Years ago, when they'd holidayed at this campsite, she'd fancied a boy who worked here. Missing her friends and bored with 'holiday activities', she'd skulked around, hoping to bump into him during one of her many unnecessary trips to the shower blocks. She'd got to know where he might be and made up all sorts of excuses to slip away from her parents and brothers so she could walk past him and maybe get a smile in return. Now she was at it again. Or was she just reliving and extending those old memories? There was no harm in enjoying a few silly moments as long as Logan wasn't already spoken for.

'Do you run this place by yourself?' Dad asked, like he'd been reading her mind.

'Yes, I do,' he said. 'I've had quite a few staffing issues recently.'

'Oh dear. And no wife or family to help you out?'

'Sadly, no. Just me.'

'That can't be easy.'

No, it couldn't, but her heart did a crazy swoop like she'd tipped off the top of a rollercoaster. Where would the harm be in watching out for Logan throughout the week? Just to please her eyes and escape into a world of fantasy. Like old times. Was she too old to behave like that? She was twenty-eight. Most people her age were either in relationships or free to pursue them. She wasn't. So, eyeing someone from afar was as far as sensible Eleanor could go.

Holiday flings led to broken hearts, and she'd had quite enough heartbreak to be going on with.

Chapter Three

Logan

Logan took Andy under the arm and assisted him into the passenger seat of a burgundy Ford MPV. Eleanor was in the driver's seat, ready for the off. He closed the door and waved. The car crunched along the gravel path through the site towards the exit gates.

He held his hair flat against the top of his head, watching until the car disappeared out of sight. That little interlude had taken up a whopping chunk of his day. The electricity at pitch eleven would still be broken, the bins would be overflowing, the shower block a mess, and the shop shut. Booking enquiries would be unanswered and no grant applications had been filled out. But so what? Andy was safe, and that was the most important thing. Across the site, his three young pals from the day before were gunning for each other again with water pistols. Their dad was stoking a mini barbecue and their mum was reading on a foldout chair outside their tent. Logan gave them a wide berth, not because he didn't want to chat, but because he couldn't afford any more time away from what he was supposed to be doing. And he'd rather not get soaked again.

Andy would be fine. The hospital staff would get him comfy. On a purely selfish level, Logan didn't want him to be so badly injured he'd cut short his stay. Not because he cared about the money – if Andy and Eleanor had to leave, he would refund them fair and square – but an aching desire gnawed at him. *Please God, any god, mountain fairy, or whatever, let me see her again.* The thought nibbled at his insides, worming into him as he unlocked the shop and nipped in. He needed to check something before he started his round. Hopping into his office chair, he woke the computer and flicked through the booking system, settling the cursor over the name Eleanor Kendrick. Seven nights. Yes, that's what he'd thought she'd said. She was leaving on Saturday. Six days left. That was a longish booking. Mostly he got people for four or five nights max. But they'd travelled a long way, after all. They must want to make the most of it.

He rested his chin on his hand and sighed. Did any of this matter? She was just someone he liked the look of. He could go on liking the look of her for another six days, then forget all about her. It had been a while since he'd had a crush this strong. In fact, he wasn't sure he ever had. He jumped up again, ready to do his rounds. Since his last breakup, he hadn't seen anyone who turned his head, so this had to be a good thing, right? It meant he was getting back to his old self.

The best way to stop thinking about Eleanor, or anything else for that matter, was to immerse himself in scrubbing the toilet and shower block. Oh, the glamour of his life. When mindfulness was a gleaming bowl and shiny tiles.

The couple he'd employed to take on the maintenance jobs had pulled out at the last minute, leaving him in the lurch and the lovely woman who'd worked in the shop had gone on maternity leave and no one had applied to fill the vacancy.

One day, his plans for this place would be more than fantasy. When it was fully staffed and he was running hiking tours, kayaking and water sports, maybe even some kind of winter sports, and he could keep the place open all year, then he could pat himself on the back and show everyone how successful he could be.

With his rubber-gloved arm down the toilet, scrubbing away, that day seemed a long way off. He'd dreamed of running Heather Glen ever since he was a teenager. Finally, he'd achieved the dream. The easy bit anyway. His new baby was in his arms. What to do with it next was the main issue. And how to afford it. If his mum could see him now, it would confirm her worst fears. After he'd done the noble son duty, studied and got himself into Cambridge University, where he'd graduated with a degree in sports science, he was now reduced to cleaning toilets. He could almost hear her tutting and placing her hands on her hips before saying, 'You really let the side down. I had such high hopes for my children and here you are throwing your life down the loo.'

Hey ho. But a guy could have dreams, right? He adored working outdoors and providing recreation for people. The drudgery was just a small stop on the path to achieving the rewards. Some of the gleam had worn off though. When the 'water sports centre' had been damaged in high winds a couple of weeks ago, it was another knock in a series of bashings for his new ownership. Rain had got in, damaging the building and the roof had caved, destroying almost everything. The centre's location on the other side of the hill from the shop and the main site meant it was impossible to staff when there was only him, but the fact he couldn't even try now doubled the irritation. The starry eyes he'd sported when he first cradled the title deeds were now strained from dealing with an overdose of waste management and sanitary cleanliness.

And electricity. *Shit.* He must check that socket before the couple at pitch eleven blew a fuse. If someone else rocked up needing electricity, and the number-eleven people were using the wrong socket, it could open a whole new book of problems. He finished scrubbing and mopping the toilet block, then jumped in his converted golf cart. Next stop: bins. He navigated towards them. Soon, the full bags were squashed together in the back of the cart. The view to pitch eleven was clear from here. No cars were parked next to it. Fingers crossed, the unhappy campers had taken a trip for the afternoon. He could attempt to fix the socket without them watching. After he dispatched the bin bags into the giant metal wheelie bin behind the shop, he collected his toolbox and grabbed a plug and cable as well. If it worked, then he'd know it was their faulty wiring, not his.

The site wasn't huge, but the cart was useful for carrying a shed load of bin bags and cleaning equipment. He didn't need it for this kind of job though. A large navy tent with sleeping pods on either side fluttered in the breeze in a pleasant spot close to the stream and surrounded by trees. It was one of the most picturesque parts of the whole site. That was Eleanor's pitch. And of course, she'd been before, which was how she knew to request that location. Logan had grown up working summer jobs here and always loved the idea of being the one in charge. Back then, there were no electric hook-ups for tents and the owners had kept chickens and sheep onsite. Campers were allowed to use eggs they found and often woke to sheep snuffling outside their tents in the morning. That was all gone, and it was more commercial now, even a little flat. He was on a mission to kick-start it. He'd jumped at the chance to buy it when it came on the market. With the owners knowing him already, he was their ideal choice.

He fiddled about with the socket at pitch eleven, testing his cable in it. 'Works fine.' He rubbed his chin. How would the unhappy campers take this? Their cable must be defunct. Probably more than his job was worth to tell them. If he lent them a working cable, that might help. His holiday job hadn't prepared him for the kind of grief people gave him when they were unhappy. He yanked out the plug. His skin was getting thicker on a daily basis. Just as well.

He returned to the office and the files. Only four hours after he started. Better than nothing. Focusing was an issue – more so than usual. His mum always insisted he had ADHD, and maybe he did. He'd learned to deal with his excess energy by keeping active as much as he could, but some days that was near impossible. Getting through his degree had been a minor miracle but he'd done it. Now he just had to get through the day and that seemed a lot trickier. His eyes and his brain kept leaping up and wandering off task. Were the grumpy campers back? Was Eleanor? A stomach flip accompanied all his rambling thoughts of her, making him fidgety. The campsite was usually quieter between eleven and three when people were away on day trips, but when that magic number hit, new arrivals piled in, and people returned. He glanced at the clock. The big hand inched towards the top, the short one bang on three. An engine grumbled outside. Right on cue. He shoved the document box aside. The rickety shop door clanked open and the first new arrivals sauntered in. End of peace for at least the next half hour. He pulled up the booking list, ready to check people in and assign pitches. A smiley couple beamed as he handed over a map and went over the rules.

'We like people to keep the noise down after nine, as this is a child-friendly site.'

Uh-oh. He spied the unhappy campers returning. With a queue of admissions and guests stocking up for the evening, he couldn't go to them. *Please don't try the electricity straight away.* They'd think he'd forgotten to sort it. Finally, he served the last customer, whipped the sign around on the door and legged it towards the unhappy campers' tent. The shop keys jangled in the pocket of his walking shorts and his feet thumped the grass.

'Hello.' He tapped on the canvas. 'It's Logan, the site manager.'

A zip whirred down. The serpent tattoo on Mr Unhappy camper's arm muscled out before the rest of him. 'Yeah? What's up?'

'Did you get your electricity working?'

'No. Your hook-ups are crap. None of them work. We should get a refund.'

'Well, I tried this cable in it earlier and it worked.' Logan flashed him a grin. The man would hate it for sure, but good cheer was free. Why not spread it around?

'Are you calling me a liar?' Mr Unhappy camper folded his thick arms.

'No, of course not.' Logan pulled himself up straight; he was a good few inches taller. 'I think you might have a faulty cable, that's all. You can borrow this one for the rest of your stay if you like. Like I said, I tested it in socket eleven and it works fine.'

'Yeah, we'll see. Thanks.' The man snatched the cable. 'It better work or I want my money back.'

'Well, why don't I hook it up and get you started?' Best to be there when they tried it. This man seemed the type to claim it didn't work just to get the cash. Logan lifted the casing. A burgundy flash caught his eye by the woods. Eleanor's MPV glided under the trees into the spot next to her navy tent. She got out of the driver's door, and Logan froze, his hand suspended in mid-air next to the socket. Her ethereal elegance shone from a distance. She almost floated around the car and opened the passenger door. Andy got out with a bit of assistance and limped towards the tent.

'Are you plugging that in or not?' Mr grumpy camper placed his hands on his hips. 'I've not got all fecking day.'

'Yeah, here.' Logan thrust the plug into the socket. 'Try that.' He flexed his fingers and waited, his gaze straying to Eleanor's tent. Damn. She'd gone.

'It's working,' Mr grumpy camper said from inside the tent.

'Great. You hang onto it while you're here. Just hand it in when you leave.'

'Thanks, man,'

'Any time.' Just as well he couldn't see Logan's gritted teeth.

Logan strode towards Eleanor's tent, ruffling up his hair with ferocious strokes. Did he look a fright? If he teased out his hair, he might appear vaguely respectable. She and her dad were sitting on fold-out chairs in front of the tent, gazing over the bubbling stream beyond, shaded by the canopy of trees. Oh, to join them. How awesome did it look? So peaceful. Easily the best spot on the site.

'Hey, how did you get on?' he asked.

They turned around and Logan's eyes zapped straight to Eleanor. She looked back and his heart crashed into an erratic rhythm. *WTAF!* Since when did he react like this to a pretty face? Seriously? People often called him a flirt or a lad. And sometimes he couldn't help himself bantering and chatting up women. He took pleasure in getting laughs from people and that pushed him into flirty behaviour, and so what? There was no harm in it, but that wasn't what was happening here. Right now, he just wanted to look at her. *Try to focus on her dad; he's the injured one after all.* Tearing his gaze away from those piercing blue eyes, he smiled at Andy.

Andy patted his leg. 'It's not broken; just a sprain.'

'I've got frozen peas.' Eleanor wrapped a packet in a dishcloth. Logan's gaze sprang back to her. 'I'm not sure how we'll keep them frozen in a tent, but he's to apply this until the swelling goes down.'

'Use my freezer. I live in the static next to the shop. Just give me a knock. I'm always about somewhere.'

'Thanks.' She smiled and her pale skin glowed pink like life was returning to her after a long, cold winter. 'Put this on, Dad.' She handed him the wrapped-up peas. Andy rested it around his ankle and she dragged their fold-up table closer.

'Here, let me.' Logan grabbed the other side. She didn't need his help. Of course she didn't. The table weighed nothing, but he couldn't stop himself. She smiled and blinked, not raising her eyes to him.

'Only time you're allowed to put your feet on the table.' She helped Andy lift his leg.

'I'm glad to hear you're on the mend.' Logan adjusted the table so it was perfectly placed. 'I don't suppose walking back down the hill really helped.'

'Probably not.' Andy moved the injured ankle gingerly from side to side. 'But I couldn't have sat there all day. It already feels better. A couple of days resting it will be fine.'

'Shame it happened on your first day.'

'I'll drive us to lots of places.' Eleanor patted Andy's arm. 'Then you won't have to walk.'

What a lucky guy to have such a caring daughter.

'Well, if you need anything else, just give me a shout.' Logan glanced between them and smiled.

'Thank you.' Andy gave him a thumbs up. 'We appreciate your help.'

'Yes, thanks.' Eleanor fiddled with her nail. 'I hope we didn't mess up your day.'

'No, you definitely didn't do that.' Their eyes connected again, and he held her gaze for a moment. Her ice-blue irises twinkled, and he caught her biting her lip. She did that a lot and every time it sent a crashing wave into his chest, knocking him off course for a moment. 'Well, I'll see you about. I hope.'

He raised his hand, then ambled back to the path. A magnetic force tugged him and he peeked over his shoulder. She was still watching. He gave her a brief smile, then picked up his pace. No use hanging about. He aimed for the shop. What was happening to him? Could he ignore the hormones, pheromones or whatever it was telling him to act? If she was someone he'd met in a bar or out with friends, he'd ask her out right now with no hesitation. But doing that here could lead down a ropey path. He'd had the odd short-term fling. Who hadn't? But not with someone like her. Nope. She was a devoted daughter with an injured dad, not someone on the pull. Interfering would be unhelpful and unwelcome. How much more sensible would it be to back off? He couldn't hook up with a guest. That wasn't a line worth crossing. Doing that was like turning to the dark side. Trouble lay that way. Dating and guests didn't marry well in this business, not if he wanted to keep his reputation and he really couldn't afford to lose it.

Chapter Four

Eleanor

The outer flysheet rustled in the breeze. People chattered and laughed in the distance, and a grasshopper hummed outside. Eleanor tugged the zip around her sleeping pod, closing it off from the main section of the tent, and snuggled into the depths of her fleece-lined sleeping bag. It was extra toastie from the hot water bottle she put in earlier. Tugging it close and nestling her fingers into the soft, plush fur cover, she let out a deep sigh. The comforting heat spread through her veins. Once upon a time long ago, she'd slept in this same pod with her two brothers, all squashed together like sardines, chatting and moaning about not having enough space, then pretending to die if one of them broke wind.

Her parents had been in the other pod, shushing them and telling them to go to sleep. The same stream babbled past, sometimes full and raging, other times just a trickle over the stony riverbed. She'd seen it in different stages at least four times in her childhood, possibly more. It was hard to recall. Memories of those happy days rolled together into one. Who could have known then how altered their family would look fourteen years later? With Mum gone, nothing would be the same again. Familiar tears leaked from the corners of her eyes. She let them flow. Over the last year, she'd cried more than a river. If tears had to come, these quiet moments alone were the best place. They washed away some of the immediate pain. The tightly wrapped blankets cocooned her in safety. She was allowed to remember, even if the memories brought sadness. Freeing her hand from its grip on the hot water bottle, she brushed her fingertips under her eyes and breathed deeply.

Grief was such a rollercoaster. Shying away from memories didn't help. Hitting them square on was sometimes more powerful than waiting for them to creep up unexpectedly. This trip was meant to help exorcise some demons for her dad too. He needed to see he was capable of holidaying without his wife. Being fifteen years older than Mum had made her loss even more crushing for him. He never thought she'd be the first to go. None of them had. She wasn't even sixty when she was snatched from them. Dad was seventy-five and where he was spritely and full of joy before, he now seemed much more his age. She couldn't lose him too. The idea struck like a dagger in the heart. *Must keep him going.* That was her task, her job, her goal and her mission. Her brothers were married and had moved away. She was the only one who could.

A patter of raindrops hit the canvas in a ragged rhythm. Chatter from other tents slowly fizzled out. The light faded. An odd cough or laugh punctuated the growing hush. She closed her eyes. Her mind wandered away from sadness and the never-ending dark hollow of loss to a brighter place. Logan's face swam clearly before her, all rugged and smiley; his calm voice whispered words of solace. An all-encompassing sense of safety washed over her; he was nearby – somewhere. Maybe she'd see him again soon. Fingers crossed. Her lips stretched into a grin and she nuzzled into the fleecy pillow. The tight hold of her sleeping bag became his arms, huddling her close. She was like a teenager again, imagining running into the boy from the campsite, maybe even stealing a first kiss with him. She almost laughed aloud, recalling one time when she'd got up early and positioned herself on top of a gate near to where he fed the chickens. When he appeared swinging his bucket of chicken feed, she pretended to have her foot stuck in the gate, so he'd help her out.

She screwed her eyelids tight shut. *Oh crikey, how cringy.* He probably thought her a lunatic. She'd only been fourteen. He'd been older. Maybe two or three years. Now, she couldn't even remember what he looked like. She wouldn't be that ridiculous again. Logan was a nice guy and, if she bumped into him, she'd enjoy chatting to him. If she had to manufacture a reason to see him, then fine, as long as it didn't involve faking a stuck foot. She'd been so red faced after that incident she couldn't look the boy in the eye. He'd asked if she was ok, maybe more. She couldn't remember; she'd blotted it from her mind long ago. The moment she'd been praying for had arrived, that second when he would notice her and talk to her. And he had. But she'd bottled it, unstuck her foot and run for it. After that, she'd spent her time ducking out of sight whenever he was around and wishing she hadn't made such a fool of herself.

Next morning, Eleanor sloshed through the wet grass with her wash bag towards the shower block. Rain overnight had left the campsite marshy. The modern addition of a log-panelled shed that resembled a Swedish sauna was an improvement on the portacabins she'd used as a teenager. They'd been so yucky. She'd come running back every night screaming about the giant daddy longlegs flying around her head.

Her dad's ankle was a little better, but he wasn't up for a long walk or anything too strenuous. He fancied a day birdwatching but the weather didn't look that great for sitting outside with binoculars.

The water was hot, warming her from the veins out. After she'd dressed in her leggings and hoody, she took the long way back via the shop, not for purchasing purposes, just for the sake of it. She glanced in the window. Logan was chatting with some customers. Her heart rate sped up and her temperature rose a notch, but she kept walking. *Don't make this infatuation too obvious.* He'd said he ran the site all by himself. It must be a big job. She worked in business administration and had done stints in project management on small-scale jobs. No denying how challenging it was. The admin for a place like this must be a full-time job, add the practical tasks, and it was a job for two, three, maybe more. But she knew nothing about him. Just because he didn't run the site with anyone didn't mean he wasn't dating. But the way he'd looked at her yesterday… That look wasn't an innocent glance from someone in a relationship. No. It was loaded with something else. She knew it because, crazy as it seemed, she felt it too. And when he'd brushed hands with her on the walk down the hill… He'd done that on purpose, hadn't he?

The rain increased. 'Oh gosh.' She pulled up her hood. Maybe she was imagining what she wanted to see. It could be utter rubbish. She'd always liked the idea of love at first sight, but her best friend, Hattie, kept reminding her it was rarely real. 'Um no, more likely to be lust at first sight,' she'd say. Eleanor could chalk it up to that. Logan was attractive; she was attracted. No mystery; no brainer.

Her dad wasn't back from his shower, so she dumped her wash bag and filled up the kettle with water from the portable canister. Here was another new thing, electric hook-ups for tents. As kids, this would have been the height of luxury, having charge points and a kettle. Imagine not having to wait half an hour while Dad boiled a tiny kettle over the stove for each hot water bottle. How much more convenient to flick a switch, but it stripped away some of the charm.

The zip whirred, and Dad's head popped through the door.

'Did you get on ok?' Eleanor said.

'Yes. My ankle seems not too bad.' He ducked inside and zipped up the door. 'I think I can walk short distances. I thought maybe we could do a whisky distillery tour. You children were always too young when we were here before and your mum didn't really enjoy it enough.'

Eleanor could understand that. Whisky wasn't her thing either, but the distillery tour sounded like a good plan. At least it'd be indoors. 'Which one do you fancy?'

'Well, I don't know. Probably one that's not too far. Why don't you look it up on your phone? You're good at finding things to do.'

'How about I go and ask at the shop? Someone there should be able to tell me a good one.'

'Oh yes, that's an excellent idea. I'd prefer a personal recommendation.'

Her insides danced the conga. What an amazing reason to visit Logan. Completely real.

She wolfed her brioche and coffee, pulled on her jacket, whipped up the hood and unzipped the tent. Thick clouds clung to the hills behind the campsite, shrouding them so they were almost invisible unless you knew they were there. She approached the shop and scanned the inside. The serving area doubled as the admissions office and Logan was seated at the desk section, his head just visible over a computer screen. No one else seemed to be inside. She'd have him all to herself. Was that good or bad? Her heart beat a little quicker. Would he guess her game? How stupid was she? A grown woman snooping around for a chance to ogle some random man. But she'd come this far. She could always pretend to need some milk if she lost the nerve to speak to him. The door swung open more ferociously than she meant it to, clattering into a nearby shelf. She lunged for it. 'Sorry.' *Eek.* Bang went cool.

'No worries. It always does that.' Logan's head jumped up. 'Oh. It's you. Hi.' He got to his feet and leaned on the counter. His smile cracked his face and his eyes linked with hers, filling with warmth like they'd reconnected with an old friend. Her heart did a ridiculous swoop like she'd thrown it out of an aeroplane window. Was she still breathing? Time momentarily stopped. 'Is everything ok?' he asked after a beat that could have been a few seconds or an hour. 'Your dad?'

'Yes, um... we're both fine.' She slipped her hood down. Camping hair never looked good, and she ran her fingers through the blonde strands before tucking them behind her ears. Hopefully, that was semi-respectable. Something about the loaded look in his eyes spoke volumes. He wasn't bothered if she had no make-up on, her hair was a fright, and her clothes damp. He was happy with what he saw – everything in his expression said so. An inferno burst in her chest, firing up her cheeks.

'Great.' His smile could power a city for a week.

She was still caught in his gaze, like he'd snared her in a lasso and was winding her in. 'I, um, do need help with something though. If you've got a minute.'

'Sure. Is it for the frozen peas?'

'No.' She let out a laugh. It relieved some of her choking nerves. 'Dad gave up on them. The swelling has gone down a lot overnight.' She blinked. Now was the time to spit out what she wanted from him. What exactly was that? All cognitive function seemed lost. Why was she here? Just to smile at Logan? 'Um... Dad wants to go to a distillery and do some whisky tasting, but neither of us knows anything about what's good and what's not. Maybe you know a good one?'

'Sure, there are loads to choose from around here.'

'Yes. That's the problem.' She edged closer to the counter. 'What would you recommend?'

'Hmm, let's see.' He sat at his computer and clicked around. 'I'll check some opening times. They don't all do tours every day. The bigger ones do but some of the smaller places don't and they're often better. You get a more personal tour and the whisky is more unique.'

'I'm not even sure I like whisky.'

'It's an acquired taste.' He glanced at her and smiled again, denting a wide dimple into his chiselled cheekbones. His lips had a perfect Cupid's bow and its shape preoccupied her for a moment. He cleared his throat. 'I don't mind a wee dram now and then, though some of the peaty ones are too strong for me. I think you'd like the Glenbriar Distillery. It's the closest and has an interesting history as well as good whisky. Or you could try Torrindhu. It's a smaller distillery and a bit further to drive to but they make one of my favourite whiskies; it's really mellow and...' He waved his hand about. 'And something. I'll leave the people on the tour to tell you, I'm useless at describing it. Both those distilleries are part of a family-run business that's expanded over the years. Either of them would be good, or both. They're not that far from each other.' He turned from the screen and faced her. Her heart was up dancing again. She could look at his smile all day, but if it was going to affect her pulse rate like this, she'd end up in cardiac arrest.

'Er... Yes, that sounds good. Are they easy to find?'

'Dead easy. Do you have satnav?'

'On my phone, yes.'

He laughed. 'I have that one too but the voice annoys me. It reminds me of my mum nagging me.' He glanced sideways. 'Sorry, was that totally insensitive?'

'No.' She shook her head. 'I don't let things like that get to me.' She couldn't afford to. There had to be a line somewhere. If she got upset every time someone mentioned their mum, she'd crawl into a cave and never come out.

'Sorry anyway.' He got to his feet and thrust his hands into his back pockets, pushing his shoulders and chest wide. Her nerve ends tingled. He was epically proportioned. A proper Adonis.

A pinnacle of manly attractiveness. And so unavailable, which, all things considered, was probably for the best. If he was on the market and touting himself as a candidate, would she find a fault and back off? Fear would kick in because he was way too handsome for her. And she wasn't ready anyway. She couldn't date right now, and she'd never been a part of the hook-up culture. It wasn't her. Her soul still hurt from her last relationship. Losing Mum was bad enough, but when it came alongside a spectacular breakup, it was like having her heart ripped out and splattered into her face. Logan was safe, someone she wouldn't see after the week was up, so looking and admiring were ok. *Yes. All good.*

He turned to the shelves behind him, running his finger along a line of books until he came to a large yellow one. 'Let's see.' He edged around the counter and stood close. Eleanor breathed him in. Her eyelids gently closed for a second as the woody-fresh and spicy aroma tickled her nostrils. 'We're here.' He folded the page open at a map and pointed, his arm brushing hers as he held it towards her. Heat seared her cheeks, but she didn't flinch or back away. She swallowed, keeping her eyes on the map. He slid his fingertip across it, tracing the route. His skin was tanned and his hands looked well-worked and strong. 'Glenbriar is just a couple of miles away, and for Torrindhu, there's a testy section – here – once you reach the glen. But it's mostly a main road. Though a main road up here doesn't mean a dual carriageway.'

'I know that.' She scraped her hair behind her ear. 'I think I can find them both. I remember visiting Glenbriar when we were here before but I can't picture the distillery.'

'So, it's just here.' He pinpointed the location and she leaned in. Then, seized by a brave – or completely mad – moment, she put her hand over his and shifted his finger, feigning an attempt to look closer. His skin was warm, like really warm, and felt so good.

'I see.' She blinked, taking her hand from his, not wanting to meet his eye.

'It's in the middle of the town and up the hill, and it's well signed.'

'Great.' She chanced a look. He was still smiling. Silence slipped over them. Oh, to fall into his arms. How irrelevant that she didn't really know him. His blue-grey eyes twinkled, dropping only fractionally from hers to her lips, telling her everything. His mouth moved slowly from a smile to something more pensive. She leaned closer, though she shouldn't – really shouldn't, but she wanted to. External forces shoved her forward.

The cranking door burst open and he looked away suddenly. 'Good morning.' How was his voice so normal? Eleanor was sure she couldn't string a sentence together right now. She was dazed. Where was she and what was she doing – or meant to be doing?

'I, um, should go.'

'Sure.' Logan gave her a brief pat on the arm. 'Have a great day. Enjoy the whisky.'

'We will. And thanks for all your help.' She met his eyes one last time, thanking him silently for everything... Like just existing and being right there so she could drop in and see him whenever she fancied.

He waved like he understood and returned behind the counter.

Chapter Five

Logan

'Enjoy your day, guys. I hope the weather holds out for you.' Logan served the penultimate customers in the queue. His focus strayed beyond the display of camping essentials to the window. The morning bustle was in full swing, campers heading off on day trips or packing up, ready to move to their next stop. A group of men carrying holdalls and large towels emerged from the shower block with damp hair and proceeded towards a row of campervans stationed at the trackside. These vans blocked the view of the lower field, so the woodland area where Eleanor was camped wasn't visible. *Eleanor this, Eleanor that*. His mind played volleyball with visions of her flying across his brain on a big, shiny beach ball.

'Ahem.' The last customer cleared her throat and Logan blinked. He couldn't stop his mind from wandering.

'That's fourteen eighty.' He pushed the card machine across the counter, still preoccupied with the goings-on outside the window. A burgundy MPV glided around the bend in the track towards the exit. Eleanor was off for the day. The reality stabbed him like a knitting needle, puncturing his shiny beach ball; all the buoyancy fizzled out, leaving him flat and useless. He took the card machine back and tore off the customer's receipt.

As soon as she left the shop, he slumped into his chair. What the hell was happening to him? Since when did Logan Ramsay get this infatuated with a woman? He had women friends and acquaintances; he met women every day through work and was no stranger to dating and relationships, but he'd never felt anything like this. Eleanor had got under his skin and fast. How, from a chance meeting or two, had he got to here? Ok, not completely chance; he engineered the one last night. But then... Could her sojourn into the shop earlier have been a similar ruse? He ran his fingers through his hair. 'Get a grip, man.'

With Eleanor gone, the tension in his nervous system shifted. He rolled his shoulders and stretched, linking his hands above his head and pushing until his fingers cracked. What he needed was a strenuous hike or a bike ride. Something to clear his brain and work his body. None of his feelings made sense right now.

He filled up the converted golf cart, ready for his rounds, trying to figure out what to do and where to start, and none of it should involve Eleanor. She was out and he could forget about her for now. Or at least forget about trying to cook up ways of bumping into her. He could do that, couldn't he?

'Christ, I've turned into an actual stalker,' he muttered. The phone inside the office rang just as he was about to put up the 'closed' sign. He dithered for a second, then nipped in and grabbed it. The answer message started. 'Hello,' he cut in.

'Good morning, it's Rachael from Highland Segways. It's about your booking for Wednesday.'

'Hey, Rachael. Is the booking still ok?'

'Absolutely. I just wanted to confirm you have everything ready.'

'Yeah, everything's good.' He rubbed his face. It was as ready as it would ever be. Though, in reality, it was a half-baked plan that could end in chaos. He'd booked it when he thought he would have staff-a-plenty to cover all eventualities. Now it seemed like just one more thing to squeeze into an already over-packed schedule. 'The field is ready and I've got the whole day booked up.' He'd even invited a couple of friends and family members to make sure there were no gaps.

'Great, we'll see you on Wednesday then,' Rachael said.

'Epic, thanks. See you then.' He replaced the phone and set off on his rounds. Before he delved into the shower block, he sent a quick reminder to his friend, Duncan, hoping he could join him for the Segway experience. He'd appreciate even moral support, though midweek probably wasn't the best time. The same was true for his sister, Sophie, and her husband and daughter, also his cousin Matthew and his girlfriend, Nina. Nina would love Segways, but she'd be working. He didn't bother reminding his parents. Imagining his mum on a Segway was an image he could do without, but she always moaned about not being invited to things or feeling 'left out'. This time, he'd given her the opportunity to join in, but he was sure she wouldn't take it. He frowned. Recently, his mum had shown a different side to her usual straight-down-the-line self, like when she'd locked his cousin Matthew in a shed at a family gathering a couple of months ago. But locking someone up so she could win a game was more her style than riding on a Segway and she'd replied to his original message with, 'If I'm not too busy', though she always was.

If she didn't show up this time, that was good; it would leave a space for Eleanor. A reason to see her again flashed on the horizon. Would she come along if he invited her?

Scrubbing toilets and mopping showers was grim work, but the glimmer of Eleanor at the end of the tunnel kept him going. Almost choking on bleach fumes, he coughed and ran outside to claim the fresh air. Ripping off his rubber gloves, he checked his phone and discovered a message from Duncan.

DOUGHNUT: Hey man, will try to make it on Wednesday. Segway sounds so cool but I'm working. Might get away P.M. Will let you know.

Logan tapped the phone. Yes, having Duncan on hand would mean more laughs, but if Eleanor was around, it could be a complication. Some flirting may occur and he'd rather not have an audience. 'Aw man.' He loaded the cleaning fluid into the cart. 'I've really got this bad.'

'Excuse me!' a shrill voice cried.

A portly woman jogged up the track, waving to him, and Logan sniffed trouble.

'Hi. How can I help?'

'The noise.' She raised both her hands in front of her in a gesture of finality.

Was she going to elaborate? He gave her a half-smile as he waited. She pushed out a pout, presumably for effect, before letting rip a huge, very dramatic sigh.

'Can you please do something about the noise around here?'

'What noise specifically?' Occasionally campers of a certain age complained about noise, but he couldn't keep everyone quiet all the time. There were limits and he only interfered if blatant rule-breaking was taking place like loud music or rowdy parties running late into the night. These were rare and usually confined to the main part of the site, close to the showers and cooking area – where both the middle-aged campers and the partygoers liked to frequent for different reasons. An annoying combination.

'All of it really, but mostly from the pitch next to ours.'

'Remind me, which pitch is that?'

'We're on twelve, so I assume it's eleven or thirteen. I don't like to get too close. Honestly, it's either music, videos, or they're at it like animals. It is not the sort of thing I want to listen to.'

Seriously? He ran his hand over his chin. Pitch eleven? His no-electricity friends. No way was he marching around there to ask them to keep the noise down when they were at it. What went on inside their tent was their business.

'Ok, well, that's not something I can do much about unless the music is at a particularly high level or going on very late.'

'It is.' The woman looked indignant. 'I think they put it on to try and drown out the disgusting noises they're making, but it isn't working.'

'Would you like to move pitch?' God knew where he was going to put her, but it seemed the easiest solution. 'I could help you move anything and re-pitch your tent if you like.' He should get an award for fastest pitcher these days.

'Let me see where first. I don't want to move too far from the toilets, but I don't want to be too close either, you know, for the smell and the constant flushing.'

Nice and easy then – close but not close. Moments like this were the ones he would like to cut from the job. His dreams were slowly evaporating in a cloud of hopelessness. How, amongst all this drudgery, could he ever succeed in running a successful outdoor centre alongside the camping? The upcoming Segway experience was a big thing, but even that seemed too little too late. He should have events like that booked in for the whole summer, but he didn't.

He abandoned the golf cart and went with the woman to the edge of the woodland pitches. 'There's this one here. It's still not too far to the shower block if you take the back path. And because you're in the woodland section, it's quieter.'

'What about electric hook-up? We still need that.'

'There's a socket just there you can run your cable from.'

'All right. We'll try it, but we have a lot of stuff to move.'

'I'll fetch it in the cart. Maybe you could start taking your tent down.'

'Well, it's a massive inconvenience.' The woman narrowed her eyes at the vacant space under the trees. 'And not at all what I expected.'

'I'm sorry to hear that.'

She carried on moaning as he left for the cart. *Money back, money back, money back* was all he heard, though she didn't use those words. Obviously, that was what she was angling for, but he wasn't giving in. He was helping her find a solution, and it would have to do.

A string of people hung around outside the shop when he finally got back an hour later. His timetable had gone to pot as usual. Maybe one day, everything would go according to plan and he'd get stuff done on time, but it wasn't this day.

'Hi, everyone.' He unlocked the door. 'Sorry to keep you. There was an emergency. In you come.'

By the time the burgundy MPV rolled back in the gates, he was shattered. He stretched and yawned, then flopped his head into his hands at his desk. He still had the late afternoon rounds to do and he hadn't started on the mountain of paperwork waiting for his attention. This was what happened every day. There just weren't enough hours to do everything. But Eleanor had returned and the tension was back too, that desire, tugging him from somewhere behind his navel, and compelling him to go find her and not waste one single second.

More customers came in and he served them, half hoping she might come and find him. But at six o'clock when he shut up shop for the day, she hadn't appeared. He nipped round the back to the static he called home and made himself a sandwich. Proper meals were a luxury he didn't have time for.

He changed into clean jeans and a fresh t-shirt, the flattest one he could find. It was a good fit. Hopefully, the creases would stretch around him, and Eleanor would notice his body more than the un-ironed state of the shirt. He pulled a Popeye pose and grinned at himself in the tiny bathroom mirror. 'Not bad, you twat.' When was the last time he tried this hard, even when he was going on a date? He kept in good shape and women usually appreciated that more than what he chose to wear.

He stuffed the remains of his sandwich into his mouth and left, trying to appear like he was on an everyday walk around the site and he was just casually passing Eleanor's pitch. Warmth hung in the air even though it wasn't bright sunshine. Hopefully, it would be enough to mean Eleanor and her dad were sitting outside. 'Knocking' on their tent would look weird – weirder even than wandering by like this? Hands in pockets? Hands out? What the hell should he do with them?

With his focus trained on her tent, he jumped as the boot of the MPV slammed and his eyes met Eleanor's.

'Oh... Hello.' She pushed her blonde hair behind her ear. Her heart-shaped face was very pale, but her cheeks glowed peachy pink and her bright eyes glittered. He should speak. *Yes, open your mouth and say something.* But what? Words failed, though other parts of his body were working overtime. A crushing desire to take her in his arms had paralysed him. He wanted to own her, worship her and make her completely and utterly his.

'Hi.' His voice squeak-croaked like a dying frog.

Her lips curled up, but little frown lines appeared on her brow. 'Are you... I mean, is everything ok?'

'Er, yes.' He cleared his throat. 'How did you get on? Were the distilleries any good?'

'Yes, they were. Whisky still isn't my thing, but I enjoyed trying it. Dad loved it. I think he had a few too many. He's exhausted now.'

'Is he? Oh dear.'

'That reminds me.' She opened the boot of the car again, and he admired her from head to foot. She was average height and slim, though, at a second glance, she seemed a bit too thin, like she hadn't eaten well for a while. Her outdoor gear was a layer he'd happily remove, starting by slowly taking down the zip in the centre of her pink hiking jacket. He bit down on his lip and internally slapped his face. *Behave.* 'We got you this.' She held up a bottle full of golden liquid, bearing the Torrindhu logo. 'As a thank you for helping with Dad.'

Logan shook his head. 'You really didn't have to.'

'I know, but we wanted to.' She moved closer and pushed it in his direction. He took it, smothering the desire to lean in and kiss her cheek.

'Thank you. This is great.' He examined the bottle. It must have cost them a lot.

'I, em...' Eleanor glanced around. 'I thought I might go for a walk; you know, do the traditional camping thing and collect some firewood. I could dry it out and maybe have a fire tomorrow. Would you like to come with me? I mean, only if you're free. Dad's too tired, you see.'

'Yeah, I'd love that,' he blurted out straight from his heart. Catching her gaze again, he telepathically told her just how much.

She nodded; he knew she understood. 'We can leave the bottle in the car. I don't suppose you want to carry it around the woods.'

'Epic plan.' He handed it back and she stowed it in the boot. She seemed to be struggling to focus on anything and her eyes kept darting back to him. *A good sign, huh?*

'Right, I'll just nip in and tell Dad where I'm going. Two secs.'

Logan strolled away a few paces, adjusting his waistband and breathing purposefully. This was it. Almost a date. He liked her; she liked him. She must like him or she wouldn't have asked him on a walk and bought him an expensive bottle of whisky. All good so far. Very good. Except for the her-being-on-holiday part. Well, screw that. This was happening now, and he was damn well going to enjoy it.

'Hey.' She tapped his shoulder.

A grin split his face and she mirrored it. For a moment, they stood smiling at each other like goofy kids. Then he put out his hand. Eleanor stared at it and bit her lip. After what felt like an eternity, she took it and he clasped his fingers around hers, savouring the warmth and contentment flooding through him. Energy and strength surged from the epicentre of their joint hands. A steadying sensation like they'd just sealed a bond that could never be broken seeped through him, making him feel completely invincible. He gently squeezed her hand and strolled towards the gate that led to the mountain path, ready to face anything and everything.

Chapter Six

Eleanor

Hand in hand, Eleanor walked through the campsite with Logan, heat blooming in her cheeks. Neither of them spoke and that was ok. Just focusing on her hand in his was enough. The way his large warm palm encased her small slender fingers flooded her with heat and joy. Without warning, he did an odd thing, splitting her pinkie finger from the rest with his so they had their own little loop but the rest of their fingers were still in a traditional clasp. The gesture seemed quite natural, but no one had ever held her hand like that. Anyone passing by wouldn't notice the subtle difference but something about it was more personal and intimate than the usual way. Just living the moment made her pulse soar. The bigger picture was a scribbled mess with too many missing pieces, but here and now, it was perfect.

'I feel like a naughty teenager,' she said as Logan dropped her hand to open the heavy steel gate that led to the path through the woods. Eventually, that path joined the Bealach Pass and intrepid climbers could carry on to the top of Ben Vrack.

He smirked, holding the gate open for her to pass through. 'I can't imagine you ever getting into trouble.'

'You're so right. I've always been well behaved, though I wish I could say that wasn't the case. I've been called a goody two-shoes more times than I can remember.' This was the most daring thing she'd ever done. She was not in the habit of wandering into the woods with strange men or holding hands with a man like she was on a date when, really, they hardly knew each other.

'Same with me.' Logan pulled a grim expression. 'I never put a foot out of line.'

'Really?' She couldn't stop herself from raising an eyebrow.

'Well...' He flicked her a wink and grinned. 'Maybe a couple of toes now and then. You have to live a little.'

Maybe he was right. Life *was* too short, but she'd never been one for taking risks. 'Running a campsite on your own is pretty adventurous.' She strolled through the gate, then turned to wait while he closed it. 'And brave.'

'Ha, yes, or stupid. It's definitely hectic. I love it though and I love this place. I've got big dreams for it.'

'Do you?'

'I sure do.'

She reached out for his hand again. He took it, doing the same pinkie move as before.

'I want it to be an adventure centre with hiking, climbing, water sports and all that jazz.' He waggled his fingers in the air.

'Amazing.' She clutched his hand tighter. When he matched the move, warmth penetrated her deep. Perfect bliss. But the heat also ignited sparks in her core, rejuvenating her weary soul.

'It sounds better than the reality. I need proper staff and hopefully, I'll get some grants, but none of it's happening as quickly as I'd like. I've never been great at waiting patiently for things to happen.'

'No?' She glanced up at him. He sounded like the opposite of her but, right now, she was channelling some of his energy.

'Nope.' He grinned at her and they walked on, stealing glances at each other while pretending to admire the woodland scenery. 'Your turn. What do you do?'

'Business administration.'

'Ouch.' He screwed up his face liked she'd slapped him. 'That sounds like my worst nightmare.'

'It's not very exciting.'

'A lot of the stuff I do isn't very exciting either.'

'Can't you hire more staff?'

'Ha! Don't get me started. I had a couple ready to take on the maintenance and daily site management but they pulled out last minute and I've not had anyone else willing to take it on. Same goes for the shop position. Louise, my brilliant assistant, left to go on maternity leave and I can't fill that post either. It's a nightmare.'

'Sounds it.' Eleanor sucked on her lip, half closing her eyes and allowing him to guide her up the winding path. Switching off her worries and concerns even for an hour hadn't been a possibility for a long time. But he was in control now. She didn't have to think, she could just while away the minutes, exist in his presence, and enjoy it for what it was. 'When I was last here, a couple owned the campsite. I don't remember their names, but Dad might.'

'Eck and Shirley. They owned it right up until I bought it. They just retired. They had Heather Glen for twenty-three years.'

'They had staff working here, didn't they? I remember a boy who helped them out, probably just during the school holidays, or he could have been their son. He always went about in wellie boots with a bucket, feeding the chickens.'

Logan laughed. 'He wasn't their son. That was me.'

'What?' Eleanor froze, tightening her grip on his hand and pulling him to a stop. She gaped at him, her pulse rate quickening. It couldn't have been him. Her brain was working overtime, summoning a recollection of the boy's face and trying to turn it into the man in front of her.

'What's wrong?' He watched her with a lopsided grin. 'I guess it's lousy that I haven't moved on in my life since I was seventeen, but hey ho.'

'It's not that.' The picture was slowly coming together; she could see the boy's face in Logan. Her first major crush blended with her latest one. 'I used to fancy you,' she murmured. Her cheeks must be beetroot by now.

'What?' He hid his face in his free hand and laughed. 'You did not.'

'I did. Or I fancied that boy. I didn't realise it was you until now. You look... Well, so different.' So much more muscly, rugged and tall, but the smile and the eyes were the same. She almost kicked herself for not noticing before, but who would have thought it?

'That's something.' He chuckled. 'I hope I've changed a bit.'

'I can't believe I'm sneaking off into the woods with the boy from the campsite. I used to dream about doing this every night in my tent.'

'No way.' He ran his fingers through his hair. 'Are you messing with me?'

'I'm serious. I once got up really early and sat on the fence close to where he... *you* fed the chickens. When you appeared, I pretended to be stuck to get you to help me down, then I was so embarrassed I ran away.'

'That was you? Wow, you've changed too, but yeah, I see it now.'

'You remember? You can't.' She must have gone from beetroot to nuclear.

'I sure do. You had super long hair, didn't you? And you wore it in a plait that went all the way down your back.'

'Yes.' She giggled, then sucked in her lip. He *did* remember.

'I secretly fancied you too,' he murmured through a smirk. 'But you had two scary big brothers hanging around, so I kept my distance. When you ran off, I thought I'd blown it somehow.'

She raised her hand to her mouth and looked away. This was unreal. 'I wish I'd held my nerve.'

'Well, it's water under the bridge now. I don't think it did either of us any lasting damage.'

She let go of his hand and stepped off the path into the lee of a tree. He followed her, snapping a twig underfoot.

Through the gap in the trees, the loch glittered in the evening sun, spreading far into the distance, banked by sloping hills and tall trees.

She sniffed and ran her fingertip under her eye.

'Hey.' Logan laid his hand on her shoulder. 'I didn't mean to upset you.'

'You didn't.' She glanced at him. 'You're right, it was a harmless crush. It's the stupidest things that set me off these days. It's not your fault; it's just the way I am since losing Mum.'

He took her hand again, softly rubbing her skin with the pad of his thumb. 'D'you... Would you like a hug?'

Through a mist of tears, she nodded. He gathered her against his hard chest and his arms wrapped tight around her like a strong protective barrier, shielding her from pain. Leaning on him lessened the chronic ache in her heart and warmth spread through her, melting the frosty pieces that had jammed in her veins and stopped her from opening up for so long. Tears fell, but they weren't just sadness and grief; happy ones mingled with them. She buried herself in his firm torso, enjoying the sense of being small and safe, inhaling his calm, manly scent.

He pulled back a little, and his thumb found the corner of her eye. Gently, he stroked away her tears. 'Oh, Eleanor. I wish I could make it better and take away the pain. But nothing can do that.'

She shook her head and gazed at him. 'I know. And this *is* helping.' His hug was the best thing she'd experienced in a long time. 'I just can't get my head around the fact that you're the boy from the campsite. I used to think about you all the time. I'd mope about on day trips, wanting to get back and see you.'

He cocked his head. 'Aww, that's cute. And good for my ego, you know?'

She blinked the last tears away and smiled. 'I fantasised you'd be my first kiss, but I couldn't escape my brothers long enough... And then that one time I had a chance, I lost my nerve.'

He ran his hand down her cheek and she leaned into it, loving the comfort it brought. 'I can't be your first, but... well, if you've got the nerve now, there are no brothers here to object.' He glanced from side to side, then raised his eyebrow a fraction. 'If you want to.'

Her heart skipped a beat, and she nodded, tilting her head to the side. Anticipation tingled through her veins. As he dipped in, she closed her eyes, cherishing every nanosecond. His lips grazed hers so softly she thought he'd changed his mind, but before she could open her eyes to check, he slipped his hand behind her head and his mouth burned hot against hers. His scent drowned her, that lush, woody, all-man fragrance. She slid her fingers around his neck, brushing against his soft hair and letting out a whimper of contended satisfaction.

The sound seemed to unlock a deeper level of desire in him, and he gently nudged her back, so she was resting against the tree. He placed a hand flat on the bark like she was his, only his, and he was guarding her. All fine with her. She was ready to yield. For the last year, she'd been the strong one, shielding her dad and her family from as much pain as she could, deflecting it or taking it for them. Now, someone was going to protect her. She could drop her guard and relax, safe in his arms.

Her heart thundered with desire and maybe she was imagining it but she was sure she could hear Logan's pounding the same rhythm. She blinked, gazing into his eyes. 'Are you ok?' she whispered.

'More than.' His palms gently glided down her upper arms. 'You?'

'All good.' She cupped his face and kissed him again, sliding her fingers across his shoulders and along the curves of his muscles, before slipping them under his arms and linking her hands around his back. The crush she had was a flickering candle next to the furnace of desire raging inside her now. She never did anything in such a rush, but she'd missed a chance years ago for a teenage kiss, and she was not going to miss anything this time. He groaned and held her close.

'Eleanor,' he whispered, still kissing her with little pecks between breaths. 'Are you sure this is ok? I mean, you said you were patient, and I'm not. Just tell me to bugger off if you want me to stop.'

'I'll do pretty much anything right now. We never know what's around the corner.' She knew that better than most. 'I'm not crazy. I'm only here for a few days, but I think I'd have regretted it if I'd let this moment pass and not kissed you.'

'Me too. Just so long as we're both on the same page.'

'Same page. This is just a kiss.' She glanced sideways. A little robin hopped off a nearby branch and skipped around their feet before flittering off. 'That doesn't mean I want to rule out more kisses for the rest of the week though.'

He laughed, resting his forehead on hers. 'A holiday fling?'

'With the boy from the campsite.'

'With a client?'

'I'll be discreet. I'll have to be. My dad definitely won't approve.'

'You're really beautiful.' He dipped in for another kiss. Eleanor savoured the taste, parting her lips and embracing every second. Life was too short to waste. Heartache might follow but it would do anyway if she gave up this chance. Their hungry lips played softly and slowly, but enough to cause a mini firework display deep in her tummy. His powerful embrace held her upright and stopped her from melting into a pool at his feet.

Light raindrops pattered through the trees, spattering the undergrowth. It started to get too heavy to ignore. 'I don't have my jacket,' she whispered through the kiss.

'Me neither.' Logan held her face and gazed into her eyes. 'I don't want to leave you.'

She placed her hands over his. 'I don't want to either, but we don't have much choice. Can I come and see you tomorrow?'

'Of course. As soon as you can. You can guarantee I'll be missing you like crazy.'

She beamed as the intensity of his look bored into hers. Everything he said was true. She could read it in him and she would miss him too.

The rain fell heavier as they walked back, but they didn't rush. They held hands, swinging them and laughing as rain splashed on their faces. Eleanor swept her arm up and dragged Logan in for another kiss. His kisses were so gentle but firm. Her wet t-shirt rubbed on his and breathing became a struggle. She trailed her fingers down his soaked back and found a way under his t-shirt to touch his skin. If she was alone, she wouldn't let him go. She'd do something she'd never done before and invite him back after a first date – if you could even call it that. But her dad would be worried, and she couldn't very well take a man back to the tent with her. Eleanor Kendrick was way too well-behaved for that. This kiss was knocking her reputation out of the park.

Logan groaned as her palms moved over him, then pulled back but continued dotting little kisses on her face like he was catching raindrops. 'Eleanor,' he murmured. 'Once we're through the gate, that's it.' More little kisses. 'We have to stop. It would just be my luck to get caught by one of the grumpy campers.'

'Is it a crime to kiss a client?'

'I can see it offending some people, so let's try and restrain ourselves, somehow.' He carried on the little kisses.

'I'm not sure I can.'

'Me neither.' He tugged her close, then leaned her back, kissing her through a laugh. She squealed and clung to him, every cell in her body exploding with delirium. 'But we need to be sensible. Ok?'

'Ok.'

'I can't believe I'm the one saying this.' He pulled her back up. 'But let's keep a cool head.'

'Ok. I'll try.'

'Let's jog. We're soaked enough.'

Eleanor stuck close to him. Their feet slapped into shallow puddles as they neared her tent. Soon they'd have to say goodbye. The canvas flapped as they drew close. He checked around, then quickly placed a peck on her cheek. She shifted her head to catch more, holding his face as rain trickled over them.

'Goodnight,' he said. 'I'll see you tomorrow.'

'Give me your number.'

'Ok, quick.' He slipped in under the cover of the trees and pulled out his phone.

She told him her number; he keyed it in and rang her. 'Now you'll have my number too.'

'I'll message you.' She stole one last kiss, then ducked around to the front of the tent. The stream babbled over the rocks as she undid the zip around the door, then stepped inside, drenched.

'There you are.' Dad looked up from his foldout seat, his head torch shining towards her like an inquisition light. 'You were away a long time. Did you get the firewood?'

'Oh.' Drat, she'd completely forgotten. 'No... It was too wet.'

'We could have left it to dry somewhere.'

'I'll get some tomorrow. I was chatting with Logan.' The heat in her cheeks was another throwback to her teenage years – not a welcome one this time. She didn't need to be embarrassed about talking to a man. Of course, *talking* was putting what they'd done in its widest form.

'Did you give him the whisky?'

'Yes, I did. Well, it's still in the car. He couldn't carry it. He was, um, doing checks and the like, then it was raining, so he dashed off, and I forgot. I'll take it to him tomorrow. He's pleased with it.' She was babbling and couldn't stop. She'd take it to him right now, but she didn't trust herself to hand it over and leave. Tomorrow would do.

June in the Highlands meant long daylight hours and, even though it was close to ten when she made the last dash for the showers, it wasn't dark, though the rain made it dim. The showers were well heated and Eleanor made the most of the toastie water, her mind zipping back to Logan and those hot kisses in the woods. What was happening to her? She'd never done anything this mad in her life. Ever. Towelling herself quickly dry, she jumped into her fleece pyjamas and pulled her waterproofs over the top, then traipsed back to the tent. Her dad was already in his sleeping pod, though it was unzipped. Eleanor bent down and kissed him goodnight as he sat propped up in his fold-out camp bed – it was an easier height for him, unlike her sleeping mat that was 'too low for his old knees to get down to'.

'Night, Dad, sleep well. I love you.'

'You too, lovely girl.' He squeezed her hand. 'I can't thank you enough for bringing me here and looking after me. You're a godsend and I don't know what I'd do without you.'

'You don't have to worry about that.' She patted the back of his hand. 'I'm not going anywhere. Night-night.' She shucked off her waterproofs, crawled across the tent and climbed into her sleeping pod. 'Thanks for the hot water bottle.' She snuggled down into her cosy sleeping bag.

'No problem, sweetheart,' Dad said.

Her eyes misted over and she cuddled in deeper. The familiar beat of rain drummed on the canvas. No, she wasn't going anywhere. And that made this week with Logan even more important. A week of something special with him was better than a lifetime of nothing, and she was ready to grab it head on. Good little Eleanor was about to embark on a holiday fling and there was no time like the present to get started.

Chapter Seven

Logan

Rain drummed on the roof of Logan's static caravan. He stared at the dark ceiling from his bed, not convinced he wasn't about to get a large drip square on the forehead, followed by more on the covers, the floor, everywhere. Like everything else on this site, his accommodation had seen better days. That wasn't what was preventing him from closing his eyes though. He took one last look at his phone. The little green dot beside Eleanor's picture had gone and her last message from over two hours ago was still the same.

ELEANOR: Night-night, sleep tight! See you soon x

Right, away it goes. He put it beside the bed. If he didn't have to be on call 24/7, he'd switch it off. How long had he been scrolling? Duncan, his mum, his sister Sophie and his cousin Matthew would not be thrilled that his insomnia had led to him messaging them late into the night just for something to do. Another cousin, Cha, who was often up late, had eventually pinged him, saying, *'get to sleep, you tosser, or I'll come round and whack you over the head. That'll put you out for the next few hours. Luv ya! x'*

He smirked at the blank ceiling. Maybe her plan wasn't a bad one. What other solutions were there for getting any sleep?

Only a few hours and he'd see Eleanor again. Only a few days and he'd be liking photos on social media with no hope of seeing the real woman for maybe as long as a year. With a growl, he rolled over and buried his head in the pillow. *We have to make the most of this.* Why was he making such a big deal out of it? It was a fling. He needed to make it the best fling ever, but how the hell could he fit it in? With all the work he had to do, it wasn't like he could sneak off on a day trip with her. Even if he could, her dad would be there. It just couldn't work, and that hurt his heart like hell.

He'd split with his previous girlfriend because of his lack of time. She wanted him to have a nine-to-five job with weekends off – a nice, simple ask in her mind. But that wasn't him. He wasn't a put-on-a-suit-and-go-to-the-office kind of guy.

With daylight hitting just a few hours after sunset, he woke from barely a wink of sleep. Groaning, he sat up. No point staying in bed. It clearly didn't want him in it. He got up and headed to the shop.

'May as well use the time wisely.' He yawned the words at the kettle. Maybe he could finally get around to filling in his latest grant application. It was a tedious data entry process he wished he'd started last night. Its soporific value was better than overdosing on Nytol.

He lost track of time, staring at the screen and trying to conjure some pizazz into the application. Whatever he wrote sounded forced. How could he explain his vision in a hundred words or less? He'd just got on a roll when there was a knock on the door. He jumped, glancing at the clock on the wall. Almost eight. Shit, that was when he usually opened the shop. Maybe someone was desperate for a morning snack. Before he was halfway across the room, the face at the door became clear and he smiled. Eleanor.

'Well, hello, you.' He opened the door and let her in. Before he could say another word, she threw an arm around his neck and kissed him slap on the lips. The softness of her skin sent charged currents through his weary body, wakening all the nerve ends and priming him for action. He rested his hands on her slender hips. So much for patience and discretion. The thought made him laugh into the kiss. Eleanor smiled too and inched closer. He held her tight, cradling the back of her head and threading his fingers through her soft hair. When her tongue found his, he moaned, now fully awake and ready for anything.

'I missed you,' she murmured, pulling back, her eyes still closed.

'Mutual.' He placed a featherlight kiss on her forehead.

She let out a whimper, then opened her eyes. 'And you forgot this.' She held up the bottle of whisky in the hand not clamped around him.

‘I had other things on my mind. Thanks again.’ He took the bottle and smiled at it. ‘I better hide this in case someone tries to buy it.’ He stowed it behind the counter, then leaned across. Eleanor took his hands in hers, beaming.

‘I wasn’t sure if you’d be here this early. I just had a hunch,’ she said.

‘I couldn’t sleep.’ He lifted her hands to his lips and kissed them.

‘Me neither.’

He smiled, holding eye contact, then shook his head. ‘What are we like?’

‘Crazy.’ She peered into the space behind him. ‘What were you doing?’

‘Filling out a funding application.’

‘For the adventure centre?’

‘I’m trying to get a grant to improve facilities at the old water sports centre, but it’s a bit of a stretch. The examples on this form are for play parks and trim trails. I’m not sure Heather Glen fits the criteria.’ He sighed.

‘Hmm, yes, I see what you mean. Could I have a nosey in the office? I’ve always wondered what it’s like in there.’

‘Sure.’ He released her and she slid around. ‘Though it’s not exciting and it’s a mess.’

She took his hand on the way past and dragged him into the back room. ‘I guess we could make it exciting.’

'You told me yesterday you were patient, discreet and a goody two-shoes.' He tugged gently to stall her. 'I don't believe a word of it. You're completely unstoppable.'

'Eek. I know. Should I pipe down? Am I being really ridiculous?'

'About as ridiculous as I feel.' He wrapped his arms around her waist and drew her close. 'I wish I could just shut up shop and spend the day with you.'

'I wish you could too, but there's also my dad.'

'Yeah, it's his holiday too. I don't want to ruin it for him.' He rubbed the tip of his nose against hers. 'It's not like I can anyway. I'm stuck here.'

'You don't sound like you really enjoy doing this.'

'I love it... Well, not this bit exactly. Office work does my head in. And I'm not fussed about cleaning toilets either. But I've had no applicants for any of the posts.'

'I wish I could help. I know some tricks for advertising.'

'Thanks, but I don't want you wasting your holiday doing dry stuff like this.'

'I don't mind. I could drop by later for an hour or so and give you a hand.'

He tucked a stray hair behind her ear. 'If you drop by later, the last thing I'm going to want to do is work.'

She leaned up and her lips met his again, warm and eager. He went with it, clutching her face, fully aware of the dangers but not caring. Moments like this were precious.

A crashing sound broke them apart. 'That bloody door.' Logan gritted his teeth and looked heavenward. 'I better go.'

'Me too,' she whispered. 'But how will I escape?'

'Out there.' He kicked a box out of the way of the back door and unlocked it. 'It comes out beside my static. Message me. I'll catch you later.'

'Ok.' She blew him a kiss and snuck out.

He pinched out his t-shirt – *bet I look a state* – and nipped into the shop. His heart sank and he hitched on his smile, coming face to face with the woman whose tent he'd moved the previous day. She narrowed her eyes a little and squinted past him towards the office door. He continued to smile. Frankly, what happened in that office was his business. How did she know that wasn't his wife he was in there with? As long as she hadn't seen Eleanor. If she had and then spotted her getting into a tent, he was in trouble. This was exactly the kind of moaning Minnie who loved to complain. He wasn't going to give her any rope. Unfortunately, he was perfectly capable of hanging himself.

'I thought you opened at eight.' She gave the sign on the door a very pointed glare.

He glanced at the clock. It was six minutes past. Three hundred and sixty seconds late. Three hundred short seconds spent with Eleanor. 'Sorry. It was open. I was just in the office. I had some business to attend to. How can I help you?'

'I don't suppose you have anything to get rid of midges. That pitch we have might be quieter, but we're being eaten alive.'

'We have a few options.' Though if it were up to him, the midges could have her, especially if it kept her out of his hair. 'Repellent spray, candles and midge nets you can wear.'

'I don't like the sound of nets.' She dismissed the idea with a flap of her hand. 'Do the other things actually work?'

'Some people have success with them.' He tapped his foot and glanced at the clock. Every second away from Eleanor seemed like wasted time. But she would be away with her dad shortly anyway. Finally, the woman chose a bottle of midge repellent. She lingered near the door like she was inspecting the hinges before finally leaving. Logan slumped into the seat behind the desk.

Typically, on the day when he'd welcome a stream of customers to divert his mind, there was no one else. He returned to the computer. Now was the time to tackle some of the paperwork before his first round at ten.

As long as he shut off his brain to external factors, he got on ok, except Eleanor was the *only* factor he cared about right now, and she was the number one thing he wanted to think about. He shifted up and down, moved things around on his desk, and attempted to make things more conducive to work with, but none of it distracted him. 'I'm seriously fucked,' he muttered. What the hell would Saturday be like when she went home? Would he just accept it once she was gone? Or should he try to fathom ways to see her again? Long distance? Could that work?

At quarter to ten, he gave up trying to work and nipped out of the back door to load up the golf cart. It rattled on the gravel around the edge of the shop as he drove it to the front. He hopped out to lock up the shop and spied Eleanor striding towards him. His heart flipped and a smile spread across his face. What a goof he must look like. Every time she was in view, he started grinning.

'Hi.' She half ran to reach him.

'I thought you'd gone out with your dad.'

'He just wants a quiet day birdwatching.'

'And you?'

She pulled a little shrug and a fake *I don't know* smile, then looked him up and down. Logan glanced over her shoulder in case any nosey campers were about.

'I'm happy to spend every second I can with you.' He took a step closer. 'Unfortunately, I have to clean the showers and the loos first. The never-ending glamour of my life.'

Her expression dulled and sadness clouded her features. 'Oh right... Well, I'll...'

'Hey.' He closed the gap between them and wrapped her in a hug. He'd do anything to make her smile, though he couldn't see that cleaning toilets would do that. 'It's a gross job, but you're welcome to join me.'

'Can I?'

'Sure, but it's not likely to be your most romantic date.'

'I don't care. I just want to be wherever you are.'

'Oh god.' A lump rose in his throat. 'You're going to make me greet.'

'That's such a funny Scottish thing to say.'

'Well, I'm a funny Scottish man.'

'You certainly are.'

He rubbed her back and placed a lingering kiss on her cheek, though his eyes scanned about for busybodies. She melted into him and he gently rocked her for a few seconds. His heart swelled with love. *Yes, love.* Shock waves ricocheted through his body, but he didn't let go. He couldn't *love* Eleanor. Not after this short a time. And he mustn't anyway. Flings were about fun not love. Love was a serious business and he wasn't good at anything serious. 'Come on, jump into my cart. I'll introduce you to life in the fast lane.'

She giggled and hopped in beside him. He started it up and they both burst out laughing as the cart trundled along the track with the two of them squashed in beside each other.

Outside the shower block, he jumped out and put up the sign warning campers it was out of order while he cleaned.

'One day I'm hoping to get some glamping pods up there.' He pointed to the field that would host the Segway later in the week. 'But the company I was dealing with went bust and I haven't found another supplier yet. It's all these things that add up and I just don't have the hours in a day to deal with them.' Or the focus and brain space right now.

'I've always fancied one of those glamping pods. Especially the ones with a wood burner.'

'Once they're up, feel free to come back.'

He caught her eye and gave her a one-sided smile, mirroring her look of dismay. Neither of them really wanted to remind themselves how little time they had.

He opened the door to the shower block. 'Oh no.' The tiled floor was covered in wet grass. 'People are so gross. I leave mops and a request to clean up after use, but I still come into a ridiculous mess every day.'

'I know. People just don't care. They think they're on holiday so it's up to someone else to clean but it's so inconsiderate.'

'Exactly.' He dragged the overflowing bin to the door. 'You can wait out here if you want. I can't put you through this.'

'No, I'll help.' She followed him in, carrying an armful of cleaning fluids. Then she pulled on a pair of rubber gloves and started humming like Cinderella as she sprayed.

'I've never known anyone who's so cheerful about cleaning.'

'It's the company.' She tipped him a wink.

'Yeah, it sure makes things a lot more fun.' He ran the water over the stall and rinsed away the cleaning fluid. As he hung up the showerhead, a hand tapped his shoulder. Turning, he barely had a second before arms wrapped around his neck. Her mouth was on his. He backed her up against the wall and devoured her. 'Jesus, Eleanor. You are definitely not a goody two-shoes. You are very, very naughty.'

She let out a little giggle, beaming like she was extra pleased with herself. Her gorgeous blue eyes twinkled. 'I've finally found my inner bad girl.'

'I like her.' He dipped in and kissed her neck. 'An awful lot. But this kind of behaviour in the campsite showers is what gets campers kicked out. I'm not exactly setting a great example.'

'I guess not, but you are fulfilling all of my fantasies.'

'Am I indeed?' He raised an eyebrow. 'Well, let's crack on with work. Once it's done, we can fulfil some more.'

They jumped into the cart and motored towards the first set of bins. 'Shit,' he muttered.

'What?'

Complaining camper woman was marching towards the shop. If she looked left, she'd spot the two of them. Logan drew himself up tall, trying to dwarf Eleanor out of sight. 'That woman is a pain in the arse.'

'Drop me here,' Eleanor said. 'I'll nip back to the woods and check on Dad. I'll come find you shortly.'

'Ok.' He pulled on the brakes and parked behind an enormous green and grey dome tent. 'Here.' Before she jumped out, he planted a soft kiss on her lips. His eyes closed and he almost forgot where they were.

'Later.' She pulled back, putting her finger to his lips. 'Patience.'

'Hello, sensible Eleanor. Pleased to meet you.' He shook her hand. 'Where have you been hiding? I've heard so much about you.'

'Stop your nonsense.' She grinned and backed out of the cart. 'I'll see you later.'

He hovered until the complaining woman got to the shop. She tried the door, then shielded her eyes and peered in the window. Logan hung back, still watching as she turned away, frowning and shaking her head. She glanced around before sidling around the edge of the shop. Where the hell was she going? That path only led to his static. She wasn't going to try his door, was she? A few moments later, she emerged, muttering to herself and marched towards the shower block.

Logan drove the cart down the path on the other side and parked at the back. So what if she was annoyed? He couldn't be bothered dealing with her right now. He opened the shop and went straight onto the computer. The screen looked bright and happy. With the prospect of seeing Eleanor again, he started typing and words flowed onto the application form. It was like he was describing it to her, the most beautiful place in the world, full of glittering potential.

Within half an hour, he was finished, and the result made him slouch back in relief. Who could resist this application? After rereading it twice, he tapped his finger on the send button and off it went. He shoved his hands behind his head and twirled the seat with his foot. Now he just had to wait... The thing he was the world's worst at doing.

Chapter Eight

Eleanor

Sunlight poked its way through the trees. The branches swayed in the breeze, making the shadows dance. Bees buzzed around the bushes, and the stream babbled alongside. Chapel Brampton, where Eleanor lived, was pretty too and had green spaces all around, but Heather Glen was so far removed from her normal world. Maybe it was the untamed splendour or the sheer unfamiliarity that made it so appealing. Everything was so beautiful. White and blue flowers dotted the dappled ground. She wanted to sing. How ridiculous could she be? This was the Logan effect in action.

She craned her neck, scanning around outside the tent for her dad. Where was he? She nipped the skin at her throat as the familiar tremors of worry started again. 'Dad!' She called in a shaky voice, nowhere near loud enough to carry into the woods. He still wasn't walking right, so he couldn't have gone too far. She set off past the tent, following the stream along a narrow path. If she followed it onwards, it met the main road to Glenbriar. Surely he wouldn't have gone that way?

She quickened her pace, marching towards the end. It quickly became obvious her dad wasn't there. The path widened and no one was on it. A car swished past on the road ahead.

She pulled out her phone. Nothing. Well, strictly speaking, that wasn't true. There were messages in abundance from people in her real life, but she didn't want to reply to them. Somehow their concerns didn't matter when she was so far away, and if she replied, she was admitting to the existence of that world when she just wanted to enjoy living in her dream world right here.

Dad had a mobile, but he was no great shakes at using it. Reception was so patchy anyway she couldn't guarantee it would ring even if she called it. She tried it, but after a few rings, it went to voicemail. She briefly checked to make sure there were no important messages but what to wear to Alix's party and the lock breaking on the office door just weren't of any interest.

Where to look now? Should she get help? Logan again? Her mind couldn't shake him even as niggles about her missing dad gnawed at her tummy.

What would her friends, brothers, and work colleagues make of Eleanor Kendrick and the holiday fling? 'They wouldn't believe it,' she told the trees as she marched back towards the tent. She could hardly believe it herself. And she wasn't done. She had every intention of seeing him as often as possible, assuming she could find her dad first. Where was he? She needed to know his whereabouts at all times, but the flip side of having him nearby meant there was no chance of a 'sleepover' with Logan. Her starved body was crying out for him. But wait. What madness was this? She was genuinely contemplating the next stage of the fling. Her goody two-shoes had been well and truly abandoned and she was strutting in with stilettoes like a catwalk pro. When had she been this physically drawn to anyone? Never that she could recall. It was new and strange and not at all like her. She'd only scratched the surface of what a relationship with him might be like. But her mind wasn't at liberty to play with the ideas. A heavy weight and a queasy niggle squashed the fluttering butterflies in her tummy. Where the hell was her dad?

What should she do now? Maybe she should walk back the other way. Would Dad have tried to get to the loch? Going over that hill was quite a climb and he shouldn't do anything too strenuous on his ankle. Her tummy rumbled. Since meeting Logan, normal things like food didn't seem important either. Her head was light and a bit dizzy. What use would she be to anyone if she keeled over? She speed-walked back to the tent, unzipped it from the bottom and pulled back the door.

'Oh, hello,' Dad said.

'Good god.' Eleanor jumped. 'You're here. I've been wandering about looking for you.'

'I came in about ten minutes ago.'

'I must just have missed you.' The tension in her shoulders lifted.

'It's so midgy out there.'

'Yes, they're annoying. I popped back for something to eat. Have you had enough birdwatching? Do you want to go out for lunch or anything?'

'I will if you want to.' He closed a book on his lap.

Her heart pulled both ways. Of course, she wanted to take her dad out for lunch, but she also wanted to see Logan, and time was so precious. 'I'll happily take you.'

'You're a good girl, but I'd be just as happy with a sandwich. If I open the flaps and let some light in, I'll read all afternoon, but that's not much of a holiday for you. I don't want to bore you, not after you brought me all this way.'

'I don't mind.' Her words tumbled out. The words she knew would lead her astray – again. *And why shouldn't I? You only live once.* 'I'm happy to go for a walk on my own.'

Dad tilted his head, his eyes mournful. 'I'd appreciate that, and if you're really sure, I think my ankle feels almost back to normal. If I rest it today, I'll be able to do something a bit more exciting tomorrow.'

'Sure.' She smiled as she took bread from the food box and cheese from the cooler. 'Sounds perfect. Let me fix you a sandwich.'

'I was hoping you'd say that.'

Dad had never been skilled in domestics. This was the practicality of life without Mum. At seventy-five, he was used to a life where the gender roles of his generation were clear. Mum had cooked, cleaned, done washing and household chores. Dad worked, brought home good money, cut the grass and weeded the garden, washed cars, and drove Mum to the shops. He'd retired at seventy and had a pension ready to see them good for the rest of their lives. But Mum's life had been cut short and Dad wasn't in a place to learn new tricks or have his situation cast back in his face. Yes, maybe, he should have learned to do all these things before, but he hadn't and that was that. Having to learn now would add too much stress and pain to the grief he was already under. Eleanor had moved back home when Mum was sick to help him with these practical jobs, as well as support him through the emotional trauma.

She set up his food for him and spent some time chatting while she nibbled a few crackers with cheese. After they'd finished, she loaded the dishes into the pop-up wash bowl. 'I might take these and wash them. I can leave them on the shelf by the sink and go for my walk. Will you be ok on your own?'

'Of course, yes. I've got Bill Bryson to keep me busy.' He patted the book on his lap. Eleanor lifted the washbowl, gave Dad a peck on the cheek and almost tripped in her rush to get out of the tent. She hotfooted it across the grass with the bowl of dishes tightly in her grip.

Goody two-shoes Eleanor had just lied to her dad. Shocking, but a white lie. She would wash up and go for a walk. But that walk would only be a few metres along the path and across the courtyard to the shop.

The sinks were in a wooden shelter along with some picnic tables, a microwave and a kettle. She'd hidden in here from the midges as a child, while her parents packed away the tent and loaded the car. She pulled up her sleeves and made short shrift of the dishes. Beside the sinks were some empty shelves, and she pushed the bowl onto one, leaving the dishes to air dry. With a feverish flutter in her chest, she drifted across the courtyard to the shop. The noisy door creaked as she entered.

'Well, hello.' Logan's smiling face peered over the counter. 'I thought you'd forgotten about me.'

'As if.' She sidled over and leaned on the surface, gazing down at him as he sat in front of the admissions screen. 'I just had to sort my dad out.'

'How's he doing? Is his ankle ok now?'

'He thinks if he rests it today, he'll be fine to go somewhere tomorrow.'

'Awesome. Do you think he'd fancy a Segway ride?'

'Er... What?'

'I forgot to say, I've hired a bunch of Segways for the day and you and your dad are welcome to come and join the fun.'

'I can't see my dad doing that... or me. I'm completely unco-ordinated.'

Logan smirked, holding his expression steady for a second before he burst into a laugh. 'If you change your mind, I'll make sure I catch you on film. Sounds like it could be entertaining.'

'Hmm, not if I sue you,'

'True.' He looked up with a half-serious face. 'But if you change your mind, the offer's there.'

She leaned in closer. 'You know I can't stand being away from you for too long, so I'll probably end up doing it.'

'You're awesome.' He got to his feet and cupped her cheeks, planting a kiss on her mouth. She closed her eyes, savouring his warm lips.

The door creaked open and he shot back into his seat, almost missing and just steadying himself on the edge. Eleanor pressed the back of her hand over her mouth to stifle a laugh, pretending to browse postcards on the counter. Logan gave her a *get-me-out-of-here* look, and she edged to the shelf by the window before she burst into a fit of giggles. What had got into her? She was hysterical. Peering out of the corner of her eye at the customer who'd just arrived, she mulled over a camping kettle. A woman chatted to two kids, then ushered them to the counter with some snacks while Eleanor continued to browse the cooking equipment and camping stoves.

As soon as the customers left, she met Logan's eye, and they dissolved into giggles.

'Oh my god.' He clapped his hand to his forehead. 'You wanted to play out some teenage fantasies. Well, there's one of my teenage nightmares right there. Fancy getting caught kissing my crush when I'm meant to be working.'

'And did you kiss a lot of crushes when you worked here as a boy?'

'Sure, hundreds.'

'Really?'

'No, course not.' He smirked. 'I didn't kiss anyone here and the only crush I remember is you. Though I still can't quite believe you're the girl with the almost-stuck foot and the long plait.'

She bunched her now mid-length hair and pulled it out to the side. 'It might still plait up, but I can't sit on it anymore.'

'It suits you just fine. And now your foot's not pretending to be stuck, it's better too.'

She buried her face in her hands. 'My none-so-subtle attempt at attracting your attention.'

'Well, you have it now. I'll give you as much attention as you like.'

Her stomach swooped at the thought of what that might mean. Just how far was he prepared to take this holiday fling? She was ready to lay herself on a plate for him. Her best friend, Hattie, might have a heart attack if she knew – she definitely wouldn't believe it. 'Who are you and what have you done with Eleanor?' she'd say.

'Would you like some help with the staff advert?' Eleanor said, flapping away Hattie's imaginary words. 'I could show you a few things.'

'I bet you could.' He clicked a little wink and beamed. She shook her head. He was really naughty... though right now, she was just as bad. 'Come round then.'

She edged around the counter and slipped behind him as he perched on the office chair. He clicked off the screen on the admissions' computer and her gaze landed on his broad shoulders. She wanted to touch them. They looked so strong and capable. Her restraint was back in Northamptonshire, and it could stay there. She sidled up behind him and placed her palms on his shoulders.

He flipped her a brief glance, raising his hand to cover hers, and she massaged along his shoulder blade, dipping in to kiss the side of his neck just below his ear. He let out a groan and dropped his head back, his eyes closing. 'Too good, Eleanor, but if that door opens, we're in the shit.'

'I know I should stop,' she whispered. 'But I don't want to.'

'Me neither.' He jumped to his feet and took a deep breath, adjusting his jeans. 'Right... um, if you go into the office, I'll show you what I've got.'

'There's an offer I can't refuse.'

'Steady.' He pulled a frown but was still smiling. 'We're already on thin ice.'

She chuckled and stepped into the office.

'I'll log you on to the laptop and show you what I have already. Realistically, I need someone to do the cleaning five out of the seven days and someone to look after the shop between nine and five – it could be shiftwork or a job-share. I advertised it before as a live-in job for a couple or two friends, but that obviously isn't working, so I'll also need a general maintenance worker.'

'Ok, let me have a look and I'll fix it.'

'You superstar.'

Logan typed in the login details and stood back to let her have the seat, which wasn't easy given that the office was barely big enough for the desk with no one sitting at it. Backed up against the bookshelves, he pointed her to the list of files and she clicked through them.

'I can make you some new ads and clarify the details. You can either print them and have them in shop windows in the village or run them online. I know a few good sites for that too.'

'Wow, great. That's so awesome. And if you work on that, I'll try to think of a way to pay you.'

'I accept kisses and all major forms of cuddle cards.'

'You're so cute and damned irresistible.' He bent down like he was going to kiss her cheek, but the rickety door banged open. 'Bugger. I better see to the customers.'

'Ok,' she whispered. She worked through the files, making them into creative ad copy using Logan's catchy wording from the original ad. He was good at that. It was his presentation that needed improving. Listening to him talking to customers just through the door was cheering and strengthening enough to make it not feel like work. She only broke a couple of times to send messages to her friends. Wi-Fi was good in the office, so she may as well make use of it while she could. She had to make some kind of effort to prove she hadn't vanished completely. She didn't tell them what she was doing and definitely not what she wanted to do. Little tingles of pleasure darted through her fingers and she smiled. If she could just keep this feeling everything would be fine, but if she thought too deeply about any of it – especially if her mind strayed past Saturday – she'd curl back into her shell and never come out again.

'How's it going?' Logan poked his head around the door.

'Come see if you like.'

He nipped in and peered over her shoulder. 'Wow, you're talented.'

'It's just my job.'

'Maybe so, but it's awesome. I would apply for that... You know, if I wasn't already doing it.' He flipped out his phone. 'Meh, look at the time. I need to do the afternoon rounds.'

'I'd like to come with you, but I think it's better if I stay and finish this.'

'Ok. I'll close the shop and lock you in. You're mine and there's no escape,' he added in a deep, spooky voice that sounded like Dracula. It set off her giggles again. She'd reverted into her teen self.

'Oh no, save me from this maniac.' She threw up her hands.

'There's no saving you,' he said in the same voice, pouncing on her from behind and wrapping his arms about her. 'I want you all to myself.' He spun the chair, so she was facing him and leaned over, bracing his hands on the arms, caging her. 'You're mine.' He dipped in and kissed her.

The depth of the kiss took her breath away, and she moaned as his tongue met hers, throwing a flame of lust into her gut. He shook the chair gently, still holding it fast, and gave a low wicked laugh.

She squealed and giggled. 'You can have me, I surrender.'

'That easy, huh?'

'Yup.'

He chuckled and the sound tickled her ear. 'I'll be back as quick as I can then.' He pressed one more lingering kiss on her lips before he left. Giddy waves crashed through her. She wanted to soak up how coveted and special he made her feel. Just part of her holiday fling. *Yes, that's it.* All part of the holiday fun. How could it be anything more?

As she continued playing about with ad layouts, messages pinged intermittently. Some of them she replied to, but she didn't want to say too much in case she somehow betrayed herself. Who would believe what Miss Goody Two-Shoes was up to? She didn't believe it herself. If her friends got wind of it, they'd want to know everything, and she didn't want that. Explaining it to herself was hard enough.

Chapter Nine

Eleanor

A clicking sound, followed by the rickety door opening, announced Logan's return. He burst straight into the office, whistling. 'You're still here then. I don't have to ride out with my hounds and search for you.'

'Not this time.'

He peered over her shoulder at the screen. 'Oh, Eleanor, what's all this?' He leaned over the seat and wrapped his arms around her from behind. 'Check this out. I honestly can't thank you enough. You're an angel.'

She put her hands over his and leaned her head on him. 'I don't mind helping.'

'But to do all this on your holiday.' He kissed her cheek. 'I really do like you. You're awesome, and I'm not just saying it because you've done all this. I just really like you.'

She bit her lip, holding back the surge of emotion building inside her. 'I like you too,' she whispered, only just managing to get the words out. They were perfectly true but didn't seem enough. *Like* wasn't strong enough for how she felt. 'I just don't want to think too hard about it.'

'Yeah, I know. Here.' He straightened up and spun the office seat around. She giggled through the mist in her eyes. 'Stand up.' He took her hands and tugged her to her feet. 'No pressure. I just wanted you to know how I feel.'

She held onto him and looked directly into his eyes. 'I feel it too, but it scares me as much as it thrills me. I don't want to get emotionally attached to someone I can't be with. It hurt too much when I lost Mum... before that even.' She gazed towards the window. 'I had a boyfriend when Mum got diagnosed. At first, he was great, but when Mum deteriorated, and I started going to my parents' house more often, he got annoyed.' She shook her head, sighing at the memory. 'I didn't prioritise him, so he left.'

'That's shit,' Logan said. 'He should have been there to support you. Selfish dick.'

'But the same thing could happen again. I have to help Dad. He's as helpless as a child. I can't guarantee I'll ever be able to prioritise a relationship.' Maybe that was why she'd let herself go with Logan. Their relationship had very set boundaries. It would end on Saturday before things could go too far and they had to worry about logistics or the future. They could enjoy the good bits for a little while.

He let go of one of her hands and ran his finger down her cheek. 'You're an awesome person, no matter what happens.'

'Thank you. So are you.'

'How about I shut up shop for the day and we go for a walk? Then if your dad asks where you went, you can tell him.'

'Ok. But do you have time?'

'I'll make time for you. This is important.'

Her chest filled to bursting point. *He's really going to do this... for me. He thinks I'm important.* She let out a giggle that verged on a squeal while inside her head a little jig had started.

'We could go to the loch; it's pretty over there,' he said.

'Anywhere.'

He took her hand and led her onto the path that wound past the static where he lived. She held on tight, her energy levels boosted by the contact. They trekked up a hill before descending through an open grassy stretch towards the loch.

'There's potential for more glamping pods up here.' He gestured across the landscape. 'But I'd need a new shower block. I couldn't expect people to walk from up here every time they needed the loo.'

'This would be a lovely place. With the view to the loch. What about log cabins? People love them. You could call them Loch Hideaways.'

'Yeah, that's an idea. They could have their own bathrooms. But I'd definitely need staff for that. I couldn't clean cabins as well as everything else.'

'You'll get there.' Eleanor patted his arm. 'You have the vision and with a little help, this place will be the best.'

'Thank you.' He squeezed her hand in his.

The loch sprawled in front of them, broad and grey, with hills surrounding it on every side.

'That doesn't look too good.' She frowned at a dilapidated old shed with rotten wood and a fallen-in roof.

'Yeah. That's supposedly the boat shed and water sports centre.' He let out a sigh. 'It kind of spoils the fact that this place is called Heather Glen Campsite and Water Sports when I can't even offer them anymore. All the paddleboards and wetsuits were ruined when the roof came off, not that it was the most watertight building in the first place.'

'That's so sad.'

'The good news is, I had budgeted for a new boathouse with proper storage, a changing area, toilets and room for a drinks machine and snack fridge. So that's going ahead in the autumn, assuming there are no more setbacks. Just a pity I'll miss the whole summer season.'

'That is such a shame.' She glimpsed a little island not too far from the shore. 'My dad forbade my brothers and me from coming here when we were kids. He said it was really dangerous.'

'I suppose it is if you wade out too far and can't swim.'

'I can swim, but there's no danger I'd be going in there.'

'No?' Logan raised his brows.

'Well, obviously. People don't swim in there, do they?'

'Sure they do. I've swum in there loads of times. It's great.'

'Isn't it freezing?'

'Yeah, but it's good for you.'

She gaped at him. 'Like shock therapy or something?'

He chuckled and rubbed her hand with his thumb, sending a thrill up her arm. 'Let's walk to the far side. There's a quiet little bay down there. It's a bit more secluded.'

'And why do we need somewhere quiet and secluded?' She arched an eyebrow. Just what was he planning? Something that would normally send her pulse flying for all the wrong reasons? But alarm bells weren't ringing and her racing mind concocted all number of exciting ideas before he could answer.

'I'm going to swim.' He flicked her a wink. 'But I forgot my costume, so we don't want any hikers getting an eyeful.'

Her eyes popped. 'Just me then.'

'I'm sure you can handle it.'

She covered her mouth, and the giggles hit her again. 'That sounds a bit suggestive.'

'Shit.' He looked away and laughed too. 'It does, doesn't it?'

They grinned at each other, still sniggering, and he led her to his quiet spot, a little glade surrounded by trees and scrubby bushes where the loch bent around, making a small pool.

'You're not seriously going in, are you?'

'Yeah, why not?'

Eleanor tapped the grass at the side of the loch with her walking shoe. 'What if you get into trouble and can't swim back? I'm not that good a swimmer; it's not like I could rescue you.'

'I'm not going in far. Don't panic. But avert your eyes if you like. Or not. I'm not bothered either way.' He tugged his t-shirt over his head and she held her breath, feasting on every curve of his chest and torso. Wow. Ok. She'd been able to visualise his shape through his clothes, but having it bared before her like this stole the air from her lungs. He was fit, really fit. Outdoor-man style, not ripped from the gym. Rugged and much more her thing. Her heart tremored as he toed off his shoes, pulled off his socks and undid the button on his jeans. She half wanted to look away, but she couldn't. Her pulse sped up. With a grin, he whipped down his jeans and boxer briefs in one go, hopping to get them off the end of his leg.

She covered her mouth as he leapt around. The humour masked her hot cheeks, hyper heartbeat, and the desire to grab him.

'So slick.' He finally tugged the jeans off the end of his legs, keeping his back to her. 'You see, I've got it all.' He rolled his eyes and facepalmed.

'I'm not complaining.' She couldn't hide her smile, eyeing his tight backside.

'Yeah, well, you're easy, remember?' He winked over his shoulder as he waded into the loch.

'My god, please don't drown.'

'I am your god and I will not drown.' He pulled up his fists and flexed his muscles as his waist sank beneath the water. 'I might freeze though. Jesus, it's colder than I remember.'

'But so good for you.' She folded her arms and raised an eyebrow.

A grin split his face. 'Come and join me.' He turned to face her and opened his arms.

'I can't. It's not going to happen.'

He sank slowly downwards until only the tips of his shoulders, his neck and head were visible. 'Then you'll have to cuddle me dry.'

'Ok. I'll try that.'

When he ducked under, her palpitations reached fever point, but he surfaced seconds later and ran his hands across his head, slicking his soaked hair back. He kicked off and swam a little way along the edge. The water rippled over his skin, making it look pale and deathly beneath the surface. She watched him for a few seconds, then stooped and picked up his clothes, turning them the right way, folding them neatly and stacking them. It seemed better than having them strewn across the grass. Plonking herself down beside the neat pile, she pulled her legs up to her chest, assuming she was in for a long wait. The thought had barely slipped into her mind when he swam towards the shore and started to wade out. Holy hell. Her heart flipped. She really got an eyeful. This was like a voyeur cam with a model tailor-made to suit her every fantasy.

Her eyes travelled upwards, taking in every beautiful inch. He was so perfectly proportioned and well-defined but real, nothing plastic looking, waxed or steroid built. Some dark hair covered his body, not excessively, just enough to look rugged. She only reached his face when he was almost upon her. He grinned and dropped down beside her, resting his elbow on his knee, his skin no longer pale but subtly tanned and shining with water beads.

'You're so shameless.' She sucked on her lip. 'Strutting about naked like this.'

'It's just a body.' He ruffled his wet hair. 'Seen one, seen 'em all.'

'I'm not sure that's true.'

'Lol. Maybe not. I don't do this for everyone, you know? It just feels ok with you.' He leaned forward and pressed his forehead against hers. She wrapped her arms around his wet body. His skin was cold, and she clamped her hands firmly into his back, trying to create heat. He shuffled closer, slid his arms around her waist, and rested his head on her shoulder. Something about the way he was lying naked in her arms was like he'd wholly given himself to her. Literally laid himself bare and handed himself up to her mercy.

'Aren't you freezing?' she said.

'No. I'm just happy.'

'Me too.' She stroked her fingers through his wet hair. He closed his eyes and gently kissed her neck, his hot breath tickling her. She smiled and sent up a silent wish. *Please let this moment last forever.*

Chapter Ten

Logan

'Let's not do anything too risky out here.' Logan huddled close to Eleanor. A slight breeze skimmed his naked skin, reminding him he should feel cold, but where her fingers clung to him, warmth burned like a firebrand. Flames consumed his insides, scorching him with an urge to hold on to her and never let go. Her proximity was generating enough heat to create diamonds.

'Ok.' The word fell like a soft kiss on his neck.

'It's not that I don't want to,' he said. 'Just doing anything out here is a bad idea. Anyone could walk past. Swimming is one thing, but... well, you know.'

'Yes. I do. So you better get your clothes on and stop teasing me.'

'Ok... But wait...' He put his hand to his lips and scanned around. 'Shit, I hear voices. Bugger it.' He grabbed his clothes, jumped up and dived behind a bush beside the loch. 'Ouch.' The twigs needled him in all the wrong places as he crouched out of sight. The voices got louder. Eleanor squealed. *What the...?* He pushed some branches back and peered through a gap.

'Oh, hello.' Eleanor had got to her feet. A dog sniffed around her. *Shit!* His boots were still on the grass and the dog had its nose in them. It checked up, then snuffled towards the water's edge.

'Good evening,' a cheery middle-aged man said.

The dog sniffed his way. 'Noooo,' he muttered. 'Shoo...'

'Lovely weather,' the woman said to Eleanor.

'After the rain last night,' the man continued.

'Um... Very changeable.' Eleanor's gaze followed the dog, and a crease formed on her brow. She edged in front of the man, possibly trying to distract his wandering gaze.

Logan pulled his boxer briefs over his ankles and his bare feet slipped on the muddy edge of the loch. *Bloody hell.* He just steadied himself when the dog bounded up and barked, its front paws down, its tail wagging. With a tug, he swiped up his briefs, narrowly avoiding the dog's curious sniff. 'Paws off,' he whispered. 'Now, go away. Shoo.' The dog leapt back playfully, then grabbed his rolled-up socks and placed them in front of him, wagging its tail, waiting for him to pick up the bundle and throw it. He bent to snatch them, but the dog jumped for them, grabbed them and sprang back, dropping them further away.

Seriously? He held out his hands, then stretched and made a grab for the socks.

'Come on, Dusty,' the woman's voice said. The dog barked and picked up the socks.

'What's he doing?' the man said, meandering ever closer to the bush. 'He's got hold of something he shouldn't.'

'I'm sure it's nothing,' Eleanor said in a shaky voice.

Logan lunged for the socks, then glanced up. Two shocked faces glared back, mouths open.

'Good god.' The woman's hand leapt to her chest.

'What on earth?' The man grabbed the dog and pulled the now drool-covered socks from its mouth.

'Er... They're mine.' Logan attempted a smile but wasn't sure his facial muscles were complying. Neither of the people were looking at his face anyway. They were both screwing up their noses and running their gazes over his almost completely naked body. The woman's eyes lingered for an uneasy length of time on his boxer briefs until Eleanor gave a pronounced cough.

Using his thumb and forefinger, the man handed back the socks with his nose screwed up. The woman continued to gape at Logan. He held his smile, but her eyes were nowhere near his face.

As the couple turned to walk away, she muttered, 'He's the campsite owner, I'm sure.'

'Disgraceful way to behave.' The man tutted as he passed Eleanor. She was rooted to the spot, her hand at her neck and an expression of utter bewilderment plastered across her face. Logan stifled a laugh, but, Christ, it wasn't funny. They recognised him.

'Oh my god.' Eleanor rushed towards him as the couple marched out of the glade with the dog.

'Oops.' Logan pulled on his t-shirt.

'I hope they don't complain.' Her eyes darted between him and the edge of the glade.

'I bet they do. Argh!' he growled. He dipped his feet to wash off the mud, then pulled on his jeans, hopping about again. 'I really need to work on this move when I'm in company.'

She giggled. 'You're funny. I just hope they don't give you any trouble.'

'Don't worry.' He padded through the grass, back to his boots. No way was he putting on those socks after their detour into the dog's mouth. 'We should get you back. What time is it?'

'Oh gosh, yes.' She checked her phone. 'It's nearly six o'clock. My dad will be really worried and he won't have had tea yet.'

'Come on then, let's go.'

She slipped her hand into his and he forgot to worry about what the people may or may not do. They kept a brisk pace, swinging their linked hands and casting smiles at each other. What could be nicer?

'This has been such a fun day,' she said. 'Apart from that last bit. I wish it could go on and on.'

'Me too.' But like everything else in this relationship, it was coming to an all too quick end.

At the edge of the campsite, he let go of her hand to open the gate. Not far off, he spotted the dog-owning couple chatting to someone else. It had to be her, didn't it? Mrs Grumpy Camper. He was ready to bet the whole business they were telling her about what they'd just witnessed. And he dreaded to think how that would go. The half-naked campsite owner hiding in the bushes near an unsuspecting female camper. Whichever way he spun it, it sounded dodgy.

'We maybe shouldn't be seen together in here,' he said, 'or maybe we should. I don't know what's worse right now. At least if they think I know you, it doesn't look like I was perving behind the bushes.'

'They won't think that. I'm sure they'll just think you were swimming and trying to get dressed out of sight. Why else would your hair be all wet?'

'Hmm, let's hope, but I'm not sure they'll see it like that. Uh-oh.'

Mrs Grumpy Camper was walking directly towards him. She had her head down and her eyes averted, but Logan knew she was coming for him.

'Make a run for it if you like,' Eleanor muttered. 'I'll say you had an emergency.'

Too late.

'Excuse me,' Mrs Grumpy Camper said in a carrying voice. 'What are the opening hours of the shop?'

'Eight until five.' He barely restrained his eye roll. 'Though it can shut at any time during the day when I'm on my rounds.' It said so on the door if people bothered to read it.

'Well, it seems to me to be shut more than it's open. I've tried several times today and it's never been open.'

'Is there something you need urgently? I can open it now if you like.'

'It's too late for that. I had to drive to the village, which rather defeats the purpose of having a shop here.'

'I'm sorry about that. But I can't be everywhere at once.' Though maybe taking an afternoon off hadn't been his most sensible move when the site was so busy.

The woman's eyes travelled over him, then onto Eleanor, and she arched an eyebrow.

'Logan does a really great job,' Eleanor said, a pink bloom firing in her cheeks. 'It's very difficult to run a place this big on your own. He's in the process of advertising for staff, but that takes time and it's not easy to get people to work out here. I'm sure you understand that.'

The woman glowered at her, and Logan covered his mouth. What was with him and these manic laughter attacks? He liked a laugh as much as anyone, but he felt kind of giddy. Was he that drugged up on love?

'I understand perfectly,' the woman said. 'But it doesn't take away the inconvenience for the paying guests. Anyway, I wasn't criticising, merely questioning. It's not my business, but if it was, I would be a bit more concerned about keeping the shop open. In fact, there are a great deal of things I'd do differently given the chance.' She turned on her heel and stalked off.

Logan tipped his head back and blew out a breath. 'And if I kept the shop open all day and didn't bother cleaning the toilets or the showers, emptying the bins or maintaining the grounds, then we can all guess what she'd be moaning about.'

'You can't win.' Eleanor brushed her hand down his arm, causing a tremor. 'I'm sorry if this was my fault. You shouldn't have done this for me.'

'I wanted to. I need downtime too, otherwise I'll burn out.'

'I know you're doing your best. What more can you do?'

He smiled and started walking again. 'You should ask my mother that. She thinks I should be doing better. According to her, this is a waste of my so-called talents.'

'Is it?'

'Yup. Remember I told you I used to live in Cambridge?'

'Of course, why?'

'It was when I was at university there.'

'Seriously?'

'Deadly.'

She swallowed and seemed to size him up with her eyebrow. 'It's so hard to get in there.'

'Exactly. You didn't expect that, did you?'

'I didn't, but not in a horrible way. I can tell you're intelligent by the way you talk, you just don't seem…' She gave a little shrug.

'Academic?'

'Kind of. And I know you don't like desk work. You said so yourself.'

'Spot on.' He snapped his finger. 'Getting through uni was tough. Getting in was possibly worse. I'm not a natural studying type. Sometimes I struggle to focus, but I did it. And I had some great tutors there, who made me want to finish and do well. It was an interesting course but once I was done, I needed to get away and go wild for a bit. So, I travelled and became an outdoor instructor, even did some ski coaching and water sports. I hate the idea of holding down a nine-to-five job in an office. This seemed like the ideal place for me. A readymade business opportunity with potential. I want to do so much here, but everything takes so long and without the staff, I'm having to wear too many hats and juggle too many balls, and I'm not really qualified to do any of them. While I'm trying to fix the small stuff, the bigger picture gets further and further away.'

'You'll get there. It just takes time when you want it all to happen straight away.'

'So damn right.' She'd read him like a book. 'I wish I had more patience but I don't. I get so frustrated with people letting me down, red tape and too many overheads.'

'I hear you. I work with people like you every day.'

'Maybe I should just hire you to do it all for me and I can nip off up a hill for a hike.'

She chuckled. 'You could hire the company I work for, though it probably wouldn't make good business sense at this stage.'

'Are you saying you're too expensive?'

'Yup.'

He put his arm around her shoulder. 'You're easy but not cheap. I like it. So, what about the Segways tomorrow? You going to try?'

'Oh dear.' She sucked on her bottom lip. 'All I can imagine is nose-diving and falling flat on my face. But I'll come and see... Though I think I'll just watch.'

'Ok.' He glanced around. People were everywhere, sitting outside of tents, cooking under gazebos, hanging up wetsuits and muddy cycling gear from the doors of their campervans; kids ran about, kicking balls and chasing each other with water guns. The idea of kissing Eleanor goodbye was ridiculous with so many chances to be caught, but the reckless spirit that lived in him wouldn't be suppressed. He leaned in and placed a quick kiss on her cheek. 'See you tomorrow. I'll miss you.'

'Me too.' She blinked and smiled, then walked slowly towards her tent, glancing back every few seconds. He waited until she ducked inside before heading back to the shop, swinging his arms, completely bereft.

Chapter Eleven

Eleanor

Water cascaded from the campsite showers and steam billowed around the cubicle. Eleanor's mind was whirring over plans for the day ahead as she lathered up her pink grapefruit shower gel. Indistinct voices chattered from other cubicles. The very idea of a Segway terrified her. How the heck did they stay upright? Didn't you just automatically keel over? For someone who wasn't even confident on a bike, there was no chance of her having any control over one of them.

But she'd managed to persuade her dad to go and watch. Kind of. He wasn't overly keen, as it would mean a lot of standing around on his sore ankle. It was improving, and she had the feeling he'd like to go somewhere in the car, but she also wanted to support Logan. The lure was so strong she didn't have the willpower to fight it. Winning her dad around was easier.

She turned off the shower, wrapped herself in a towel and made a point of squeegeeing the floor. She would do anyway, but knowing it helped Logan made it time well spent. The voices sharpened and she tuned into a conversation. She stopped mopping, clutched the pole, and pressed her ear closer to the door.

'I caught him in the act or very near. Almost completely naked, I nearly died of shock.'

'Wasn't he just swimming?'

'No, he was with a girl.' The voice lowered. 'I think she was about to take off her clothes too. Utterly shocking behaviour in public and, I'll tell you what else, she's a guest. I saw her coming out of a tent last night.'

'Dear, dear. That's probably why this place has gone to the dogs. If the owner's more interested in having it off with the campers than actually running the site, then it's no surprise.'

'There's been a real decline since he took over.'

Eleanor took a deep breath and dried herself. The talking women split into cubicles. So the news was rampaging along a camping busybodies' grapevine. Poor Logan. Eleanor closed her eyes and held her face. *What am I doing?* Was it really worth chasing around after him when it could ruin his business? Not to mention the heartache. *Why can't I just stop and be sensible?* Where had her good sense gone? The desperation to see him again was like a hunger she couldn't satisfy and it was eating up every rational objection. *How can I go somewhere with Dad and miss Logan and the Segways?* Her stomach twisted uncomfortably. She wasn't sure she could get through the day without seeing him. It was that bad.

When she was dressed, and the other showers were running, she made her escape. As she crossed the site, a large green van rolled up the path towards the wide-open field where Logan wanted to put the glamping pods. Highland Segways was emblazoned across the van's side along with a blown-up photograph of a model couple gliding along a rugged track in front of wild mountain scenery. Like it was that effortless. A close-up of her face in the mud would be what they'd get if she had a go.

'If we're going to be watching this thing, I should take my chair,' Dad said as she ducked into the tent. 'Is it like a race or something?'

'No, it's an experience. People can have a go on them.'

'Oh dear, no. I'm not going on one.'

'Me neither, but I'd like to go and have a look.'

'Seems a bit silly. What's the point of just watching other people?' He folded up his chair. 'I think we'd be better using the day doing something more interesting.'

'Like what?' She packed away her wash bag.

'All the things we planned to do before we came.'

Of course, he was right. Why was she planning on wasting a precious day of the holidays watching strangers making fools of themselves? A pain cleaved her chest and she willed it away. No time for pointless regrets. This holiday was for Dad, not for her to behave like a stupid teenager with a crush. 'Yes, of course. It's silly.' She sucked in a deep breath. Now was the time for sense to prevail. 'What shall we do instead?'

'I'm not sure. What made you want to go to this thing anyway?'

'Oh, nothing really. I was talking to the owner, er, Logan, yesterday, and he suggested I might like to. I thought if your ankle was still giving you grief, you might not want to go too far, so I said I might, but it's fine. He won't mind. So, where shall we go?' She pulled her biggest smile out of the bag and tried to make it sincere. She didn't let any of the bitter disappointment eating her inside show on her face.

'I wouldn't mind a trip to the Falls of Briar. Maybe we could do that this morning, then grab an early lunch and come back and watch some of the Segway things later.'

'Sure. Let's do it.' Eleanor unzipped her sleeping pod. 'I'll just pop on a different top. It's a bit warmer than I thought.' She climbed in, closed up the pod again, and pressed her fingers to her lips. Her heart and mind were racing. Sitting on top of her sleeping bag, she bit back a ridiculous tidal wave of emotion. None of this was like her at all. Maybe it was nothing to do with Logan. Perhaps the pain of being back here had found its own outlet, and while she thought she was handling it, maybe she wasn't. Coming back was supposed to be a chance to purge some of the grief and relive happy memories. But that was never going to be all roses. The reminder of happiness always brought new sadness. Was Logan just a subconscious diversion she was clinging to, so she didn't have to face the ache in her heart?

She pulled out her phone and messaged him.

ELEANOR: Sorry, won't make it this morning. Dad wants to go to the Falls of Briar and I can't really say no. It's unfair not to. I might be back this afternoon and will try to drop by. Will miss you. X

She sent it, and a tear spilled from the corner of her eye. It stopped midway down her cheek, almost as if checking if it was needed, then continued to her chin. If only Logan was here to comfort her. Wiping away the tear, she took off her sweater, pulled on a lightweight top and crawled out of her sleeping pod. 'Ok, let's get going.'

They jumped into the car and she drove towards the gate. Over at the field, she spied Logan talking animatedly to a woman with long, curly hair. Bitterness stabbed her square in the chest.

'I don't know if I ever told you,' Dad said. 'Your mother and I once considered moving up here. There was a lovely little cottage not far from the falls. I'd like to see if it's still there.'

She vaguely remembered hearing the story before, though she didn't imagine it had ever been a serious consideration. The idea of her family moving to the highlands of Scotland was crazy. Dad had lived his whole life in Northamptonshire. Mum was originally from Devon and, after her marriage, had been happy to stay in the village of Chapel Brampton with her husband. The highlands were great for holidays, but neither Mum nor Dad would have wanted to make this their forever home. They had too many ties and connections to do that. *Just like me.*

If some miracle happened and she found a way to be with Logan permanently... How would that even work? Her mind whirred through a rolodex of ideas – and problems, barriers, and objections. Other than him, she'd have no one. No friends, family, or familiar faces. The shops were a long drive away, so were the amusements. And things she enjoyed, like the odd day trip to London, would be out the window. She and her friends frequently hopped on a train to take in a West End show or for retail therapy in Oxford Street. She couldn't exactly do that from here. Just as well none of this was real. *Must take care and remember this is just a holiday fling.* Though she wasn't completely sure how that would work either. *Take the fun, then run; don't over invest emotionally...* All much easier said than done.

The Falls of Briar were only about ten minutes away by car. More adventurous people than her and her dad walked to them from the campsite, but with Dad's ankle, it wasn't even a possibility. From the car park, it wasn't a long walk. She took her dad's arm and together they descended a well-kept path, flanked by trees on either side. A thunderous rushing increased as they made their way down. As the falls came into view, she gasped. So impressive. Her shoulders and chest were tight, and she wasn't sure she wanted to go too close to the rail around the large, paved viewing area, not because she thought she might fall in and get swept to a watery grave, but because memories were dancing before her. She'd been terrified of this place as a child and hid behind Mum on the viewing platform as spray leapt up and hit their faces. She could almost see it in her mind's eye, playing out like an old film, a bit blurry and not too detailed. Sorrow threatened to engulf her, as it always did when she remembered those tender mother-and-daughter moments she'd never experience again. She bit back tears. *Must be strong.* But her shaky insides craved the strong arms of Logan. Even if she let her heart crack and spill out cold tears of regret, he wouldn't push her away but hold her until everything was ok. Why was she thinking such things? Those arms weren't going to be near enough to do anything with her after Saturday.

She made her way to the edge of the platform and leaned on the railings. There was little wind and no spray today. The damp on her cheek was from the deep agony of wishing her mum was still here. If she was, Eleanor wouldn't be. There would be no need for this holiday, and she would never have connected with Logan again. Perhaps it was fate after all. Was it a message from her mum? A gift from beyond the grave? Eleanor didn't believe in anything like that. It didn't change the reality, did it?

'Here.' Her dad held out a shiny five-pence piece.

'What's that for?' She squinted at it.

'Throw it in and make a wish. That's what we always used to do.'

'Isn't it bad for the environment?'

'I shouldn't think so. Go on. Make a wish.'

She took the coin and held it between her fingertips until the cold metal warmed up against her skin. A little robin landed on the fence in front of them and Eleanor blinked. Those birds were so brave and bold. Her mum used to say, 'when robins appear, loved ones are near'. Fresh tears welled at the thought. Mum might have believed robins were messengers from loved ones who'd departed and were now at peace, but that was nonsense. Still, it brought an odd sort of comfort, imagining that somehow, she still had a link to Mum. She fingered the coin. What should she wish for? What did she want at this precise moment? Wishing her mum back was beyond the power of this little coin. Wishing for a future with Logan seemed selfish and pointless. But what about Dad? She could wish for his happiness. The robin took off with a twitter and flittered to a nearby bush. With a little flick, she tossed the coin into the crashing water and took a deep breath, thinking with all her might. *Please, let dad be happy again.* The coin vanished with a dizzying speed. She stared into the swirling depths below where it landed. Foam whirled around the top of the almost black water in an unbelievably calm pool, considering the amount crashing into it from the falls.

Turning to her dad, she smiled. 'Done. Now, your turn.'

Dad remembered coming to a café in Glenbriar a short drive from the waterfall. 'We used to go there when you were little on wet days for a hot chocolate or ice-creams if it was warm,' he said. 'Don't you remember?'

Eleanor shook her head. 'Kind of.'

'Oh, now slow down here.' Dad flapped his hand as she rolled the car along the winding road. 'This is the house we once considered buying. Such a pretty location.' He craned his neck to look into the garden. 'You can probably hear the falls from the window. That would have been nice to wake up to every day.'

'It is cute,' she agreed, though it looked a little too small. Two dormer windows on the roof told her there probably weren't enough bedrooms for three children and she and her brothers would have ended up fighting nonstop. She carried on down the road and into the pretty little town of Glenbriar. It had undergone some modernisation since she'd been here as a teenager and there were new houses dotted around the outskirts. It had always been busy in the summer, with lots of cafes and ice cream shops. She'd already passed through it on the way to the hospital and the distillery. It was nice to stop for a proper look, though she couldn't shake the FOMO on what Logan was doing. An antsy sensation gnawed at her chest.

The Cosy Bean Café was the place her dad remembered, and it was still there, but with a modern-looking sign. Eleanor couldn't remember what it had been called when she was last here, but it seemed to have changed hands and been renamed.

'It's been done up.' Dad peered in the window and frowned. 'It doesn't look as nice as it used to.'

Grey-painted dressers laden with tea sets and cake stands lined the panelled walls, giving it a country feel. The wallpaper was a modern take on William Morris with bright pops of fuchsia flowers. All in all, it looked perfectly pleasant. 'Let's see what the food's like.' She pushed open the door. A woman only a little younger than herself greeted them.

'Table for two?' She led them to a window seat and pointed out the daily specials board.

'It's all gone a bit fancy,' Dad muttered.

'I don't really remember what it was like before.' Eleanor looked around. As most of the clients seemed closer to her dad's age than her own, his attitude surprised her. Raking in her bag, she quickly checked her phone. Reception at the falls was non-existent, but now a string of messages appeared. One from Logan caught her eye straight away, and she flipped her thumb up the screen to open it.

LOGAN: Miss you too but keep your dad happy and don't worry about the Segways. Hopefully see you later, have a lovely day. X

She smiled at the words, like he was there in front of her. He didn't sound annoyed or upset. Not that she expected that. So why did it feel like she'd let him down? Maybe it was the throw-back to Mark, her previous boyfriend. Everything she did for her mum was a letdown in his eyes. But Logan wasn't like that, or he didn't seem so. He'd shown nothing but understanding.

She glanced up. Dad lifted a Perspex display holder and read through the various ads. 'This is all new.' He peered over his glasses. 'Everything's changed since we were last here.'

'It was quite a long time ago. Fifteen years, I think.'

'Yes, I suppose. It just doesn't seem that long ago.' He passed the display holder to her, and she scanned through the info.

'There's a social club for the over sixties. You should go to that.'

'Don't be silly.' He shook his head. 'I can hardly go from home.'

'I guess not, though I thought they might have something you could join in with this week.' She ran her finger down the advert. 'They do lots of things that you enjoy.'

'Hmm.' He scratched his chin and looked at the menu. 'I don't think I'd be confident doing anything like that without your mother. It just wouldn't be right.'

'Maybe.' She checked out the menu. 'But it might be just what you need.'

He grumbled at the suggestion and she let it go. There was no point in pressing the subject.

The order seemed to take an age to come, though it probably wasn't that long. She checked the time on her phone over and over. The Segway experience was on all day, but every second spent waiting for her lunch was a missed moment with Logan. She snatched her phone and tossed it into her bag. This had to stop. The whole point of this holiday was to spend quality time with her dad and all she was doing was wishing it away.

The jitters of agitation however weren't so quick to dispel. By the time they got out of the café, she was an inexplicable bag of nerves. What had brought this on? Did she have some mental disorder? Maybe she should go back to counselling. She'd had it after Mum died, but maybe she'd given it up too quickly.

When they finally turned back into the campsite late in the afternoon, she spotted a group gliding around on their Segways. How effortless it looked from here, but she was pretty sure it was anything but. She'd tried to roller skate once and couldn't even stand up. Then there was the ice rink where she'd clung to the barrier for the whole hour before being knocked over seconds before her time was up. She'd never been back.

'That looks very silly.' Dad frowned over at the Segways. 'I'm not sure what the point of it is.'

'Me neither.' But it didn't stop her from leaping out of the car, ready to go over straight away.

'Aren't you going to come in first?' Dad hovered his hand in front of his face, covering a yawn. 'And have a rest?'

'No, really, Dad, I don't need a rest. You can if you like.' If he did, then she wouldn't have to worry about him.

'No, no. If we're going to do this, let's get it over with. I'll just get my seat.'

She covered her face and rubbed her cheeks with her palms. 'Getting it over with' wasn't exactly what she had in mind.

They headed towards the field, Dad with his collapsible chair under his arm, Eleanor craning her neck to catch a glimpse of Logan. He was talking to a group at the fence and looked over at them. A broad grin split his face. He excused himself and made his way over. Heat blasted her cheeks and she crossed her fingers. *Please don't let Dad notice.*

'Hey.' Logan strode up to them. 'Good to see you both. How's your ankle, Andy?'

'Not bad but not good enough to go on one of those contraptions either. You'll forgive me if I give it a miss.'

'Of course.' Logan gave him a gentle clap on the upper arm. 'They're definitely not for everyone. I've had a go though and they're lots of fun.'

'Well, Eleanor seems very keen, so I'll just park my seat here and watch.'

'Oh... Um, I'm happy to watch too.' She fiddled with the hem of her t-shirt.

'That's not the impression I got.' Dad undid the clip on his chair with a little smile. 'She's been desperate to get back for this. Don't be shy on my account. I know you want a turn; I can tell. So off you go. I'll watch.' He opened his chair and parked himself down on it.

Logan grinned at her, warming her to the core, but she frowned at her dad. She'd obviously made herself a right pain, so much so he'd read something completely different into the situation. That hadn't been her real reason for wanting to come back, but it was definitely for the best that he hadn't guessed the truth. She didn't exactly want him to know what she truly desired. Her eyes locked back on Logan, telepathically transferring all the information he needed to know. His responsive smile told her he understood.

'Great,' he said. 'Come with me and I'll get you on board.'

She swallowed. 'Ok, let's do it. Are you sure you're ok, Dad?'

'Yes, yes. Perfectly. Off you go and have fun.' He settled himself in the seat.

Eleanor followed Logan towards the gate.

'I'm glad you came,' he said over his shoulder.

'I don't really want to go on one.' She jogged to fall in step with him. 'I just wanted to get back to see you. I'll stand on one, then chicken out.'

'Oh, come on, Eleanor. Where's your sense of adventure?'

'All of this is adventurous for me.' She lowered her voice and drew closer to him. 'I've just abandoned my dad for a holiday fling.'

He chuckled and shook his head. 'You're awesome.' Leaning in, he added in a whisper, 'And beautiful and wonderful.'

'Shh.' She play-slapped his arm. 'I'm serious.'

'So am I.'

The group on the Segways was coming closer.

'That's Rachael.' Logan indicated the curly-haired woman she'd seen him talking to that morning. She was directing the riders. 'She'll sort you out.'

'Oh god.' Eleanor's eyes widened. 'I'm really not good at this kind of thing. I know I'll make a mess of it.'

'Hey.' He draped his arm around her shoulder casually but with a meaningful glance. 'I have faith. You can do this. I'll come and help you.' He let his arm fall as she glanced at her dad sitting some way off on the other side of the fence. Dad's brow was slightly furrowed and his lips were pursed. A prickle of unease ran down her spine.

Rachael assisted the people off the Segways and thanked them before handing them over to Logan. He produced feedback forms from a box in the corner and asked if they'd mind filling them out. Eleanor bit her lip, staring at the odd two-wheeled devices. So many things could go wrong.

'Can Eleanor have a quick go on one before the next group?' Logan approached Rachael. 'She's been helping me out in the office and I promised her a shot.'

Eleanor crossed her fingers behind her back, hoping Rachael would say no.

'Of course, no problem. Over you come. Have you done this before?'

'No. Definitely not. I'm the most uncoordinated person in the world.'

'Don't worry.' Rachael took a helmet from one of the handlebars and passed it to her. 'They're easy to ride and very intuitive. It's difficult to fall off one unless you're going far too fast.'

Even stepping onto it, Eleanor was sure it would topple over, and she would fall flat on her face. She buckled the helmet extra tight. Logan gripped her arm as she balanced herself and when he let go, she inhaled sharply, but nothing happened. The Segway was upright. Rachael pointed out the controls and Logan stood by. Eleanor should pay close attention to everything Rachael said. It was important, after all, but all she could concentrate on was the heat coming from Logan. The appearance of the sun was making her physically warm, but his presence was warming her from the inside out. If she went 'bum over kettle' as her dad would say, Logan might not be able to stop it, but he could help pick up the pieces and help her back together again; that counted for a lot right now.

Logan slipped on a helmet, jumped onto another Segway and grinned. 'I'll drive alongside. You'll be fine. You'll love it. Come on.'

Swallowing hard, Eleanor started up and rolled forward. Almost holding her breath, she powered on with him easing along beside her. Soon she was level with her dad, and he waved as she passed by. She didn't dare wave back. Her knuckles were clamped on the handlebars. An odd swooping sensation filled her tummy, part nerves, part unexpected enjoyment. She chanced a glance at Logan and he beamed back.

'I knew you could do it.' He tipped her a wink. 'You're a brave woman.'

'Not really.'

'Yes, really. You're doing something you were terrified of not fifteen minutes ago, so you can pat yourself on the back, though maybe wait until we get back to the start. It might be jinxing it to lift a hand.'

'Yeah, I'm definitely not letting go.'

As they approached the far end of the field, he pulled a little closer and said, 'You've made my week. Whatever happens from here on in, these are great memories.'

She nodded but couldn't reply. This holiday was supposed to be reliving old memories and celebrating the past but, instead, she was making new memories. Neither was helping her move on or face the future. Life after Saturday was like a black tunnel leading to an unknown destination, and she didn't want to think about it. She couldn't bear to turn her mind in that direction even for a second.

After an amazingly smooth circuit of the field, she was ready to get off, despite him begging her to do another lap. 'No, really. That was my limit.'

'Ok. Well done.' He patted her on the back as she stepped off, then leaned in and brought his mouth close to her ear. 'Can you hang about? Or are you going somewhere else?'

'I need to see what my dad wants to do.'

'Ok.' He pressed a tiny peck on her cheek. She didn't dare to look in her dad's direction. What would he think if he'd seen Logan kiss her?

'Hopefully catch you later.' He chapped her arm and she thanked Rachael. Her legs were a little wobbly as she strolled through the gate.

A tall young man walked her way. Looking beyond her, he shouted, 'Hey, Berry Boy!'

Eleanor jumped and turned to spot Logan waving to him.

'Doughnut! You made it.'

She half watched him and the man clap each other's shoulders as she made her way to her dad.

Dad had his arms and legs folded and was still wearing a frown. 'That young man is very familiar with you.'

'Oh... Is he?'

'You know he is. I saw him kiss you on the cheek.'

'He was just being friendly.'

'Hmm. I hope so. He seems a nice enough boy, but a little flirtatious. Getting tangled up with him would be very silly, if you ask me.'

'Don't worry, Dad. There's no question of that.'

She crossed her fingers behind her back again. She hated lying, but what else could she do? Admitting to falling for a guy after just a few days was ridiculous enough. The fact he lived so far from her home was the icing on what was already a very messy, but annoyingly tasty, cake.

Chapter Twelve

Logan

Duncan placed his hands on his hips and looked Logan up and down, a grin spreading from ear to ear.

'Who's the girl?' he asked.

'What girl?' Logan pulled his most innocent face.

'The one you were all whispery with just then.'

'Eleanor.'

'Care to elaborate?'

'No, shh.' Logan held a finger to his lips. 'She's coming back.' He eyed her nipping through the gate towards the box where he had the evaluation forms stowed. 'Hey.' He ignored Duncan's smirk and unmasked curiosity. 'Are you ok?'

'I forgot my bag.' She stooped, lifted her bag and straightened up, smiling with a pink tinge on her cheeks.

Something nudged him on the upper arm and he heard a cough. Duncan was grinning like an idiot, clearly expecting an introduction.

'Eleanor, meet my friend, Doughnut.' He flourished his fingers in Duncan's direction.

'Doughnut?' She arched an eyebrow. 'Is that your real name?'

Duncan stretched out his hand to shake Eleanor's. 'No, my real name's Duncan.'

'Exactly,' Logan said. 'Dunkin', like the doughnuts.'

'Oh dear,' she groaned. 'That's terrible.'

Duncan and Logan looked at each other and laughed. 'Yeah, it's lousy, isn't it?' Logan said. 'He tries to repay me with Loganberry and Berry Boy, but it doesn't have quite the same ring.'

'So, are you here for the Segway experience?' Duncan asked.

'I didn't plan to be, but I had a go. I'm here on holiday, camping for a week with my dad.'

Unabashed interest spread across Duncan's face. He lifted his left eyebrow and the corner of his mouth in tandem. With a glance at Logan, the words *you sly dog* flashed into his eyes.

Logan shook his head and turned away, only to focus on two new arrivals storming across the campsite. 'Oh my god.' His jaw dropped. 'What are they doing here?'

'Who?' both Eleanor and Duncan said, turning around and following his sightline.

'What you been up to?' Duncan chuckled, covering his mouth but barely suppressing anything. 'Your mum looks like she means business.'

Logan's parents were making their way towards the field. Duncan might mistake the expression on his mum's face for something untoward, but that was what Rowena Ramsay usually looked like, except when she'd had too much to drink. She was the woman of two faces. The day-to-day look was the determined, get-the-job-done face she had on right now, while the intoxicated one was full of mischief. A Jekyll and Hyde transformation if ever there was one.

His dad, Iain, trailed along in his mum's wake – as he had done throughout his life.

'That's your mum?' Eleanor said quietly.

'What's she doing here?' Duncan asked.

'I invited them, but I never thought they'd show up.'

Rowena muscled through the group gathering at the gate for the next Segway session. She had on a bright yellow top, a purple gilet and a pair of very large sunglasses that always made her look slightly waspish. She marched up to him. 'Well, son, this seems fairly well organised.' She reached up on tiptoes, kissed his cheek and stared around. 'Not bad at all, but it might be better if you were at the gate welcoming people.'

'Hi, Mum,' he said. Duncan turned away, snorting with laughter. Eleanor hovered, clasping her hands and chewing on her lip. 'And Dad.'

'Hello, son.' Iain gave him a soft pat on the arm.

'I didn't think you'd actually come.'

'You invited us,' Rowena said. 'And I told you we'd try, though we're exceptionally busy. Still, we made it.'

'You did. Well done.'

'Oh, hello, Duncan.' Rowena fixed her gaze on him. 'You're here too, are you? And hello.' She pulled a wide smile at Eleanor. Logan hoped it didn't look too intimidating. His mum had a kind heart, but she could be so damned overbearing at times. She'd spent his childhood petrifying his friends – and most of their relatives too.

'Hi.' Eleanor held up her hand in a little wave.

'Are you Duncan's girlfriend?'

'Er, no. I'm Eleanor. I'm just on holiday.'

'Oh. And are you enjoying it?'

'Yes. Very much.'

'She's been helping me out a bit.' Logan's gaze shifted between the two women. Rowena's questioning was so forceful it was almost aggressive. He also needed to justify Eleanor's presence to her. Otherwise, more probing questions would follow. 'Her dad had a bit of an accident and was out of action for a day or two and she kindly helped me with the advertising for new staff.'

'Oh, Logan. Expecting people to work when they're on holiday. Did he pay you properly?' Her focus snapped back to Eleanor.

'I got this experience for free.' Eleanor beamed, then blinked and switched her gaze to Logan. He silently thanked her diplomacy.

'Hmm.' Rowena drummed her fingers on her oversized handbag. 'I'm not sure it's such a great reward. I fail to see the thrill of these things, but Logan knows best when it comes to trends in the world of adventure sports.'

'Thanks, Mum.' That was gushing praise from her. 'So, I'm guessing you don't want a go on them?'

'Of course I do.' Rowena slipped her bag off her shoulder and tossed it onto a patch of rough grass by the fence. 'We didn't come all this way to mope around.'

'Er... Ok. Well, there's a group gathering just now. I'll go and chat to them. After their session, I should be able to get you on.' He glanced at Eleanor. 'Sure you don't want a second go?'

'Positive. I better get back to my dad.'

'I'll walk you to the gate.' Almost subconsciously, he put his hand gently on the small of her back as they ambled towards the gate. With a brief check over his shoulder, he whispered, 'I can't believe my parents and Duncan showed up. I invited them in case nobody else booked. Now I've got loads of bookings and they showed up too. Talk about everything happening at once.'

'You're doing great.' She nudged him with her elbow. 'Everyone's enjoying it.'

'I hope my mum didn't scare you. She can be intimidating.'

She grinned and shook her head. 'I can see that, but it's fine.' Andy was at the gate holding his chair all folded up. 'I think Dad might want to leave. I'll have to sort him out.'

'Ok, catch you later.' Logan held his palm on her back a second longer, resisting any other kind of physical contact, ignoring how much his body craved even just a brief hug or a peck on the cheek, and squashing the deeper urges burning him up inside. He joined Rachael to welcome the latest group and help them get set up.

As the group set off, he drew back, keeping half an eye on where Eleanor was and the other on his mum. He didn't need to watch Rowena; her voice carried across the field and her laugh resonated over everything else. Eleanor and her dad had vanished from sight and Logan withdrew to the box of evaluation forms and started organising them.

'So, how are you keeping the shop open with all this going on? I saw it was shut, so I assume you haven't got any staff yet.'

He straightened up to find Rowena frowning, hands on her hips and one foot tapping.

'Nope. I haven't found anyone. I've closed it for the day. I've had a sign up all week saying it'll be closed, but if anyone needs something urgently, they can find me here.'

Rowena shook her head. 'I'm not sure that's the best way to run a business.'

'Probably not, but I can't be everywhere. I can't magic more staff out of thin air. That couple letting me down at the start of the season threw a big spanner in the works. That's what Eleanor was helping me with; her job is helping businesses through tricky times.'

'I still can't believe you made a guest help you.'

'I didn't make her. She offered.'

'Well, she seems nice. Is that her over there?'

He glanced to the far side of the field, where Eleanor was strolling with her dad around the outside edge. 'Yes. She's with her dad. They lost her mum, and this is a nostalgia holiday for them.'

'How terribly sad. Poor girl. I'll have a chat with her when they come back around.'

No point asking her not to. When Rowena got an idea into her head, there was no stopping her, but he hoped her attempt at kindness wouldn't backfire and make things worse.

It didn't take Eleanor and Andy long to get to a place in the field where Rowena could reach them. She dragged Iain over to the fence and Logan watched with a helpless sensation in his gut as they chatted with the Kendricks. Should he go over or leave them to it? Perhaps it was better if he had nothing to do with it.

They were still chatting at the fence when the Segway group finished up. Duncan sidled over and sat in the grass, waxing lyrical about his latest cycle ride. 'Come with me next time. It was a freaking ace route. I went with a guy from work who's almost as big a fanatic about bikes as you. You should come. You'd love it.'

'Sounds awesome.' Logan crouched in the grass, resting his elbows on his knees. 'As soon as I get cover sorted here, I'll be able to take a few days off for stuff like that.' And he needed to. Apart from a short break at Easter when he had to ask the previous owners to cover for a few days, he hadn't had a day off for ages.

'So, what's the story with Eleanor?' Duncan tossed some grass in the air and glanced over at the fence.

'It's like I said, she helped me out a bit.'

'Oh yeah? What else you been getting up to?'

'Nothing.'

Duncan's eyebrow was almost level with his hairline. 'I knew it would happen one day.'

'What?'

'That you'd start getting it on with the campers.'

'That is not what's happening. What do you think I am? Some kind of creepy dude who stalks the tents at night?'

Duncan laughed. 'No, man. I just smell chemistry. You and her have the hots for each other.'

'Even if that's true,' he muttered, so only Duncan could hear him. 'There's fuck all I can do about it. She's a paying guest. It wouldn't be right.' Damn cruel twist of fate.

'If she's up for it, why not go for it?' Duncan gave Logan's leg a punch. 'She doesn't seem the type to roast you on the socials if it all goes tits up.'

'Shut it. I need to debrief this group.' He leapt to his feet and grabbed a stash of forms. At this moment, being 'roasted on the socials' was the least of his worries.

As the latest Segway group left in a gaggle of chat and laughter, Rowena appeared and ran her finger over the Segway like she was trying to find a vein. Logan frowned. 'Mum... What are you doing?'

'Hush. Just checking they're up to standard.'

He pulled a grin and gave Rachael a half-shrug, hoping she understood he had no control over anything that came out of his mum's mouth.

'So, can I get on?' Rowena said.

'Sure.' Rachael handed her a helmet.

Duncan approached, swaggering a little and flipping his hair as Rachael showed him to a Segway. Logan took his turn to raise an eyebrow.

'I think I better go around with them.' He lifted a helmet. From the corner of his eye, he spotted a man in an orange high-vis jacket, standing close to the entrance to the field. Beside him was a smartly dressed woman chatting with some of the people who had just finished their Segway experience. That was the same man he'd seen a few days ago. Logan's shoulders tensed. Something wasn't right about this, but he had to get this ride done before he checked it out.

He pulled on the helmet as Rachel began her safety brief and explained the controls.

For a woman who expected everyone to hang on her every word and do exactly as she bid, Rowena was amazingly lax at not listening to anyone else. All through Rachael's chat, she fiddled with the controls, adjusted her helmet, or shook her head like she was being told to do something highly unreasonable. Logan wished the ground would open and swallow him. If he'd behaved like that, she would have murdered him, but for her… He shook his head with a long sigh. His focus strayed to the gate. The man in the hi-vis had gone. Or so it seemed. Logan squinted into the gathered crowd. Was the man in the middle of it? Why did it seem more than a bit suss?

As soon as Rachael gave them the go-ahead, Rowena zoomed off and Logan's eyes popped. She sped ahead, screeching.

'Mum!' he yelled.

But there was no stopping her. The screams and squeals were apparently whoops of delight. She roved forward like she was on a fairground ride.

'Dear, dear.' Iain shook his head, moving along sedately behind. Not for the first time, Logan wondered how his parents had stuck with each other this long. They were passing the fence close to where Eleanor and Andy were standing. Both of them had their hands at their mouths like they were trying not to laugh.

Logan drew up beside them.

'She's a brave lady,' Andy said, watching Rowena career forward.

'She's insane,' Logan said.

Eleanor's hand was still clamped to her mouth when she said, 'I hope she doesn't fall off.'

'I bet she does.' He half closed his eyes. 'And she'll blame everyone else.'

'She's very adventurous.' Andy watched her progress around the field.

Logan had to check what his mum was up to, but his gaze didn't want to budge from Eleanor. She smiled at him with a coy kind of expression, like she was inviting him to leave this mayhem on wheels and find a quiet place where they could be together. Alone. What utter bliss that would be. Not just a few stolen hours, but real time together without having to worry about anyone else or the ticking time bomb of Saturday's departure hanging over their heads. Sadly, it wasn't possible anywhere other than in the world of dreams.

Chapter Thirteen

Eleanor

Eleanor couldn't stop laughing as Logan zoomed off to check on his mum. Rowena looked like she was having the time of her life, grinning from ear to ear, and whizzing around, causing happy havoc on her Segway.

'Very nice people,' Dad said. Eleanor smiled at him. He'd obviously been touched when Rowena and her husband had made their way over to speak to him; their friendly inquiries had been just what the doctor ordered.

'Are you ok watching?' she asked. 'Or would you prefer to go back to the tent?'

'I'll watch a little longer. It's very amusing.'

Eleanor silently thanked Rowena. She might be loud, but her fussing over Dad and now her entertaining antics had brought him round in a way Eleanor couldn't have managed on her own. Now she had the perfect opportunity to watch Logan without arousing suspicions of anything untoward. They did a final lap around the field, Rowena lurching ahead and careering forward like she didn't have a care in the world. Logan and Duncan followed, exchanging looks and shaking their heads, but still grinning like they couldn't quite believe their eyes. Iain had given up and was at the gate, talking to Rachael. Another group started to mingle for the next session.

'I think this must be the last group,' Eleanor said. From the centre of the assembled people, she spotted a man in an orange hi-vis jacket emerging. He was short but very broad and he was talking to a smartly dressed woman, who nodded and tapped at her phone.

'They'll have difficulty getting her off.' Dad was still observing Rowena.

Iain headed towards them, perhaps purposefully avoiding watching his wife's antics. His focus was definitely not on her. He beelined for her dad and joined him and Eleanor.

'So, is this your first visit in some years?' Iain leaned on the fence, smiling.

'Yes, it's nice to be back,' Dad said, 'though I see a lot of changes.'

'Good ones, I hope.'

'Just different.' Dad let out a sigh. 'It's the same everywhere. Technology moves along apace. When we first came up here, it was like coming to the end of the earth. Now, it doesn't feel quite so remote. It looks like it in places. I mean, the scenery is still wonderful, but with phones and messages and all that, it isn't quite the same. My phone bleeps with messages from my sons and Eleanor's still keeping up with friends every few minutes.'

Eleanor gave a little cough into the back of her hand. It probably looked like she'd been messaging her friends, but really it had only been Logan. Her friends knew nothing about what was going on here.

'I'm happy to leave the phone in the tent,' Dad continued, 'get my binoculars and go and watch the birds.'

'You enjoy birdwatching?' Iain said. 'I do too. Have you seen a capercaillie?'

'No, never.'

'They're very rare these days. People thought they'd died out a few years ago, but we still see them occasionally. They're very bad at taking off and landing and make a terrible noise when they do. We heard one on a family holiday years ago when the kids were young and got a terrible fright. We thought a plane had crashed in the woods, turned out to be a bird.'

Dad chuckled, but Eleanor lost track of the conversation. Rowena was finally off the Segway. She handed her helmet to Rachael and gestured about like she was telling the younger woman how to do her job. Logan exchanged a weary look with Duncan. Rowena spotted Iain and waved, beckoning him over. Only Eleanor saw her.

She cleared her throat and tugged her dad's arm. 'Sorry to interrupt, but I think Iain's wife wants him.'

Iain turned around. Rowena pointed to all three of them one by one and beckoned again.

'I think she wants all of us,' Iain said.

They made their way towards the gate. Rowena had started up a conversation with Duncan when the smartly dressed woman who'd been hanging about with the man in the hi-vis approached her. The woman was still talking to Rowena when Eleanor, her dad, and Iain reached them.

'Well, personally, I thought it was a wonderful entertainment,' Rowena was saying. 'I quite fancy one of them for doing the shopping.'

Duncan pulled a weirded-out face behind her back and Eleanor bit back a laugh.

'What do you think of the facilities onsite in general?' the woman asked.

Rowena opened her mouth, then closed it again, arching a fairly impressive eyebrow. 'Who are you?' she asked.

The woman didn't reply but gave a little smile.

'You're not with the Segway experience, are you?'

'Just an interested party,' the woman said.

Rowena squinted at her before her focus shifted and landed on the man with the hi-vis, who appeared from the centre of a crowd of people. Eleanor was watching him too. He pulled a face and glanced at his feet with a slight cough, then turned away like he was trying not to be seen, which was difficult given his choice of outfit.

'Malcolm McManus.' Rowena narrowed her eyes. 'What are you doing here other than stirring up shit, as usual?'

Iain winced, and Duncan sniggered, but Rowena glared at the man in the hi-vis.

'Is this his doing?' Rowena asked the smart woman. 'Are you with the press? Badge out and let me see it.'

'I am, but...' The woman glanced at the hi-vis man, but he didn't catch her eye.

'Well, please leave,' Rowena said. 'Unless you're going to write a glowing report on today's activities. But if Malcolm's involved, I see that as highly unlikely. Now the gate's that way.' She peered at the woman, then at Malcolm like an imperious headmistress.

Malcolm McManus narrowed his eyes and gave Rowena a death stare before he turned and lumbered off. The woman gave a curt smile and followed him.

'What was that all about?' Duncan asked.

'When we lived in Glenbriar years ago, Malcolm was a first-class troublemaker.' Rowena tugged her cuffs with an irritated pout. 'I doubt he's changed. He wraps everything up in a cloak of "working for the community" but he's just a sad man who needs to get a life.'

Eleanor glanced at her dad, hoping he wasn't offended by this outburst, but he was smiling.

'Oh, I know the type,' he said.

'Malcolm's wife is even worse, as I recall,' Iain added.

'That silly bitch,' Rowena said, and Duncan nearly fell apart behind her. 'She once reported me for taking a photograph in the park, saying I was illegally photographing children because her son was playing nearby. He was behind me and there was no way he could have been in the picture. I was zooming in on a pretty bee on the flowers. But she was desperate to get anything on me. I had the police at the door about it. Utterly ridiculous. But that is the kind of idiot we're talking about.'

'Why was he dressed like that?' Eleanor asked. 'Does he work for the council or something?'

'Oh no. I doubt he has a legitimate job. He didn't used to.' Rowena pulled a face. 'He wears that jacket because it's like a magic key. He puts it on and goes anywhere he wants. People just think he's a maintenance worker. Honestly, he knows every dodge in the book. I dread to think what he's doing here, but I'm sure it won't be anything good. Now...' Rowena clapped her hands and beamed. 'How about after this last group, we all go back to Logan's for a meal? It's not very big but it'll do.'

Dad nudged Eleanor with a slight frown, his expression asking if Rowena was extending the invitation to them.

'Should we leave you to it?' Eleanor asked.

'No, no, you're invited too.' Rowena beamed at her, then her dad. 'Least we can do after the help you gave Logan. And I'm sure Andy would like to dine out of the tent for a night.'

'Indeed, it sounds good,' he said. 'If you're sure, and Logan doesn't object.'

'Of course he doesn't object.' Rowena flapped the idea away. 'I didn't bring him up to object to good manners.'

'Good, good,' Dad said.

Eleanor traded a look with Duncan. 'Sadly, I can't hang about,' he said. 'I bunked off work early to do this. I need to catch up on stuff this evening.'

'Yes, you better do that,' Rowena said. 'I wouldn't want you sacked because of Logan. Now, let's see, where is he?'

'He's just sorting the last group.' Duncan pointed to the people assembled by the Segways.

Eleanor leaned on the fence, half listening to Rowena as she chatted to Dad, but mostly watching Logan. His cheery laugh echoed as he helped the last few people onto the Segways. She flexed her fingers, trying to ward off the burn of envy that came as she spied him chatting to Rachael once the group had taken off. But though he gesticulated enthusiastically and smiled loads, she saw no more than professional regard in his eyes. Nothing compared to the blazing looks he gave her, the ones full of promise and desire. Almost as if drawn by a magnet, he glanced over right at her. A warm smile split his face and he tipped her a little wink before returning to his conversation, a little quirk still on his lips.

When the last group finished, Logan and Rachael packed the Segways away, chatting together for a while before Rachael got in the van, tooted, and drove off. He gave her a wave, then made his way over.

'Phew.' He ran his hand across his brow. 'What a day. It went ok though. No one asked for a refund anyway.'

'It certainly seemed popular,' Rowena said. 'Now, I've arranged for us to have dinner in your caravan. Duncan can't make it but the rest of us can. I hope you have some good food available.'

Logan raked his fingers through his hair, ruffling it up, and stared at his mum. 'Right. I'm sure I'll find something to feed the five thousand. You sure I can't tempt you as well, Doughnut? One more won't make much difference. See if we can squeeze six into the old caravan?'

'Na, you're fine, Berry Boy. I need to head. It was nice seeing you all and meeting you, Eleanor. I hope you enjoy the rest of your holiday.'

'Thanks.'

He clapped Logan on the shoulder and left with a little wink in his direction.

'Well, let's all go to the caravan,' Logan said. 'Though I think we should sit outside; it'll be more spacious.'

'As long as there aren't too many midges.' Rowena flapped her hand around her head.

Logan rolled his eyes, then found Eleanor's, and grinned. Her chest filled with warm liquid at the look that promised so much. But there just weren't the hours in the day or week to do everything her heart wanted.

He directed them to a picnic table near his static and behind a fence panel that screened the campsite from view. 'I'll light some magic candles,' he said, 'and test their midge-repellent powers. Would anyone like a drink?'

'Oh, yes,' Rowena said. 'Iain can drive.'

'Whisky, Andy?' Logan raised his eyebrows in his direction.

'I wouldn't say no, but just a small one. Too much whisky knocks me out cold.'

'Eleanor?' He smiled at her again, making her want much more than a drink.

'What do you have?'

'Do you like Prosecco?'

'Yes, I do.'

'Oh, good.' Rowena patted her arm. 'We can share a bottle.'

Logan disappeared into the caravan and returned moments later with a tray of glasses, a bottle of prosecco, one of whisky, a can of beer and a Coke. 'Does everyone like spaghetti Bolognese?' He set the Coke in front of his dad with an apologetic look. 'It's probably the quickest and simplest thing I can make.'

'And messiest.' Rowena peered at her yellow top as if imagining a red stain appearing in the middle.

'I could do it with pasta twists, if you prefer.' He arched an eyebrow in her direction.

'Whatever suits the majority.' She gave him an airy wave. Logan scanned around and everyone else agreed.

'Right, I'll fix that up.'

Sharing a bottle of prosecco with Rowena translated into Eleanor slowly sipping hers while Rowena topped hers up over and over. Her cheeks got redder and her voice louder. Logan dotted in and out, checking on the food and casting wary glances at his mother like he expected her to go off like a bomb at any second.

'Right, it's almost ready.' He stepped out of the static caravan and surveyed the table.

'Do you want a hand bringing it out?' Eleanor asked.

'Yes, thanks.'

She pushed back her chair and edged out from under the table, half expecting someone to stop her. This was the moment she'd been waiting for all day. Her moment alone with him. No one spoke, so she made her way up the whitewashed wooden steps and into the compact kitchen area.

He held the door, waiting. The second she crossed the threshold, he pushed the door and caged her with his arms, pinning it shut. 'Oh my god.' He breathed hard, pressing his forehead to hers. 'I can't stand this.'

'What?'

'Not being able to have you.' He leaned in and touched his lips against hers. She flung her arms around his neck and pulled him closer, drinking in his kisses, savouring every stolen second. He slipped his hands around her back, fixing her against him. 'I want you so damn much.'

She inhaled the warm cooking smells as she fed off his mouth. He was hotter than anything in here and she needed him. Lust overrode everything. She barely remembered where she was or what was going on; she just wanted to get closer, suck him in, and feel him encompass her. His strong embrace held her firm and she was safe, surrounded and happy.

'I think the bolognese is burning,' he muttered.

'It's not the only thing.' She reluctantly released him.

'Too right.' He loosened the neckline of his t-shirt, crossed the small space and stirred the pan. 'I guess we should dish this up.'

'I guess.' She straightened out the hem of her pink t-shirt and he directed her to a cupboard filled with an assortment of mismatched crockery.

He half glanced at her as he decanted the bolognese onto a serving dish, but looked like he was trying his best to focus anywhere but on her. She knew why. Every time she looked at him, she had the mad urge to leap on him and have her wicked way with him. Never had she had it this bad.

On the worktop, his phone vibrated. 'Shut it.' He leaned over to silence it. 'Shit, I better take this. Hello.'

She took the serving spoon from his hand and continued decanting the bolognese. Trying to concentrate, she blinked, but her gaze was continually pulled back to him. He frowned and seemed paler than usual. She couldn't hear exactly what the voice was saying, but it sounded like a sharp female tone.

'So, how long can you extend it for?' he asked, then winced at the reply and made eye contact with her, pulling a hopeless face. She sunk her teeth into her lip. This had to be bad news.

'I guess that wasn't good,' she said as he ended the call and laid the phone back on the worktop.

'Nope.' He let out a sigh. 'This place just isn't making money fast enough. That was the bank. Apparently, they've been trying to call me all day. Such joy.'

'But this place is really popular. Business will pick up in the summer, won't it?'

'It was popular fifteen years ago. When you were first here, it was great, but so much has changed. The previous owners were lovely and amazing people, but as they got older, they let things slip. I can't blame them; it's hard work. Unfortunately, they lost a lot of business from regulars who wanted more for their money, such as sites with more electric hook-ups, better washing and cooking facilities, and glamping pods. I've started the ball rolling with upgrades, but it means more money going out than coming in. I need the bank to extend my loans, but they're not keen or able.' He rubbed vigorously at his face. 'I'm trying really hard, but it feels like I'm barely scratching the surface.'

'I'm so sorry.' She held his arms. 'I wish I could help.'

'Don't worry.' He let out a sigh, gripped her arms in return, and stared deep into her eyes. His grey-blue irises were dull, but slowly their twinkle returned, and his pupils widened. 'Come on, let's get this food out.'

She let him go and picked up a stack of plates. Together, they ferried the crockery and the food outside before taking their seats. Her insides squirmed with uncertainty. Not just for herself but for him. When she left in a few days, his troubles wouldn't be hers, but she couldn't see herself switching off. How could she? This wasn't good. She didn't want to care. Making his affairs important to her was a bad idea and could lead to complications. Her heart was already fragile. This was a fling. A superficial entanglement to pass the week with. She knew people who did this kind of thing all the time and never looked back.

'Well, this has been a lovely day.' Rowena lounged back, patting her stomach. 'We don't normally encourage Logan to mix with the guests.'

He rolled his eyes and Eleanor barely restrained a giggle; she needed it to burst the pod of gloom building up inside her.

'But the two of you seem like old friends.' Rowena lifted her glass. 'Maybe it's because you've been coming here for such a long time.'

'With a big gap,' Dad said. 'But that's very kind of you to say so.' He clinked his glass on hers.

'Logan, do you know why Malcolm McManus was here today with someone from the press?' she asked.

'Who?' He frowned.

'Don't you remember Malcolm? The man in the hi-vis? He lived near us when we were in Glenbriar.'

'Oh, him. I knew I'd seen him somewhere before.' Logan leaned his chin on his hand and rubbed his cheek with his forefinger. 'He was hanging about a couple of days ago.'

'What did he want?' Rowena asked.

'Something about planning permission.'

'That sounds like Malcolm,' Iain said. 'He objects to anything and everything unless it directly benefits him.

'Oh, great.' Logan let out a sigh. 'But why were the press with him?'

'I don't know.' Rowena narrowed her eyes. 'But he probably told them porkies and was hoping they'd write something horrible to have you closed down. It wouldn't even surprise me if he did it to get revenge on me.'

'Why would he do that?'

'Because I didn't take any of his nonsense. He was always up to something and I wasn't afraid to stand up to him. He didn't like that. So whatever happens, don't cave. You better not sell up because of him. You've only just taken the place on, for goodness sake.'

He opened his mouth and Eleanor held her breath, thinking he might swear or snap, but he flapped his hand in front of his face, holding off a yawn. 'Sorry, folks. I'm knackered.'

'Me too.' Dad mirrored his yawn. 'I need my bed.'

Rowena glanced at her watch. 'Yes, we should probably go.'

Eleanor eyed her dad. 'I should get you back to the tent.' She lifted his limp wrist. The tiredness was just his age, but it caused a further spasm of dread. He'd always been an active man, but every day he lost another piece of that and since Mum had died, the losses had seemed more rapid.

'Thank you.' He stifled another yawn. 'It's the whisky. It knocks me out.'

'Should I help clear up first?' Eleanor glanced at Logan. His gaze was far away, and she was certain he was dwelling on Rowena's words, the call from the bank, the press visitor, and the future of the campsite.

'No, definitely not. I'll clear up. You relax.' He scraped back his seat. 'It's been awesome having you all.' His grin almost made it to his eyes. 'Hope you get a good rest, Andy.'

'Thank you ever so much. It's been a wonderful day.'

Eleanor said goodbye to Logan's parents and left them hugging their son as she took her dad's arm.

He may be ready to fall straight into a long and sound sleep, but she was wide awake. She glanced back just before they turned out of sight of the fence and caught Logan's eye. He sent her a smile laced with unspoken desire, and it struck her deep in the core. She wished she could go straight back to his waiting arms.

Chapter Fourteen

Logan

Logan threw the plates into the sink, sighing as he rolled up his sleeves. What the actual fact was going on in his life? How had he gone from a promising student to a defunct businessman in less than ten years?

As the water gushed into the basin, he braced himself. A hammering on the door made him jump and almost crack his skull on the overhead cupboard. His heart thrummed with excitement. Was it Eleanor? Could she have put her dad into the tent and come back? Would she?

He took the three steps across the caravan and pushed the door open. Instantly, he stepped back. The angry face and stiffly folded arms definitely didn't belong to Eleanor. One of the grumpy campers glared back. It wasn't the woman who'd been complaining all week, but he thought it might be the one he'd seen her talking to.

'Is everything ok?' Why was he bothering to ask? Her face pretty much told him the answer.

'Not really,' she said with a deep frown. 'I've tried calling the emergency number and, as always, the shop is closed, so this is a last resort.' She looked him up and down.

'The shop was closed for a special event today and, I'm sorry, I haven't heard any calls. What's the problem?'

'There are some extremely noisy people behind us. They're shouting, they have music playing, the kids are screaming and some of the language they're using is a disgrace. You need to move them along. It's unacceptable.'

Logan's insides recoiled. Confrontation was one of his least favourite things and it rarely solved any of the problems. Clashing campers were the bane of his life.

'Sure, let me chat with them.'

The woman gave a curt smile and set off at a brisk pace. He followed her across the site. As they drew closer to her tent, he spotted the source of her annoyance, and his insides contracted even further. What looked to be a perfectly normal family were cooking a meal outside their tent. A youngish teen was on a phone. As he got closer, he realised it was emitting music. Two other slightly younger children were pushing and teasing each other. He pulled in a sigh.

'Listen, they're not really making that much noise,' he said.

'If you had to put up with that for over an hour, you'd change your tune.'

'All right. I'll have a word with them, but they're not breaking any rules. This is a campsite and there'll always be some degree of noise from the other campers.'

'And yet it said on your website this is a quiet and peaceful location.'

'Well, the location is peaceful.' He pulled out his best smile, and the woman narrowed her eyes.

'I'll leave you to sort it out.' She ducked around behind her tent and disappeared inside.

Just great! He approached the family with a smile, pushing his hands into his pockets, hoping to appear relaxed and calm, not pissed off, because it wasn't their fault. 'How's it going, folks?' he said. A man flipping burgers at the fold-out barbecue looked up and the woman beside him frowned halfway through ripping open a packet of rolls. Logan flashed her his biggest grin and her expression morphed into a confused smile.

'Fine, ta.' The man glanced around, no doubt wondering what the hell he wanted.

This was ridiculous. He couldn't give them a ticking off for making too much noise when they were just having a good family time. 'Just doing my rounds,' he said. 'Someone mentioned there was a lot of noise going on. Have you been bothered by anything?' Was that the stupidest thing he could have said?

'No.' The man and woman shook their heads at each other.

'I don't think it's noisy here at all,' the woman said. 'We've been to campsites where it's been like a full-on riot. This is a great place.'

Logan nodded. 'Epic. I'm glad everyone's obeying the rules. We tend to keep the music down after nine, though some people think that's too late and others too early.' He put out his hands. 'Can't win. Anyway, have a nice stay, guys.'

They gave him a wave as he walked on. Now, he'd have to speak to some other people or it would look like he'd singled them out. He beelined for another family with young kids running around in their pyjamas and struck up a similar convo with them before ducking back towards his static. Whatever he did would never be enough for the moany campers. He'd had at least one every week since he'd arrived.

He pulled his phone out of his back pocket and spotted a message that made his gut swoop.

ELEANOR: I don't know about you, but I'm not in the least tired. Dad's fast asleep and I'm thinking about maybe going for a walk. Want to go with me? X

Logan changed direction towards the woodland pitches and thumbed a reply on the hoof.

LOGAN: Sure I do. I'll be at your tent in ten seconds X

As he approached, he heard the zip and a second later, Eleanor came around the side of the navy blue canvas. 'Oh.' Her hand leapt to her chest. 'You really are just outside. How did you get here so quickly?'

He pulled a face. 'Trouble with the campers.' His grumpy mood slid from his body as he scanned her smiling face. Simple beauty and effortless elegance radiated from her clear skin and piercing eyes. She'd pinned back her blonde hair in a messy camping up-do, and he was certain she wasn't wearing any make-up. Her natural loveliness burrowed its way deep into his soul where he welcomed it. With just a little nurturing, he could help her heart to grow and thrive again. She'd suffered a great trauma, but he could nourish her with love. The only problems were time and geography.

'Oh no. What happened?'

He held out his hand. 'Let's not worry about it. Let's not worry about anything.'

She slipped her palm into his and he split her pinkie from the rest of her fingers and linked his through it. Her skin was cool, but a pleasant warmth blossomed from the connection. He clasped her tightly, keeping his eye out for nosey campers.

'When I was in high school,' he said, 'I once saw my chemistry teacher in the supermarket holding hands with the German teaching student who helped out in our language classes. I don't know who was more embarrassed, him for being seen, or me for seeing him. I kind of know how he felt now.'

She chuckled. 'I guess I'm as off-limits as a student.'

'Yup. I mean, technically that student was probably twenty, and he wasn't that much older. I guess, maybe twenty-six or twenty-seven, but to a high school student, that's totally scandalous. I think quite a lot of the people on this campsite might think the same about the owner and a camper.' He looked at her and smirked. 'But I don't really care what they think anymore. It's a free country and it's not like I'm committing an offence.'

Of course, it could damage his reputation, he knew that, but for some reason, his brain was deliberately bypassing the thought.

'Maybe.' She tugged at his arm. 'But I think we should walk through the woods and not through the middle of the campsite. Just in case.'

'Yeah, that makes sense.' He let her pull him through a gap in the trees close to another tent and onto the path that ran alongside the stream. The water rushed across the pebbles. They trod along the grassy path. As they got further from the campsite and deeper into the woods, they had to shuffle through overhanging ferns and bracken and the path got so narrow it almost disappeared.

She let go of his hand and waded ahead.

'Do you know where you're going?' he asked.

'Not a clue.' She turned around and chewed her lip. 'Kind of like my whole life at the moment.'

He tilted his head, then raised his hands to cup her face. 'I can sympathise. I haven't been through what you have, but I don't know where the path I'm on is leading either. Most days, I just feel like I'm wandering aimlessly, getting deeper and deeper into something I don't know how to get out of.'

She slid her arms around him, and he held her against his chest. 'Me too,' she said. 'My life used to be simple. I had a job, a boyfriend, and a plan. Then Mum died and everything went up in the air. Nothing's clear any more. I still have a job but it's something I do on autopilot. I don't love it, but I don't hate it either. I just turn up and get the work done. I don't dare make plans for my future because I have to be there for Dad. But it scares me because I know one day he'll be gone too. I hope it's not for a very long time, but by that time, it'll be too late. You know, too late for me to live my own life.'

She shook in his arms like she'd let out a silent sob. He gently rubbed her back. 'I get it,' he whispered. 'It's a tough call. An impossible call. You want to do right by him but also by yourself.'

'Exactly. And maybe things are still too raw for me to see what to do but it's stifling. I don't resent doing it; I just feel trapped.'

'You're so kind to your dad. I know he appreciates it, but you deserve to be happy too.' He leaned in and kissed her gently, a comforting peck on the cheek.

Her hands coiled around his neck, and she moved her mouth to meet his. It was firm but soft. Her lips parted slightly, and he moved in gently and slowly. Passion boiled through his veins and he glided his hands down her back, resting on her waist and holding her close. He couldn't get enough of her. She let out a soft whimper, sliding her fingers up his back and over his shoulders. Their lips moved perfectly, tasting each other. Her fruity lip balm was divine. He drew her closer, desiring to be all over her, inside her, and joined to her all at once.

He groaned onto her mouth, and their tongues brushed together, sending bolts of lust ricocheting through him. He forgot where he was; the world was spinning out of control. 'I want you so badly,' he said. 'I know it's crazy. I'm not a fool. I know who you are, where you live and every worldly complication, but I can't stop myself from wanting you.'

'Same.' Eleanor threaded her hands deep into his hair. Her pale blue irises were bright and glistening, but full of need and understanding. 'The future can change in an instant. Who cares what tomorrow brings? Life is full of surprises and things we don't expect. I want what I can have right now. And this is making me happy.'

He rested his forehead on hers. 'I feel exactly the same.'

She breathed slowly and deeply, her chest nudging him as she did, sending his brain haywire.

'Let's walk back to mine.' He took hold of her hand. 'It's safer than doing something we regret out here.'

'Ok.' Before he could move, she pushed up on her tiptoes and kissed him again. Holding her close, he joined in. So much for moving.

She pulled away and giggled. 'This is fun, isn't it? Naughty, but fun.'

'Very naughty. But, come on, let's walk back.' He flung his arm around her and guided her gently forward. Insects hummed dizzy tunes in the bushes and trees. The fading evening sun cast its light through the tree canopy, catching the leaves and making dappled shadows, despite the time being almost nine-thirty. His body thrummed with unfulfilled need and he gripped Eleanor's hand tight. For the next few hours at least, she was his. All his. And he was hers. One hundred per cent.

Chapter Fifteen

Eleanor

Eleanor pushed an overhanging branch off the narrow path and edged past. The branch sprang back.

'Woah,' Logan said.

She whipped around. 'Oh goodness, sorry. I didn't mean for that to hit you.'

He burst out laughing. 'No permanent damage done. If I'd known you were going to attack me, I wouldn't have come.'

Awareness pumped through her as he grinned at her. His gaze travelled from her eyes to her lips and down before returning to meet hers. She swallowed, then held out her hand. He took it and gently squeezed it before they carried on to where the path emerged through the trees back at the campsite. If she went back to his caravan with him now, things were going to get heated – very heated. She wasn't one to throw herself into things like that, but good girl Eleanor was on holiday. This was the time to live and love. At this moment, there was so much she loved about

Logan and she wanted to make the connection physical. If he could make her feel whole and wholly loved even for a little while, she was going to grab it and cling on for dear life.

'Oh shit, no,' he muttered, letting go of her hand.

'What?' She tensed, flexing her fingers and trying to ignore the wave of hurt. Why would he let her go now? Was he having second thoughts?

'It's Mrs Grumpy Camper,' he said through gritted teeth.

Eleanor followed his sightline and spotted the woman who'd grouched at him the day before. A small dog snuffled around her feet.

'What is she doing?' Logan peered forward through a gap in the branches.

'It looks like she's examining the electric hook-up.'

'Yeah, but that's not her pitch. Seriously, she is such an annoying busybody.'

'Can we avoid going past her?'

Too late. A branch rustled as Logan pulled back and the woman glanced towards them. If it had looked dodgy before, surely this was even worse. After the naked-by-the-loch incident, now this. How could it appear like an innocent meeting? Eleanor fiddled with her hair. *Eek.* Was it mussed up? Would something in her look give away how raw and love crazed she felt? The woman squinted at them.

'Let's go back, so we don't have to pass her,' Logan whispered, tugging her in the other direction. They returned along the line of the stream rather than cutting back into the site. A few more minutes and they'd be at her tent. Not really where she wanted to go, but she didn't speak in case the woman was still watching them.

'Make it look like you're going back to your tent. I could have run into you,' he whispered. 'Sneaking about like this is horrible but I don't trust that woman. I can see her making a fuss, and I wouldn't want her to go to the press or anything like that. I don't need any bad publicity and she looks the type to cause trouble.'

Eleanor chanced a glance around. The woman was still hanging around one of the hook-up points with the dog and, though she wasn't watching, Eleanor was pretty sure she had them in her peripheral vision and wasn't going to let them out of sight. As they approached the tent, Eleanor winced at the sound of her dad snoring. Normally, she lived with it and didn't even notice, but hearing it from outside was weird. 'I didn't realise Dad snored that loud.'

'You hear all sorts around here,' Logan said. 'That's actually quite quiet compared to some.' He bent down slightly as he skirted her tent. 'Do you still want to come back to mine?'

'Of course I do.'

'Then give me five minutes. I'll go back and you follow. Cut round by the shower block or something. Then, if the nosey parker is still watching, she'll hopefully be thrown off course.'

'Ok.' She grinned. 'I shouldn't really be enjoying this, but it's quite fun, isn't it? I wish we'd done this the first time round; it would have brightened things up no end.'

'If we'd done it then, we'd have got into big trouble. At least now we're adults and capable of making informed decisions...' He raised an eyebrow. 'Allegedly.'

'No second guessing, Logan.' She prodded his arm. 'Now go. I'll follow you in a bit.'

He straightened up and peered over the tent. Apparently seeing nothing, he ducked back down again, placed a quick kiss on her cheek, then ran towards the main office area and his caravan. She watched him, trailing a finger along her lip. Hanging about even for five minutes in this state of anticipation was torturous. Unzipping the tent, she ducked inside. Her dad was still snoring like a walrus. She grabbed her wash bag and decided to make a quick freshen-up trip to the showers. That way, she could genuinely be seen to go in. Good thing too, as the nosey woman was walking back towards her. Eleanor cast her a brief smile and sped up.

She hadn't bothered with make-up all week; campsites didn't exactly demand that level of perfection. Her skin was always pale, but this evening her cheeks looked rosy. She pulled down the neck of her t-shirt, checking herself in the tiny mirror. What would Logan make of her? She wasn't a seasoned pro when it came to this kind of thing. Well, goody two-shoes types tended not to be. Still, he'd been attracted to her from the off. He'd said as much. The Eleanor he'd met was the raw, unmade version. No point in changing that now.

She had a quick wash, slapped on some moisturiser, and sprayed herself. *That's as good as it gets.* She tidied her hair behind her ears, then stepped outside. The sun was dipping behind the trees. Checking around, she didn't catch any sight of the nosey woman, so she snuck around the back of the block and across the gravel area in front of the shop, then around to Logan's caravan. The door hung open and clattering ripped through the still evening. He cursed from inside and water poured down the wooden steps outside. What the hell?

'Logan.' Eleanor sped up and peered inside. Towels and old sheets were spread across the floor and a barefooted Logan was tramping them down. 'What happened?'

He shook his head with a look of disgust. 'I left the bloody tap running. Can you believe it? I was washing up when another complaining woman came knocking earlier and I forgot. I just followed her out. Now, I've got this mess. Everything is bloody soaked. Under the sink, the floor right the way through. I'm such an idiot.'

'I'll help clear it up.'

'I'm sorry.' He lifted a dripping towel and threw it onto the ground outside. 'This is hardly the romantic night I had planned.'

'Life never goes to plan.' She removed her shoes and socks and tiptoed up the sodden steps, placed her wash bag on the work surface and started bailing water out the door. Logan mopped up the puddles with the already sodden towels and sheets.

'That's all my spare bedding too.' He bundled up a sopping pile of wet fabric. 'What a mess.'

'It looks like a clear night. Once we've got the water mopped up, we can hang all these things out and let them drip. You'll ruin the washing machine too if you put them in this wet.'

'I'll be washing them for the next week.'

A brief niggle flickered in her mind. She wouldn't be here next week to find out if he'd ever got it all washed, but she forced her brain in a different direction. He'd pulled everything out from under the sink and lined up the bottles and utensils along the compact work surfaces. Eleanor dragged some of the drenched sheets outside and flipped them over the whirligig. Its strings sagged under the weight.

'Right.' He patted some towels on the floor under the sink. 'That's about as much as we can do. What a nightmare.' He scanned down himself and frowned. 'I'm soaked.'

'You look like a plumber who's had an accident with a leaky pipe.' She did a quick recce over her own clothes. 'And so do I.' She stepped inside and wrapped her arms around him, anchoring her fingers in the back pockets of his jeans. 'It doesn't really matter though, does it?' She pulled him closer, rubbing against him and letting every nerve end enjoy the pressure. 'I mean, the general idea is that we take off these clothes anyway... isn't it?' She tilted her head and invited him closer with her eyes.

Very gently, he ran his fingertips along her cheekbones, stroking her hair behind her ears. 'Indeed, naughty Eleanor, that sounds perfect.' He dipped in and kissed her. It was beautifully soft and considered, but hot and promising at the same time. 'Just like you.' Before she could reply, he captured her lips again, pinning her to his chest and sending a zing of warmth through her. She drank him in, loving how his hands held her in exactly the right place. An overwhelming sense of contentment flooded through her like he'd refitted a missing piece of her heart.

He slid his hands down her body, grazing her breasts and settling on her hips. Then, he guided her backwards through the caravan. It was almost dark now, but she wasn't afraid of being blindly moved around a strange place. Her trust in him was implicit. He wouldn't let anything happen to her – only the things she wanted. When the back of her legs touched the bed, she sat, and he joined her. He'd pulled the curtains over the little windows and the bed seemed to take up most of the space. Gently, he lowered her onto her back and moved on top of her, stroking her cheek and caressing her neck with kisses. A giggle of contentment escaped her, and she hooked her leg around him, drawing him closer, enjoying his full weight pressing against her, warming her to the core. He was divine. She coiled her arm around his neck and kissed him urgently. They needed to get out of their clothes really soon. He ran his hand around her waist, sliding her walking trousers down her hip, then he pulled away slightly. 'Are you sure you want to do this?'

'Yes. Very sure. Let's get these wet things off.'

'An offer I can't refuse,' he said, the smile in his voice clear.

He moved off her and, in the dimness filling the compact sleeping area, she watched him slip his t-shirt over his head and cast it onto the floor. As he unbuttoned his jeans, she pulled off her top and moved closer to him. She shuffled out of her trousers as he wrestled his jeans and boxers off. It was weird, but she'd never actually undressed in front of a man. The darkness covered her modesty, but a keen sense of awareness prickled on her bare skin. When she and Mark had been together, sexy times always started and finished in bed when she was already in her night-clothes. They didn't change or get ready in front of each other. In fact, Mark had made a point of getting ready for bed in the bathroom. Logan was so at ease in his own skin. He hadn't cared about being naked in front of her the day before at the loch. How silly was it for her to be sitting here, shivering and feeling like her arms were too small to cover everything? Self-doubt needled her exposed body.

'Hey, you must be cold,' he whispered, finding her again, his hot breath falling on her neck and his warm palms clasping her upper arms. 'You're shaking. Are you sure you're ok?'

'I think so.'

'We're only doing this if you're sure.' He backed off.

'I want to.' She pulled him back. 'I really do. I just feel a bit shy.' The last word came out with a nervy giggle.

'That's ok.' He gently stroked the back of his hand down her cheek. 'We'll take it easy. We only do what you're happy doing.' He placed a soft kiss on her collarbone close to the strap of her bra, then he gently slipped both straps down, lowering her bra slowly, until the pads of his thumbs grazed her nipples. She gasped and whimpered as he continued kissing downwards.

Tingling and delicious sensations flooded through her system, so much so she almost forgot that her arms were hanging uselessly at her sides. Her neck had lolled to one side as she knelt on the bed with him moving his lips over her body, finding sensitive places to kiss.

Slowly, she raised her hands onto his shoulders, gliding them downward like she was forming a mind map of his beautiful body. She'd seen everything yesterday when he'd waded out of the loch, but now he was fully aroused and she wanted to touch him.

He groaned, and she slipped her fingers downwards. Their mouths melded in a deep and passionate kiss.

Months of pent-up emotions furled inside. He was so good at kissing; his mint fresh taste was utterly divine. He gently moved her, so they were side by side, not letting her go and holding her the whole time. His palms rolled over her body, waking the sensitive nerve ends. An all-encompassing warmth and safety cocooned her. When his fingers slipped between them, stroking the very top of her thighs, finding her most intimate place, she held her breath, her body coiling as the tension built, desperate for release. Logan held the key.

'Eleanor,' he whispered through his kisses. 'You're beautiful, so, so beautiful. Your hair… That smell of blossom. I love…' The word landed softly on her neck. 'I love it. It's so, mm, gorgeous. Everything about you is gorgeous.'

His whispered words in her ear and the intense friction his fingers were creating sent her over the edge. Hot and shaky, she convulsed in his arms.

'It's ok.' His voice was low and quiet, and he stroked her hair, holding her sated body against his hard chest. 'You're beautiful. And safe. Everything's good.'

She curled into him, still breathing raggedly, and for a long time he didn't move, he just kept her close. Gradually her energy returned and her fingertips grazed his hot skin, trailing a path down his side and curving around his backside.

'Hold on.' He lifted one arm off her and leaned away. She heard him shuffling around the flip-up cabinet next to the bed. 'One minute.' He moved away from her. 'Housekeeping break.'

She giggled into the pillow at the sound of him opening a packet and getting ready. When he moved over her, his heat was incredible. She wanted nothing more than to snuggle in close. It had been a while since she'd done this and a twinge niggled her tummy, even as he held her tight. What if she tensed up and couldn't? But this was Logan, and every cell in her body trusted him to be gentle.

He whispered in her ear again and his broad palms radiated heat across her back. 'You're so special to me, so, so special. There's no one like you. There's never been anyone like you.' He peppered kisses onto her neck. 'I've never felt like this about anyone else.' His breathing grew rapid and Eleanor, so engrossed in his words and kisses, suddenly realised he was nudging gently inside her.

'Oh god.' She wriggled slightly and gasped for air. They were together, joined exquisitely. Fully relaxed, she allowed herself to enjoy the sensation, wrapping her arms around his neck and holding him tight. He didn't move for a moment but pressed his forehead against hers. They were one, nothing else, just one whole being.

'You're everything,' he murmured, moving gently. 'Everything. Everything I've ever wanted. Needed. Everything.' The words came in fits as he moved.

A rush of emotion poured over her, so strong she almost cried.

'Oh, Logan. I love... love this.'

'Me too. I love everything about you.' He pressed his lips hard against hers and his fingers found her most sensitive spot. She gasped, channelling her energy into kissing him. Then, without warning, she fell over the edge into delirium. He kept moving, his breathing ragged, until his hot body collapsed on top of her. An enormous sigh escaped her lips, and she nuzzled into his neck. She could stay like this forever.

But of course, she couldn't. The moments rolled on. Logan shifted into a more comfortable position, keeping her in his arms.

'You're the best.' He placed a kiss on the top of her head. 'Just the best.'

'I'd like to stay.' She ran her finger up and down his spine.

He held her tight, gently kissing her brow. 'You're welcome to.'

'But I can't. If my dad wakes up and I'm not there... Well, he'll panic.' She held her breath, waiting for a huff or something derogatory. The kind of thing she used to get from Mark. 'It's not because I didn't enjoy it or anything.' The need to justify herself burned like a hot poker.

'It's ok.' Logan carried on placing light kisses on her forehead, his warm hands splayed on her back. 'I understand. Let's just chill for a few more minutes, then I'll walk you back.'

'You don't have to. It's not far.'

'I know, but I want to. I want to spend as much time with you as I can.' He caressed her hair off her face. 'I'm happy to walk you.'

She forced her eyes to stay open, but with his gentle kisses and the way he was stroking her, it was difficult. She could so easily close her eyes and nod off into a dreamy sleep. But the reality was, she had to move, face the cool air, get dressed and go back to the tent. It was like getting up on a dark winter morning and having to go to work when all she wanted to do was cuddle up on the sofa and watch TV.

Eventually, she dragged herself away from him, sat up and rubbed her arms, suddenly cold. She had to do it. Walking away was the only option and this would serve as good practice because, come Saturday, she'd be walking away for good.

Chapter Sixteen

Logan

Water dripped from the corners of the sodden linen hanging on the twilit whirligig beside Logan's static. He threw himself onto the steps and sat with his head in his hands. A light breeze fluttered the canvases close by. The campsite was asleep. Eleanor was safely back in her tent and he was alone.

His body and mind were weary, but even if he went to bed, his eyes wouldn't close. Less than an hour ago, he'd been snuggled up close with Eleanor and he could easily have drifted into a deep, contented sleep. Now, it was like he'd been ripped from his body and thrown onto a cold pavement to starve. It wasn't her fault. Christ no. If anyone was to blame, it was him.

'Fuck's sake,' he muttered, getting to his feet. He threw off the shorts and t-shirt he'd put on to accompany her across the site and flung himself onto the empty bed. Eleanor should be there, but he'd agreed to a quick fling, and that was what he'd got. Why the hell did she have to be so perfect? Could it not have been mediocre? A vague attraction that fizzled out come morning?

'Ugh!' he groaned, throwing his head deep into the pillows. He'd done it now – committed the cardinal sin of falling for her. A love like he'd never believed possible burned his gut.

The relentless light of the Scottish summer meant by four in the morning sun was streaming in the window and the birds were chirruping like crazy.

There was no going to sleep now. He crawled out of bed and filled the kettle. The floor was still damp and the mess of utensils from the soaked cabinet was still covering every available surface. Yawning, he waited for the kettle to boil, his hand pressed to his forehead as he scanned the chaos. Where to start? He must look like a complete basket case living like this.

'Just shit,' he muttered as he poured steaming water into his coffee mug. Even if the impossible was to happen and Eleanor wanted to try and make this work, he wasn't exactly a good investment. Who would want to live in a caravan? He shook his head. Maybe he needed to flip the solution. What if he sold up? He could move to Northampton and be with her. Surely he could find something to do there. It wasn't like he'd been the master of knuckling down to a steady job so far, as his mother kept reminding him.

He sipped his coffee slowly. Restless energy bubbled and fizzed inside him. How would it be if he just stormed round to her tent and told her... 'Tell her what?' He glowered at the coffee, and it swirled calmly. 'That I love her.' He snorted. What had happened to him? Since when was he such a sap? But it was true and he wanted her to know. Her being so close was killing him. She was just a short walk away and it had to stay that way. She had her dad and he was her priority. Logan needed to keep that at the forefront of his mind. Whatever he did, he couldn't compromise the relationship she had with her dad.

He slammed down his mug and started putting things back in the cupboard. Pools of water still lingered, and he dabbed them up with the damp towels. No one would be using the site laundrette this early; he could take all the sodden towels and sheets and bung them in before the campers turned up. He loaded them into the back of the golf cart and trundled towards the communal area. The laundry room was chilly as it faced away from the rising sun. A torrent of drips pattered across the lino as he heaved the soaking items to the machine. If the campers had made a mess like this, he'd have been seriously hacked off, but as he'd be the one clearing it up anyway, it hardly mattered. He filled all three machines and set them off. The way his luck was going, he'd come back in an hour to find them exploded. None of them sounded too healthy. Like nearly everything else on this site, they needed replacing.

He opened the shop and the office. If Mrs Grumpy Camper or one of her friends decided to come for an early morning spree, she'd be very happy. He was open at five thirty, not many campsite shops could boast that! Between her and some random villager who had it in for Rowena, Logan was doomed. If Malcolm McManus had persuaded a reporter to write a shitty article about the site, there was plenty of material. Shop closures, damaged buildings, an owner pulled in all directions like Stretchy Man. Not exactly the cheerful, fun, family experience he advertised.

Hidden amongst the papers with all the grant applications, he pulled out a letter he'd forgotten about. *Aw, man.* He shook his head as he read it. The previous owners had applied for planning permission to build a house in a deserted area of woodland close to the main gate. This letter granting the permission had arrived a few weeks before. Too late for them and too pricey for him. Maybe this was what Malcolm had been asking about. Not that it was any of his concern. Logan pulled in a deep breath. Was there any point in worrying about it? The possibility of stopping a man like that when he was hellbent on causing trouble was less than nil.

Getting up this early meant he could crack on with work without interruptions. Not physical ones anyway. Distracting thoughts of Eleanor inveigled their way in, but he was able to deflect them enough to work his way through the backlog of applications. The site alone didn't qualify for much, which was why he needed to develop the outdoor centre. He sat back and steepled his fingers, trying to work out how best to word his problem. Without the outdoor centre, the campsite couldn't be classed as a recreation facility so didn't meet the requirements for the grant, but without money to start up the outdoor centre, he'd be forever floundering with a dead loss. Or it felt like it anyway.

A heavy rattle of the rickety shop door caught him unawares and his eyes flicked to the clock. Was it eight already? No. Only just after seven. A smiling face peeked around the door.

'Morning.'

'Eleanor. Hey.' He stood up and she came in with a shy smile; her cheeks were pink and glowing. Everything about her just made him want to scoop her up and hold her close. Edging out from behind the counter, he opened his arms. She let out a little giggle before resting on his chest. That sound reminded him of the night before and sent another tremor of desire through him. He wrapped himself around her and kissed the side of her head. 'What brings you here so early?'

'Could you sleep? I couldn't.'

'No.' He stroked her hair. 'Not a wink.'

'Dad got up early, so I did too. He thinks I'm having a shower. I better not be too long. I just really wanted to see you.'

'I'm glad you came. I've missed you.' He let out a sigh. 'I don't think I can stand you being so far away when Saturday comes. I know it's breaking all the rules but I can't just forget you exist.'

'Well... I had an idea.'

He pulled back and looked at her, a grin growing on his face. 'Me too, but you first.'

'I know it's not ideal.' She put her hands up to explain. 'But how about I do some virtual work for you? I can set things up remotely and help you with some of the paperwork. Then we get to keep in touch, and I don't feel like I'm just leaving you in the lurch.'

He frowned, then looked towards the door. 'I thought...' He trailed off. Her solution was neat and tidy, tied with a bow, and would mean they could talk online from hundreds of miles away, but it didn't come close to filling the gap in his chest. He needed her much closer than that. But perhaps it was a good starting point.

'You don't want that?' she said. 'I don't want you to think I'm interfering.'

'It's not that. Of course, I'd appreciate your help and I'd love to stay in touch... But, Eleanor, don't you want more than that?'

She compressed her lips and looked around with wide eyes, almost like she wanted to escape, but she didn't move. 'It doesn't matter what I want.'

'Yes, yes, it does.' He gripped her arm and looked her in the eye.

'No, Logan. I'm not free to do as I please, not in the way you want. I have my dad. It's a fact of life. I know it sounds crazy, and it's hard to understand, but I have to think of him first.'

'Hey, it's not crazy or hard to understand.' He ran a hand up her arm. 'I didn't mean that. I know you have responsibilities, and I absolutely don't want you to leave your dad. All I meant was that I thought... You know, we could find some way we could be together without it affecting your dad.'

She let out a sigh. 'How?'

'I'm not sure.' He rubbed his forehead, but she took hold of his wrist and tugged it away from his face. Holding it firmly, she leaned up and kissed him. He tilted his head and returned it, slipping his free hand around her waist. Slowly and gently, he played with her lips. She released his wrist and wrapped her hand around his neck. Their bodies pressed together, repeating the dreamy friction they'd created last night. Fleeting imaginings of Mrs Grumpy Camper walking in or Eleanor's dad burst into his consciousness but were quickly dismissed by the rush of euphoria brought by each passing second.

Her sweet perfume tickled his senses, and he drew her closer, completely forgetting where they were or what they'd been doing before.

'I can't hang about today.' She pulled back with a sigh and composed herself. 'I promised Dad I'd take him somewhere.'

'Sure.' Logan took a steadying breath. 'Sure.' Stepping back, he flexed his fingers.

'I'll try and come back later. And I'll message you.'

'Yeah. Ok.' His feet had turned leaden. He stood rooted, watching her cross the shop. 'I really want to talk about where we go from here.'

'We will. Soon. I just can't hang around. Dad's waiting.'

'Ok. You have a great day. I'll see you later.'

At the door, she turned back and gave an almost apologetic smile. 'Bye.' She waved. Was that a tear in her eye?

He'd known this would happen. Had to. But it didn't prepare him for the crippling pain in his gut. He threw himself onto the seat and leaned back with a groan. Eleanor hadn't given him a chance to explain his idea. She'd deflected him with the kiss. And he knew why. She was protecting her heart. How could he blame her? She'd been through a huge trauma and her life had been upended. The thought of changing again was scary. Even if he followed her to Northampton, there were no guarantees. He didn't want to be a millstone around her neck. She had enough people to be looking after; she didn't need another hanger-on. If he couldn't find a buyer for the site or a job in Northampton, then he'd be even more useless than he was just now. She didn't need that in her life.

But he wasn't going to give up that easily. As if someone had flicked a switch and turned on a light in his head, he sat up and flipped open his emails. He searched for the local estate agent who'd dealt with his buyout of the site earlier in the year. There was no harm in a valuation and maybe just a little test to see what the market was like.

It had been a lonely dream for the past few months and now he'd found someone who brought sunshine into his life. If he was with Eleanor, they could make new dreams. Together dreams. He gazed out the window at the site that had been part of his life since he was a teenager. Fond memories would always remain in his heart, but he alone couldn't bring back what had been here before. The previous owners called it a family-run campsite, but he couldn't say that. He was a one-man band and not even a very competent one.

His mum would murder him slowly and publicly if he gave up on another job after such a short time, but these were exceptional circumstances. Selling up would give him some capital to live on while he looked for something else and that would leave him free to follow Eleanor to the ends of the earth.

Chapter Seventeen

Eleanor

Eleanor unzipped her tent and snuck inside. Her dad wasn't back yet, and she folded up some clothes and pushed them into her luggage bag, swallowing down a lump in her throat. Soon that bag would be packed, the tent down and squashed into the car boot. They'd be driving home and Logan would be nothing but a memory.

'Stop,' she muttered. 'Just stop.' This was exactly why she should have listened to the goody-two-shoes voice and done nothing more than ogle him from afar. He didn't belong in her real life but cutting off his affection would be like slashing a vein.

And where had her dad got to? He'd been ages. He usually took a while at the showers, but a familiar tension spread across her shoulders as she returned her bag to her sleeping pod. What if he'd slipped and hurt himself? Or had a heart attack?

At the door of their tent was a little canopy where they'd left their foldout chairs. She slumped into hers. Why could she not stop worrying all the time? Her nerves were in such a constant state of flux, she'd almost forgotten how to relax. Except with Logan. He somehow coaxed out the best in her. She leaned her head in her hand and sighed. Without her dad, she would be as enthusiastic as Logan about forging something new for the two of them, but it wasn't that simple. And now she'd hurt him. The light in his eyes had flickered and died when she'd told him she couldn't change the status quo.

None of his objections would be new. Mark had said everything to her the previous year. He'd told her how she was wasting too much time on her parents and not living her own life. 'He didn't need to tell me.' Tears welled along her lower eyelids. Her life was forfeit but what else could she do? Leave her dad to starve? Expect him to pay for someone to 'look after' him? A stranger who he'd be uncomfortable with when he was already living with intense grief? How could she justify it? How could she live with herself? If she and Logan were somewhere together, living the dream, could she really be happy knowing how she'd left her dad? Or he would have to move in with them. Not exactly ideal, and what if something went wrong? What if Logan tired of the arrangement and they split? How could they cope with another upheaval? It was all so pie in the sky for a man she'd only met a few days ago.

Must be sensible. Stick to the original plan and treat this as a fling. With time, she'd forget. Surely. One week would become nothing in the swirling vastness of time.

She lifted her phone and scrolled through it, checking some of the messages and chat groups she'd been ignoring. A friend would be welcome. Someone she could offload to, but she didn't dare tell anyone what she'd been up to. Not yet. Maybe in ten years, when it felt like something from another life, she might confess. A tear trickled down her cheek. Ten years without Logan was like being sent to prison for a decade... make that for life because she wouldn't ever have him for keeps.

Her best pal, Hattie, had sent her a string of photographs from a party at the weekend. Hattie had a perfectly normal life, a perfectly normal boyfriend, and perfectly normal plans for the future. Eleanor could imagine Hattie's reaction if she mentioned Logan, or the reaction she'd have after being scraped off the floor and resuscitated, because she just wouldn't believe it.

ELEANOR: Looks like you had an amazing time. We are too. The campsite is different from how I remember it but I'm enjoying it. Dad hurt his ankle on our first day here, so we haven't done as much as we'd originally planned. The week has flown by. X

Each sentence seemed to beg for something more, even just a little hint at Logan's existence. But she couldn't.

'Ah, you're back.' Dad came around the corner, smiling. 'I bumped into a very talkative lady on the way back from the showers, otherwise I'd have been here about ten minutes ago.'

'What was she saying?'

'That she wasn't very pleased with her stay. I said we'd had no difficulties and found it pleasant enough, but she's had some trouble with noisy people in the tent beside her. She said the owner wasn't very sympathetic. I find that hard to believe. He seems like a kind and thoughtful young man to me. He couldn't have been pleasanter providing a meal for us yesterday, and very nice parents too. But this woman reckons he carries on in a distasteful way with the campers. Sounds like a lot of nonsense to me.'

Eleanor swallowed and forced her face into neutral. 'Why would she say that?'

'Said she saw him running off into the woods with someone and apparently he shuts up the shop so he can carry out his liaisons. She seemed like a bit of a gossip to me. I don't see Logan behaving like that. He's got his head too well screwed on to be so silly. Doing things like that would get him a very bad reputation and I'm sure that's not what he wants.'

'True. I'm sure he doesn't either.' She let out a sigh as her dad ducked into the tent. Her soul ached for Logan and was feeling all sorts of love for him. Despite all her insistence it was just a passing thing, her heart was taking some convincing. She was a fling novice, so compartmentalising the emotions was difficult. Calling it a day now would be the best course of action, especially if people were starting to notice. She didn't want to compromise Logan, but she also didn't want to stop seeing him. Getting to her feet, she stretched, but her breathing was ragged. He was just over there, a short walk across the site, and even the idea tormented her.

A reply pinged in from Hattie.

HATTIE: I was beginning to think you'd vanished! I guess you don't get good reception up there in the wilds of Scotland. Send me some pics. Sorry to hear about your dad. Next time, leave him at home and we'll go somewhere more exciting. How about Tenerife? You need a break. X

Eleanor rolled her eyes. No one got it. She couldn't just leave him at home. It was like leaving a child. Ok, her dad would survive better than a five-year-old, but surviving wasn't the life he deserved. He deserved to be happy. His future had been ripped from him and throwing him out to fend for himself was adding salt to the wounds. She knew what people said behind her back. *'She should leave him to it. It's his own fault if he can't cook, should've learned, shouldn't he? Instead of expecting his wife to do it all. It's come back to bite, but Eleanor shouldn't be the one having to do it now.'*

And she didn't have to. Her dad wouldn't stop her if she wanted to move out. He'd put on a brave face, but she knew he'd die inside. Half of him had already gone with Mum. She couldn't bear it if he gave up completely. And how long would he last on his own? All the will to live would be sucked from him. She wouldn't be the one responsible for that. No. When the time came to say goodbye to Dad, and she hoped it was a long time away, she wanted to know she'd done everything she could to ensure he'd had the happiest life possible after Mum.

Another message from her eldest brother, Jamie, caught her eye. She'd dismissed it earlier among several group chats.

JAMIE: Hi Els, how's the hol? I've got some news I want to tell you, but you need to keep it under wraps for the moment and don't tell the old man. I know how worried he was when Harry went off to Hamburg and when he hears this, he'll probably go ape. I've been offered a job in New Zealand!! Linz and the kids are super excited about it. I've always dreamed of moving out there, but it was job dependent. It'll freak Dad out, so I've got to think of a way to break it to him gently. Just thought I'd keep you in the loop. Enjoy the rest of your week. J. XX

Eleanor stared at the words and her heart contracted. Harry had moved to Germany shortly after Mum had died and Dad had taken it hard, especially with his grandkids going too. Jamie was in London and that was close enough to go and visit him, Linz, and their two boys. But going to New Zealand? Dad wouldn't travel there and that would mean all his grandkids were hundreds or thousands of miles away. He'd be gutted. Jamie had talked about New Zealand before, but she hadn't grasped that he'd been so serious. Perhaps losing their mum was the catalyst. Maybe he'd decided if he didn't just do it, he never would. Should she do the same? Was this the moment to step up and do something crazy? But what exactly? How on earth could she just give up her life? And for a man she hardly knew.

The tent opened and she shoved her phone under her leg as her dad stepped outside. 'It's such a beautiful day,' he said.

'Where shall we go? We've only really got today and tomorrow left. Saturday will be mostly packing up.'

He didn't have to remind her.

'I feel like I've spoiled this holiday with my daft leg. It's a pity too because I don't think I'll be back here for a long time, maybe ever again, and I still don't think I've seen everywhere I want to.'

'Then pick somewhere you really want to see and let's go.' Her heart trembled under the weight of her brother's news, her dad's prediction that this would be his last visit to Scotland, and Logan... Everything surrounding Logan – the pain of not being with him, the guilt of having been with him when she should have been taking her dad everywhere he wanted to go, the idea she'd somehow contributed to the downfall of his business by behaving in a way so unlike herself, and the agony of having to leave him come Saturday.

'I fancy going to a lovely little place we went to years ago. There's a lochside path and an osprey hide. It had some beautiful scenery.'

'I'm happy with that if you are. Do you remember how to get there?'

'Yes, yes, I'm sure I do.'

Dad grinned and hummed cheerfully as he packed up his binoculars, ready for their day out. Eleanor made a quick trip to the toilets before they left. Should she nip in and tell Logan what they were doing? Or maybe just message him later? Honestly, this was impossible. On a normal trip, there was no way she'd bother telling the campsite owner where they were going, but this wasn't a normal trip, and the owner wasn't just some random person. He was someone she was connected to on a deeper level. Someone she'd had amazing sex with the night before. Someone she'd almost said 'I love you' to. And it wouldn't have been a lie. She'd only stopped because wasn't it completely the wrong thing to say during a heated encounter? Even if he'd said something similar to her. But love? Love changed everything. She couldn't afford to let it in, but at the same time, it was all her aching heart wanted.

She peered through the window to check there was no one in the shop, then burst in, unintentionally loudly, through the rickety old door.

'Hey.' Logan glanced up from behind the counter. 'You're back. Is everything ok?'

'Yes.' She moved to the counter and leaned on it. 'Dad wants to go to see the ospreys today.'

'Oh, wow. At Loch of Dairvin?'

'Probably. He seems to know where it is.'

'It's not far from Thistle Lodge. Do you know it?'

'Should I?'

He chuckled and her chest filled with warm bubbles. His smile could undo her. 'It's a big fancy building with turrets, looks like a castle. My family has a reunion up there every three years. We were there in April. My mum was... Well, you saw what she's like. She was up to some hijinks.'

'Oh my, she's funny.'

'In the head.' He huffed out a sigh. 'But hey, you enjoy yourself.' He leaned over and took her hands in his.

'Logan...'

'I know, now's not the time. We'll talk later. I'll miss you.'

'I will too but—'

The rickety door burst open. He let go of her hands and cleared his throat. 'Yes, that'll be fine. I'll put your name down for that date.'

She smirked and tried not to giggle. 'Thank you.'

'Any time. Have a great day.'

'Thanks.' As she turned round, she saw one of the grumpy campers scanning over the fridge and screwing up her face. Apparently, something she wanted wasn't in stock.

Eleanor couldn't do a thing to help except get out. If some of the busybodies were whispering about him and damaging his reputation, it was the kindest thing she could do. With the briefest glance back, she left the shop. What should have been joyful excitement about a day trip to a beautiful place was replaced with a wash of sadness. She wanted to curl up in a corner and cry. Instead of helping her heart with a harmless fling, she'd done the opposite and now she had to live with the consequences.

Chapter Eighteen

Logan

Hostile eyes watched Logan as he busied himself at the counter. Mrs Grumpy Camper opened the drinks fridge, then cast him the evils.

He could sense her more than see her. Making eye contact was like inviting a confrontation and he didn't want that. She didn't speak or even make a sound, but something was bubbling below the surface like a monster in the loch about to crash out and drag him under. Should he whistle? The tension was so thick he could hardly breathe. Finally, she banged a carton of milk and two chocolate bars down in front of him.

'Lovely day.' He scanned the milk carton, making sure his voice was breezy.

'Hmpf,' she muttered.

Or not. He picked up the chocolate bars and scanned them. 'Anything on the cards for today?'

'We're walking to the Falls of Briar.' She sniffed, still not looking at him. 'It's always been a favourite place of ours.'

'Lovely. I hope you have a good day. Would you like a bag for these?'

'No, thank you.' She narrowed her eyes and looked him up and down. Was she fighting back a tirade? *She's like my mum.* A wry grin spread across his face, but his chest was heavy like someone was loading bricks on it.

Rowena would go utterly mad if she knew what he'd done last night. *My son and one of the guests!* He could almost hear her screaming and giving him many, many pieces of her mind. But she was the one who'd invited Eleanor and Andy for a meal, which didn't seem like her. And she'd enjoyed their company. That brought a more genuine smile to his face. Mrs Grumpy Camper glared at him and he realised he was grinning at her like the Cheshire cat. What would she make of that? She might hit the nail squarely on the head by thinking he was drugged up on love. *Bet she thinks I carry on like this all the time.*

'Bye,' he said as she stalked out without looking back. She didn't even bother to reply. 'And good riddance,' he mumbled once the door was firmly shut.

Now what? Another day without Eleanor. Well, he better get used to it. After Saturday, this would be life.

He returned to his desk and quickly checked his emails. One from the estate agent caught his eye and he opened it.

Dear Logan

Thank you for your request for a valuation on your commercial property. We would be happy to carry this out for you at a convenient time. Please let us know when would suit.

Kind regards

Emelie Bright

Logan slouched back in the seat and reread it, though it changed nothing. Why would it? He ran his hands through his hair and tossed back his head. Everything was a mess, and he didn't have the energy to deal with it. He was doing exactly what Rowena expected him to and giving up the minute the going got tough. But the other option was to give up on Eleanor. With a long sigh, he tried to focus, but she filled every space in his mind. When she went back to Northamptonshire, she wouldn't exactly be leaving the planet. But he didn't want her to disappear back to her normal life, thinking she didn't deserve happiness. Her solution was fine to be going on with, but it wasn't what he wanted from her. What would change for his business? Having someone to talk things over with would be great, but could it make this venture any more of a success?

'This is impossible.' He leaned on his hands and Rowena's voice tutted in his mind. She'd pushed him through Cambridge and he didn't have anything to show for it in business or life. All he wanted was to be happy. He'd deliberately swerved away from office work but following dreams hadn't brought the joy he wanted. Now his only dreams were about Eleanor.

How would it be if he waited until she came back, swung round her tent and told her? 'Told her what?' he asked the screen. 'I love you, Eleanor?' Maybe he should announce it in front of all the gossiping busybodies and her dad. How very Ryan Gosling – not to mention inappropriate and mortifying for her. He closed the email. If selling up was a viable option, he needed to know he had a chance with her in the long run. No point in selling off a business concern only to discover his appeal didn't last outside the boundaries of the campsite.

He flipped the sign on the door and locked up, ready to do his rounds. A cough behind him made him jump. A couple with two teenage kids stood by the golf cart. The man looked at his feet and edged behind his wife in a completely pointless attempt to get out of sight.

'Can I help you?' Logan asked.

The woman signalled for her husband to take the two children out of earshot. 'Sorry,' she said with a sheepish smile. 'I don't want them to overhear. That's one of the problems with campsites. You hear everybody's business from inside their tents whether you want to or not.'

'Yes, that can happen,' he said. Something about the woman's sweet voice was verging on sickly and he suspected she was sugaring him up before dropping a blow.

'So, we've got a very noisy couple in the tent beside us.'

He cringed. Not again. Did people think he enjoyed knocking on campers' tents and asking them if they would mind shagging quietly? He waited, trying to hold a smile he knew didn't extend to his eyes. The woman flexed her fingers like she was selecting the right words.

'The lady is a total gossip,' she said at last. 'She spent a large part of last night talking when we were trying to get to sleep.'

'Oh?' That wasn't what he expected.

'Yes. And quite a lot of it was about you. At least, I think it's you. Are you the only owner?'

He nodded and his heart sank. He was pretty sure he didn't want to hear what was coming next.

'She seems to be collating a volume of stories about you.' She gave him a wry look. 'I just wanted to make you aware. Some of it could be damaging but hopefully she was just chattering and not actually going to do anything.'

He ran his hand down his face. 'I'm not sure I want to know, but what was she saying about me?'

'Stuff about being caught naked in the woods with a woman and visiting tents at night for... you know.' She gave a little shrug.

'It's amazing how the truth gets warped.' He glanced around and sighed. 'None of that is actually what happened. So, if you're worried, please let me tell you what she said is a distortion of facts. Someone saw me wild swimming, which I assume is where the naked in the woods thing came from and I've been helping a woman and her father this week. He fell and hurt his ankle and I've been keeping an eye on them, hence the tent visits.' *Wow, great spin on the truth, man.* He was a pro at this. Sure, he'd crossed a line with Eleanor, but not in public, and not in her tent. They'd been consenting adults in a perfectly reasonable place.

'Of course,' the woman said. 'I believe you. I just wanted to let you know what was being said. Sometimes forewarned is forearmed.'

'Thank you,' Logan said. 'I hope you're having a good week.'

'We are. Hopefully, you don't think I'm interfering.'

'Not at all.' He checked his watch. 'But I should get on.'

He seethed all the way up the path in the golf cart. That meddling woman. Not the one who'd told him. That was nice of her to let him know. But the rumours were spreading faster than the bubonic plague. *Christ, why are people so interested in my personal business?*

The shower block was an absolute midden. 'People are so fucking gross.' He slammed the mop into the bucket. He wasn't cut out for this.

'I need help,' he muttered, pouring half a bottle of bleach down the toilet. 'In many ways. Mostly for not thinking things through.' He covered his mouth, almost choking on bleach fumes.

His hands reeked of bleach for the rest of the day. Would Eleanor be back in time for him to see her, or would they return late? She'd probably go straight to bed. He yawned and his shoulders sagged. He didn't want to spend a night without her. Ever. A cavity opened in his soul.

Light rain started to fall when Logan set out on his evening rounds. He generally didn't do a big clean too late because so many people were using the shower blocks then, but he liked to check it before clocking off. It could be a gamble, especially in the ladies', and he always gave plenty of warning. If he timed it around dinner time, he was usually safe. Occasionally, a mum with very young children would be making use of the quieter time. He banged loudly on the door. 'Hello, I'm here to check the toilets. If anyone needs a minute, can you give me a shout?' He kept his ear to the door. None of the showers were running. He poked his head around. 'Is anyone in? I'm coming in to clean.' There was no reply. He put the yellow warning sign outside the door and entered, picking up the usual paper towels that missed the bins, and people overused even when there were hand dryers.

He gave the toilets a quick blitz. As he shut the cubicle door, a hushed voice spoke from outside. 'Logan, are you in there?'

'Is that you, Eleanor?'

She pushed open the main door and stepped inside. 'I didn't want to come in when I saw the sign.'

'It's just me.' His eyes feasted on her, gorging on everything from her windswept hair and rosy cheeks to her slim-fit leggings and muddy trainers. He needed to drink her all in so he had an excess to keep him going when pickings were lean. But no amount of looking could sate his appetite. He needed to tell her how he felt. And he would; he wasn't afraid to do it, but a public toilet wasn't the right place for it. Maybe if he kept looking, his eyes would tell her everything. 'I missed you,' he said.

She nodded; her lips pressed together like she was trying to hold back a dam. The door framed her still figure. Her arms hung by her side, and she made no attempt to move towards him. He wanted to scoop her into a tight hug, but he stank of bleach and was wearing rubber gloves.

'Are you ok?' he lifted the bucket and emptied the water down the drain.

'Yes.' Her voice was very high and almost too breezy.

'Did you have a good day?'

'We did, thanks. We saw the ospreys. Dad was so thrilled.'

'Fantastic. That must have been fun.'

'Dad was in his element. We stopped at the Loch View Hotel on the way back. You know, the pink place.'

'Yeah. The owner's great. Briony. We were going to get a deal up and running where campers got money off food there and her guests got money off water sports. But then the roof caved in on the boat shed and, boom, no more water sports.'

'I'm so sorry about that. We met her, she seemed nice. I think Dad fancied her.'

Logan frowned. 'What? She's about my age.'

'I know.' She stifled a laugh or was it a sob? 'But Dad can be very charming.'

'Epic,' he said. 'Go Andy.'

She smiled and he got the impression there was more she wanted to say, but the words didn't come. She just gazed at him, her eyes glassy and her lips flat. Lips he'd like to kiss if he didn't smell so strongly of disinfectant.

'I need to finish cleaning,' he said. 'Then I'm free as a bird. Do you want to come round tonight? Or do you need to be with your dad?' Her dad was the most important thing in her life and he accepted that and understood her reasons. But it didn't stop him from crossing his fingers and praying to the goddess of love and lavatories to please let her say she wanted to see him tonight. *Please, please, please.* Time was running so short and there was so much he wanted to tell her and show her. So, so much.

'I'll try.' She let out a sigh. 'Dad's quite tired, so I might be able to slip out.' She swallowed. 'I'm just not sure how sensible it is.'

'Please try. I need to talk to you. Just not here and smelling like this.'

'Ok.' She held his gaze, parting her lips slightly. He leaned in and kissed her cheek without touching her with his gloved hands.

'Text me,' he said.

'Ok. Is it safe for me to go to the loo now?' She grinned and looked him up and down.

'Safe and very clean.'

She giggled and headed into a cubicle.

He pushed open the outside door. Coming across the grass ahead was the gossiping grumpy camper who was spreading all the shit about him. How he'd like to have it out with her, but he didn't dare. He lowered his head as he filled up the golf cart, hoping she'd walk on by. Then he remembered Eleanor was inside. If the woman saw her straight after she'd seen him, she might put two and two together and get eighty-nine. Should he talk to her or divert her? Was that worse? Maybe if she just went in, she would miss Eleanor. Logan wanted the ground to open and swallow him whole.

Chapter Nineteen

Eleanor

Eleanor turned off the tap and shook the excess water from her hands as the main door to the toilet block opened. She half expected it to be Logan again, but it was one of the gossipy women. Eleanor flicked her a small smile. The woman narrowed her eyes, tutted and shook her head as she went into a cubicle. *Charming.* Eleanor dried her hands at the blower and stepped outside. The golf cart had moved to the men's side and a toilet flushed inside. Logan must be in there.

The desire to see him burned so deep inside her she rubbed her sternum. Her chest was so tight she might be having a heart attack. Everything in her soul propelled her towards him, screaming at her to seize him with both hands and spend every second with him, enjoy every moment, cherish every kiss, every touch, every word. These last few short moments together were precious, just like those last weeks with her mum.

The swelling of bitter pain rose in her chest, almost cracking her ribs and splintering her heart. She let it come. Tears weren't a weakness, they relieved some of the pressure. It was ok to remember the past and be sad. Words from counsellors and well-meaning friends spilt into her brain, justifying the emotional pain she was letting engulf her. She needed to get away from here before she became a wreck in public. She wiped her eyes on the back of her hand and took a deep breath. *Right. Back to the tent.*

The door of the men's toilets opened and Logan stepped out, picking up something from the back of the golf cart. He did a double take as his gaze latched onto her.

'Eleanor. What's wrong?' He ripped off his gloves and discarded them, then closed the distance between them. She hit his chest and tears flowed freely, leaking from the corners of her eyes and rolling down her cheeks. He held her firmly against him, splaying his hands on her back and gently stroking her as she sobbed. Nothing would stop it. She just had to let it all out. But the strength of his hold, the warmth of his body and the comfort of his embrace were so much better than doing this on a pillow in a cold, empty bed. She wasn't alone. If she needed a prop to hold on to, he would be there, supporting her when it all got too much.

His hand caressed her hair, and he gently kissed her forehead. 'Oh, Eleanor. This is all so hard for you.'

'I just can't bear it. This is what I'm like. Some days, I'm fine, then all of a sudden something will set me off. I just started thinking of my last few days with Mum.' She pushed more tears away and sniffed.

'Oh no, hang on,' he muttered.

She peered up at him, but he rotated, taking her with him.

'What did I say?'

'Nothing, sorry. It's not you. It's that bloody gossip. She just came out of the loo. But never mind that. Let's sort you out.' He rubbed her back. 'Just let it all out. Tell me anything you want. I might not be able to do very much but I'll listen.'

'I don't need to talk about it. Remembering is enough, but thank you.' She sniffed. 'For being here.'

'Well, I can do that. I'll stay with you as long as you need me.'

Forever? What would he say to that? She'd been through the logistics and objections hundreds of times. His willingness couldn't change the facts or alter her position with her dad, it just put Logan in a precarious position and she didn't want to do that. He shouldn't have to sacrifice anything for her when she couldn't give him what he deserved in the long run.

'Thank you.' She snaked her arms around his middle, loving his strong abs and how good it was to be this close to him again. 'Tell me about the gossip you saw coming out of the loo.' The sorrowful wave subsided, returning to its dormant place in her chest. 'She came in when I was washing my hands and gave me a filthy look.'

'She's just a nosey old hag.' Logan cradled Eleanor's face. 'Another camper came to me this morning and said she'd overheard her talking about me, saying I'd been caught naked in the woods with someone.' He half laughed and she chuckled too.

'They got that right.'

'Ha, yes,' he said. 'It's all grown arms and legs.'

'My dad said something about that earlier too.' She gave an apologetic frown. 'So... Did she see us?'

'Probably.' He let her go. 'But it doesn't matter. Your need is greater than hers. She'll be gone soon and she can take her rumours with her.'

She swallowed, not wanting to remind him she'd be gone soon too. It wasn't like he could forget, and he probably didn't want to be reminded. She certainly didn't. Being in denial was so much easier.

For now.

She couldn't even bring herself to mention the business idea or ask him if he'd considered it any further. After purging herself of so many tears about the past, the need to live in the moment had burst out and grabbed her again.

'I should get back to Dad and check he's ok. If he is, I'll come and see you.'

'Ok.' Logan ran his thumb down her cheek. 'Are you sure that's ok? Won't he mind?'

'I'll tell him I'm going for a walk. He won't mind that. If I tell him the truth, he'll have a fit. He likes you, but I don't think he'd understand.'

'And you're ok now?' He gazed into her eyes with such an expression of love that she nearly lost the ability to stand. It shocked her to see the strength of his feelings so plainly and so strongly. And she returned it, but that hardly helped.

'Yes. I'm fine. I'll message you.'

'Ok.'

He slipped his fingers through her hair and gently tugged her towards him, placing a long, lingering kiss on her lips. Eleanor melted into him, prickles of desire needling her all over.

It could easily have gone on but they both pulled away before it got too heated. 'Well, if the busybody's peeking round the corner, at least we've given her something to gossip about this time.'

'Naughty.' She gave his upper arm a fake slap. He raised an eyebrow and grinned.

'Take care.' He stroked her cheek. 'And hopefully see you soon.'

She hurried back to the tent, not catching sight of any of the nosey parkers on the way. The rain was getting heavier and people were packing up cooking equipment and ducking indoors.

Her dad was sitting inside the tent with the door open, watching the rain falling in the stream and tapping his finger on the arm of his foldout chair. Something about his expression struck her as odd. A nervous tension spread through her veins. Had he somehow found out about her and Logan? How could she square it with him? In his eyes, she was above reproach and never put a foot wrong. Sneaking around a campsite with the owner and visiting his caravan at night didn't fit with that image, and her dad would never understand. No matter what she said, he'd think it despicable behaviour. She didn't want to disappoint him.

'Is everything ok, Dad?'

'Not really.' His eyes were still fixed on the stream.

She swallowed. What should she do now? This sad disappointment was worse than a confrontation or his outright anger. 'Why not?'

'I've just this minute come off the phone to Jamie.'

'Oh.'

'I took the opportunity to call and see how he was while you were out.'

'And...'

Her dad fixed her with narrowed eyes and a frown. 'He told me what he apparently already told you.'

Eleanor bit into her lip and looked around the grey interior of the tent. 'I didn't tell you because he said not to. He wanted to tell you himself.' And so much for him not wanting to spring it on Dad in the middle of a holiday. He appeared to have done exactly that. Sometimes Jamie exhibited the common sense of a blobfish.

'And now he's done that, though apparently he didn't want to either, but at the same time he didn't want to keep me in the dark. Honestly, I don't know whether I'm coming or going sometimes.

How can he talk about moving to New Zealand? After all we've been through?'

Eleanor slumped onto the floor and crossed her legs like a child in preschool. 'I don't know. He talked about it before... before Mum died.' She ironed a crease on her forehead with the palm of her hand. 'Maybe it's just put things in perspective for him. Maybe he thinks if he doesn't do it now, he never will.'

'Yes, yes, I get that. And maybe I'm just a selfish old man, but I feel as if I've been robbed of my wife and now I'm going to be robbed of a son and my grandchildren. It's not like I can just nip down the road to see them if they're on the other side of the planet.'

'I know.' She took his hand and rubbed the wrinkled skin on the back. 'It's not being selfish, it's being honest. That's how it feels to you. But how it feels to Jamie is that if he stays, he'll have missed an opportunity.'

'That's true.' He shook his head and sighed. 'The world's changing so much and sometimes I feel left behind.'

'Well, you've still got me.' A heartstring twanged in her chest, reinforcing every reason why she couldn't be with Logan. If she left her father, he'd be heartbroken. She couldn't. And there was no solution other than the one she had now. She couldn't expect Logan to slot his life into this. No matter how much they fancied each other right now, the reality would soon hit. They couldn't live as a couple without the old troubles arising again. Logan would tire of her always putting her dad's needs first, just as Mark had. Mark had been fine at the beginning too, but resentment had grown quickly.

Also, the logistics were unfathomable. How could she uproot her dad and bring him up here away from everything he knew? And Logan couldn't abandon the place he'd poured his heart and soul into.

'I'll make some food.' She wanted to say not to worry, but she couldn't. Her dad would worry anyway, just as she would. When Jamie left for New Zealand, the family would be set adrift again. At least with him not far away, he was on call in an emergency. Not that she'd ever needed him, but he was part of a wider support network. He was the only other person she could trust with Dad. The only person who could give her respite. Otherwise, it was just her. Every day she had to be back to cook meals or at least make sure there was something easy to heat up if she was going to be late. Dad had learned to use the washing machine and that was a blessing, but cooking was beyond him. Wasn't it? Or was she just enabling him and using him as a prop, so she didn't have to think too hard about the future? Maybe so she didn't allow herself to properly feel the loss of her mum. Such big thoughts sent shivers through her body. But she still couldn't imagine herself moving away and leaving him.

'I think I'll have another early night,' Dad said. 'These long days tire me out.'

'Ok.' Eleanor lit the camping stove under the canopy at the front of the tent. She couldn't ignore the chance. If Dad was happily tucked up in his sleeping bag, she could go to Logan without arousing any suspicion. She filled a pot with water and set it to boil.

'Any ideas where we should go tomorrow?' Dad asked. 'For our last day. Such a lovely place. We only ever scratch the surface really.'

'I'm not sure. What do you fancy?'

'My ankle is a lot better, so I'd quite like to go for a walk. How about we drive up to the Dalarvin Wood? The paths there aren't too taxing and it's very beautiful.'

'Yes, sure. That sounds great.' She tipped half a bag of pasta into the pot. She normally enjoyed all of these things, but now it just felt like time away from Logan. Why could she not stop thinking like that? She was obsessed... Or in love.

They ate quietly at the little table inside the tent. Raindrops pattered on the canvas and Dad yawned. He was still obviously brooding about Jamie, staring into space and tapping his fingers, showing no inclination to read or divert his mind. Maybe he was just emotionally exhausted, trying to fathom what life would be like when his eldest son left the country. His world was in tatters again.

After dinner, he went to the showers and Eleanor cleared up, then messaged Logan.

ELEANOR: Dad's wanting an early night but he's not feeling great. Will explain later. As soon as I get him sorted, I'll come over as long as I'm sure he's fine. Hope that's ok. XX

She'd barely stacked away the remaining crockery when a message pinged back.

LOGAN: Of course it is. Come whenever you're ready. I'll be here, but if you need to stay with him, then do. That's more important XX

The tent zip whirred down and Eleanor stowed her phone in the back pocket of her jeans as Dad ducked in. 'The rain's getting quite heavy,' he said. 'I hope it eases off before tomorrow. I don't fancy a walk in this quite so much.'

'Let's hope it goes off. It's nice listening to it on the tent though, so I don't mind if it falls overnight.'

'Yes, it's very soothing.' Dad stowed away his wash bag. 'Now, you sleep tight, young lady.' He bent down to climb into his sleeping pod.

'I'm going for a walk first. It's a bit early for me.'

'Well, don't stay out too long.' He pulled open his sleeping bag and smoothed it along the camp bed. 'You'll get soaked and it's never easy drying clothes in the tent.'

'I'll not go far. I just need air.' She leaned over and kissed his cheek. He gave her a hug, then climbed into his pod and zipped it up. The tent was reasonably tidy, but she busied herself, folding their jackets and arranging the remaining food, listening as her dad shuffled into his sleeping bag. Through the canvas, she saw his reading light pop on and heard him open his book. She let out a little sigh. She'd hoped he would go straight to sleep.

'I'm just heading out now,' she said. 'Night-night.'

'Night. Don't be too long.'

She ducked out of the tent and zipped it up. Raindrops splashed from the trees above and she pulled up her hood. As she headed towards Logan's caravan, doubt raced through her system. Would Dad wait up? She couldn't be away too long in case he panicked and what flimsy excuse could she make up for staying out? No one in their right mind would go on a long walk in this.

She arrived at Logan's door and knocked. He opened it, grinning broadly. 'Hey,' he said. It was oddly dark inside, but a flickering light was bouncing off the wall as she stepped in. She lowered her hood and glanced around. The curtains were drawn and on the table beside the door, some candles flickered.

'This is so pretty.' Her gaze travelled over the neat interior. The night before, she'd been so intent on helping clean up the water mess and getting down to other business she hadn't taken much in. In the ambient light, she saw a cute little sofa area at the opposite end of the bedroom, where she'd spent most of her time the previous night. Heat flared in her cheeks. Who would believe it? She'd managed to miss this wonderful space because she'd been so desperate to jump into bed with Logan.

'It's a lot better tonight as the floor's dry. The rug in the living area was utterly saturated, so I've chucked it out and some of the flooring is warped. What a mess. Not the kind of place I'd like to welcome you to.'

'I don't mind, Logan. I think it's cute. You've made it so homely.'

He took her hand and gave her a weak smile. 'Not as cute as you. Has to be said, cheesy as it may be.'

'Listen, I'm really sorry, but Dad said not to be long. I think he might wait up for me and I don't want him to know I'm here. He wouldn't get it and he's just had some news from my brother that's unsettled him.'

'Oh no, sorry to hear that. Is someone ill?'

'No, nothing like that. My brother, Jamie, dropped a bombshell. He's moving to New Zealand with his family. My brother, Harry, is already living in Germany. Dad just feels like everyone is leaving him.'

'Ah, bless him. That's tough.' Logan ran his thumb down her cheek. 'You best get back to him. If you want to sit for a bit, that's cool, but go back as soon as you need to.'

'I'll stay for a little while.'

He led her to the little sofa area, and she fell quite naturally under his arm as they sat. She kicked off her shoes and curled her legs up beside her. How easy would it be to stay here? Sighing, she nestled in, letting Logan caress her hair. The question she should be asking was: how difficult would it be to leave?

Chapter Twenty

Logan

Logan held Eleanor in his arms, running her hair between his fingers. He closed his eyes and rested his lips on her forehead in a half kiss, half sigh. She didn't have a lot of time here, so every second was precious. Raw lust would have him jump her, but he wasn't a caveman. Even this tender moment was precious and calming. Having her here so close, so present, so his.

'Would you like a drink?' he murmured onto her forehead. 'Or anything to eat?'

'Just you.' She looked up and slid her hand around his jaw. Their lips met and he kissed her like there was no tomorrow because, really, there wasn't. Every second in her presence had to be used to the full. She crawled onto his lap and straddled him, wrapping her arms around his neck. 'I don't have long and I don't mind what we do, but I don't think I can resist you.'

He laughed and his sides ached. Eleanor grinned back, her shining face so beautiful his insides soared to a new high. That was what her smile did to him. He slipped his hands around her waist. 'We don't have much time.'

'I know. I want to be with you, like properly.'

'I want that too, but I don't want to rush.'

'Please...' She glanced around hopelessly. 'My body is aching for you. Is that ridiculous?'

'No, I know exactly what you mean. I just don't want you to think I'm only in this for the physical side of things. I'm really not. In fact, I want so much more.'

'Me too.' Before he could say another word, she kissed him again, pushing open his mouth and brushing her tongue against his. The touch sent wild sparks through him, and he forgot what he was trying to say. Words didn't matter any more. Nothing did. Just Eleanor.

They made out like crazy teens before finding their way to the bedroom section at the opposite end of the static. Logan's hands flailed around, searching for furniture to guide him as he couldn't stop kissing her long enough to look where he was going.

He sat on the bed and she climbed over him. Their bodies entwined and she drew as close to him as she could, taking his face in her hands and kissing him deep. He responded by matching her need.

His hands roamed over her smooth skin, caressing her and teasing her most intimate place until she squealed. She chased his mouth, seeming to crave more kisses and he obliged. It didn't take long to coax her into a frenzy and she shuddered with pleasure. He held her, peppering her neck with kisses. 'I've never met anyone like you.' He kissed her some more. 'No one. I've never had such an instant connection with anyone.'

'Me neither.' She took in a slow, calming breath. He held her tight against him, loving the closeness.

'Was that enough?' he said. If her dad was waiting, he didn't want to keep her too long, even if he could hardly bear to let her go.

'No.' She pulled back and looked him in the eye. 'I want all of you.'

'Ok. Give me two seconds. Housekeeping break.'

She giggled. 'Do say that to all the girls?'

'There's only you.' He grinned, shifting from her hold and leaning over to open the flip-up cabinet beside the bed.

'I meant before me.'

'I can't remember anyone else. You're the only one who matters.' Keeping protection stashed away was either very optimistic or just being prepared for every eventuality. Whichever it was, he was glad. He got ready, then returned to her with a kiss.

'You're the only one for me too,' she said. 'Nothing has ever been this good.'

She clambered over him again and he smiled onto her lips. So much for the reserved, good girl she claimed to be. When she eased herself onto him, he let out a groan of satisfaction, taking a moment just to savour the deep physical bond between them, consummating the intense love boiling in his heart. This wasn't the time to tell her, but he could show her how much he cared for her, wanted her, adored her. He'd had quickies in his lifetime – not with the campers – but this was different.

He resumed pleasuring her and showering her with kisses as he gently rocked inside her. 'You're the most beautiful person I know. I love... the way you make me feel. Everything. Oh, god, you're just so... oh, good.'

Their kisses grew ragged, then Eleanor's breathing caught and she shuddered, crying out again, 'Oh, Logan.'

Hearing his name on her lips set a fire in his belly; his body yearned for the ultimate release. Their face-to-face position, with her still in his lap, was deliriously intimate. The heat from their bodies could start a furnace. Her sensual lips sealed his and she tasted sweet and addictive. The fresh scent of her body mist went straight to his head and a surge of need slammed into him. He pulled out of the kiss for air before a thrill of hot blood shot through his veins and he thrust deep, racing to the pinnacle. He let out a rough moan as he crested the wave, riding it out as the fires inside raged, then gradually subsided. Her soft fingers clung to his shoulders, pinning him close. He let every tingling sensation work its way through his bloodstream, aware only of the deep warmth of her hold and her hands gripping his shoulders.

They cuddled together for a few moments, letting the world settle. With the fires of lust tempered, the glow of the aftermath crept in. This was pure gold. Eleanor's touch was alchemic.

Nothing else could kindle feelings like this. So raw, yet whole and utterly precious. She moved first, sliding off him. He kept one arm around her and flopped back, his head falling into the gap between the pillows. What felt like a goofy, love-drugged smile spread over his face and she rolled on top of him. He wrapped his arms around her, clinging to her, and kissed her, cherishing the warmth and affection of the moment, soaking up the spiritual bliss and holding her tight against his hot chest. A thin sheen of sweat stuck them together like glue, fastening them in a position he wanted to stay in for a long time. It wasn't the comfiest, and it probably looked ridiculous, but it was dreamy.

He closed his eyes, splaying his hands on her naked back. Was this the moment to say the words? He'd waited all day and he really wanted to tell her. But he knew the rules. Never say those three little words during sex with a new date... What about after? And surely, she was more than a date, though technically they hadn't even had a date yet. So, maybe he could screw the rules and just say it.

Eleanor peeled herself off him and sat up, hugging herself. In the flickering candlelight, she looked suddenly naked and alone. He hauled himself out of the pillow den and sat up too.

'Eleanor, I—'

'I need to go.' She swallowed. 'I hate running out on you like this. I really do but I've already been away longer than I meant.'

He stretched out to touch her arm, but she'd already climbed off the bed. She ran through the narrow doorway, past the little kitchen and into the sofa area. After tidying himself up, he caught up with her as she was pulling on her clothes.

'I've been thinking about your idea,' he said.

'Great. And you want to try?'

He gave a little shrug. 'Working with you is better than not seeing you at all.'

'That makes me feel a bit better.' She fastened her bra and smiled.

He nodded.

'We're going to the Dalarvin Wood for a walk tomorrow.' She tugged her top over her head. 'I'm not sure how long we'll be, especially if it rains. Maybe if we're back early, I could come over.'

'Of course.' He rubbed his hand over his face, trying to think rationally. 'I have a cousin who's working at Dalarvin just now.' The bizarre thought filtered through the cold, lonely ache within. If only he had a good reason to go and see her, then he could perhaps run into Eleanor at the same time, but how could he leave the campsite?

'We might run into him then.' Eleanor flopped onto the sofa and put on her socks.

'Her,' he said. 'She works for the Forestry Land Trust. Their site offices are at Dalarvin.'

Eleanor raised her eyebrows. 'I think I've seen the building.'

'Yeah. It's at the south end of the wood, but you know to park further up for the woodland trails, yeah?' Why were they talking about this? He just wanted to have Eleanor in his arms again.

'Yes, I do.' She tied her laces and got to her feet. 'I looked it all up and we have a map.' She stood for a moment, gazing at him. He was buck naked and exposed, but he didn't care. She could have every ounce of flesh she wanted. 'So sorry about this.' She pushed up on tiptoes and kissed his cheek. 'I hate running out on you. I feel like I'm using you.'

'No. I totally get it.' He held her for a few too short moments.

Standing naked at the door, he watched her run across the campsite in the rain. Sure, he got it, but did it mean he had to like it? If he wanted her, this was what life would be like. He jumped under his covers and threw his head into the pillow. His thoughts mused back to his cousin, Cha. Maybe he could drop in and visit her. A completely crazy idea. But he hadn't seen her for a while and this was a new job. She hadn't been in position long. When she'd mentioned where she was working in a message the other night – before telling him to get to sleep – he hadn't clicked just how easy it would be to nip up and visit her. Why not? If the busybodies moaned about the shop being shut, he could say he was checking on a family member. Because he was a family orientated kind of guy. Surely they couldn't object to that? But while he was there, he would find a way to run into Eleanor.

By the time he woke up the next morning, the plan was fully baked in his mind. His guilty conscience made him open the shop half an hour early; it was a small gesture and didn't make him feel any better. Of course, he shouldn't be doing this, but it was one day. Not even that. Just a few hours in his life and come next week, he wouldn't have this chance. If he wanted time with Eleanor, he needed to make it, and he couldn't see another way.

He printed out a sign for the door: *shop closed due to family emergency*

Surely that was enough. Or was it too much? If he thought any more about it, his head would explode. This was Eleanor's last full day and he had to make the most of it.

A string of messages had passed between them over the course of the night, most of them with her apologies for how the night had ended and her annoyance that her dad had been fast asleep when she got back, so she needn't have rushed away. He'd half-hoped she'd come back but he knew deep down she couldn't do that. He'd steered the messages on to her plans for the following day and discovered they planned to leave about ten. That gave him time for a quick round of the site and a clean, then back to the shop to check for last-minute customers. At ten past ten, he spotted her car driving out of the gate. He grabbed his waterproof jacket, shoved the sign on the door and locked it.

Before any grumpy campers, or his own conscience, could stop him, he jumped into his pickup and headed out of the gate. It was about a twenty-minute drive to the wood, but each second increased the pain in his chest. His stomach roiled with guilt and the minuscule bowlful of porridge he'd forced down for breakfast was pushing to get back out again. He tapped the wheel. *I shouldn't be doing this.* He should be back at the site, manning the shop and looking out for trouble. But surely he was entitled to some time off? This was no different from doing a supermarket run. Except that was a necessity.

He pulled into the car park and spotted Eleanor's car straight away. It was empty and she and her dad must have chosen one of the paths. Now the problems started. Which path? And why had he thought Cha would be here? She'd be at the office or maybe on a site visit. He couldn't claim to be visiting her if he didn't even know where she was. He opened his boot and sat on the tailgate. This was where a mind messed up on love got him.

Birds twittered in the trees overhanging the car park and branches swayed in the light wind. Somewhere in the distance, a louder sound droned. Was that a chainsaw? He pulled on his walking shoes, slammed the boot and set off in the direction of the noise. The hills and the trees distorted the sound, and he ploughed aimlessly up a track, stopping every now and then to get his bearings. Messaging Cha wasn't an option; signal was crap up here. But there was the off chance if he met a forestry worker, they might know where she was. Like the tiniest chance in the world.

The wood opened up beside the path, and the valley sprawled away. The River Briar snaked through the glen and felled trees lined the hillside of a secondary path not far away. He walked quicker and his chest lightened as he spotted a figure in bright orange overalls and a hard hat wielding a chainsaw. From under the figure's helmet was a long, blue ponytail. *Cha*. No way. This was too easy.

He just stopped himself from calling her name – she'd never hear him from here – and broke into a run, veering off the path onto the smaller one and jogging down the hill towards his cousin.

'Cha!' he called as he approached. A weird rush of helplessness mingled with relief flooded him. He wanted to hug her, knowing everything was ok. She was a safe person, a friendly face, someone he'd known forever and who would understand if he went to pieces.

She turned around and lifted the thick visor on the front of her hard hat. 'Logan? What the hell are you doing here?'

He marched up to her. She obviously realised he was about to grab her as she put the chainsaw down. He threw his arms around her. 'I just wanted to see you.'

'See me? How the hell did you know where I was?' She patted his back and chuckled.

'I didn't. Well, you said you were working here in your message the other night, but I thought you were doing office work these days. Didn't you ditch the tree surgery for something more settled?'

She pulled back and cocked her head. 'Are you having a laugh? Me, settled? But, yeah, you're right. But we've had a spate of people being off sick and the work up here is on a tight deadline, so I'm doing a bit of moonlighting to help out. It's quite nice getting a break from my desk.'

'I can't imagine you at a desk, little cuz.'

'It happens occasionally.' She removed her helmet, shaking free her long, blue hair. Her reputation as the wayward one in the family was misplaced. She could be strong-willed, sure, but as far as career goals went, she was way ahead of him.

Her brow creased and she looked him up and down. 'Something weird is going on, isn't it?'

'How do you mean?' Logan thrust his hands into his pockets. *Rumbled already.*

She tilted her head and folded her arms. 'It's obvious. There's no way you would just turn up here. Come on, tell me what's going on. You're not in some activist group, are you? Have they sent you to stop us from cutting trees? You know what I do is actually to help preserve the forests?'

He clapped his hands and glanced around. 'Yeah, I know that. It's nothing like that. I just fancied a walk and I hoped I'd run into you. I can't believe it was this easy.'

She looked at her watch. 'I could take a break for a bit and walk with you. My boss, Nick,' – she pulled a face – 'is expecting me back in the office later, so I better not take too long.' Stooping, she picked up the chainsaw, then crossed to a nearby van and packed it in along with her helmet and gloves. 'We could go through the woods up there to the little loch. It's cross country but it's quick.'

'I don't mind cross country.'

'I know. That's why I suggested it.' She prodded him and they set off at a fast walk. She beckoned him to follow her up a deer track on the other side of the main path and they scrabbled up through the undergrowth into the trees. 'How's the campsite?' she asked.

'Busy.'

'Who's looking after it today?'

The guilt seared in his chest. Of all the questions she could have asked, it had to be that one. 'No one. I just needed a break. I've had some tricky customers this week and I had to step away.'

'Sometimes it's the best way.'

Crashing through the bushes, they pushed their way to the top of the hill, then scrambled down the other side. The loch was in view and, even on an overcast day, looked stunning. The hills curved around. Logan and Cha hit a thick patch of trees before stepping out onto the path. He brushed himself down, then looked up. Today's timing just got better and better. Who should be walking towards them but Eleanor and Andy? Shit and double shit. He so hadn't thought this through. What must it look like? And he'd have to talk to them. What would Cha make of that?

Eleanor's eyes had zoned in on him and uncertainty flashed across her face as her gaze flicked to Cha.

Logan cleared his throat. 'Hi.'

'Oh, it's you.' Andy's focus travelled over both Logan and Cha, taking in their messy clothes and lingering on Cha's overalls.

'This is my cousin, Cha.' Logan directed his words at Eleanor, watching as relief flooded her face. 'I just nipped up to see her.'

'Oh,' Eleanor said.

'These two, Eleanor and Andy' – Logan turned to Cha – 'are guests at the campsite.'

'Hi.' Cha gave a little wave, but her eyes wandered from Eleanor to Logan, and she pressed her lips together as if suppressing a laugh.

'Well, it's nice to bump into you,' Andy said. 'We'll leave you in peace.'

Eleanor gave Logan a pained smile and he nodded. These were the crumbs he had to survive on. As they carried on around the lochside, Cha tapped him on the upper arm.

'Interesting,' she said.

He ruffled his hair, still watching Eleanor.

'Did you plan that?'

'No.'

'Really?' Cha put her hands on her hips. 'That look she gave you. I think she fancies you.'

He glanced away, chewing his lip, but couldn't stop his mouth from curling up.

'Thought so.' Cha raked up her hair, letting it fall around her shoulders. 'And you fancy her.'

'Yup. I do.'

'Bloody hell, Logan. Do you think you're still a teenager? Do you normally go about crushing on the campers?' She peered at him with steely eyes. 'I know you set this up. Or you at least hoped to bump into her.'

'Ok. Yes. I did. But no, I don't do this all the time. She's a special case.'

'So are you.' She rubbed his arm with a smirk. 'Very special.'

'Shut up.'

She chuckled. 'Look, you've had your eyeful. Let's walk.'

He fell in step with her, going the opposite way from Eleanor. His heart twisted and pulled, willing him to go back. 'It's worse than that.'

'Is it? Explain.'

'I slept with her. Twice.'

'What the fuck?' Cha stared at him, shaking her head, her eyes bugging out. 'Are you insane? Isn't that against some kind of code?'

'Probably. I wouldn't normally but I really... care about her.'

'Do you know her? I mean, is she a regular or something?'

'No. I only met her a few days ago.' Telling her they'd met as teenagers would only muddy the waters further and he was already wading through a swamp of his own emotions.

'Ok. So, she's just a hook-up really.'

'No. She isn't.'

'There's nothing wrong with that, Logan. It's allowed.'

'Yeah, I know. But that isn't what's happening here. I'm serious. I've never met anyone like her before. What the hell will I do tomorrow when she goes? I can't stand it.'

'Oh, Logan.' Cha's expression softened and she opened his arms to him. He folded himself into her, letting her hug it out. 'I don't know what to suggest.'

'Me neither. I'm completely lost.'

Chapter Twenty-One

Eleanor

Eleanor fidgeted with her phone in the pocket of her walking trousers. Her feet dragged on the path and she tried to gee up some enthusiasm from the scenery. But Logan was back down the path, walking in the other direction. Why was he there? What a mystery. Just nipped up to see his cousin? A likely story. *Obviously, he came to see me.* She pressed her lips together. Silly man. Didn't he know this was her life? She couldn't spend time with him and it had led him to this. It changed nothing. They'd had a few more seconds looking at each other but now it just amounted to more heartache because she couldn't go back and spend time with him. It would have been better if he'd stayed away. She was messing up his life for him and it had to stop. If she'd stayed sensible this week, none of this would have happened. He'd abandoned his campsite to see her. The knowledge someone cared enough about her to do that was overwhelming, but it wasn't right. He had a job to do and she was distracting him.

'Very odd that.' Dad glanced behind. 'I wonder what he was doing here? Seems an odd place to run into him.'

'He said he was visiting his cousin.'

'Hmm. I'm not sure I believe that was his cousin.' Dad frowned. 'I'm starting to think the rumours about him have some foundations in the truth. The way they came out of the bushes looked very suspicious.'

'I don't think so, Dad.' *Great.* Now her dad thought Logan was putting it about too and if he ever got wind of the truth, it would be almost impossible to shift his mindset. He'd just never understand. Would he? She sucked her lip and looked at him. No. She couldn't tell him. Saying it out loud would sound ridiculous.

They found a place to sit at the edge of the loch and Eleanor pulled off her rucksack and spread a picnic rug on the ground. Dad grumbled a little as he sat. 'These bones are getting old and stiff.'

She pulled out the sandwiches she'd packed, and they ate in silence. The wind picked up, whipping the trees behind them and sending long ripples over the loch.

'Oh dear,' Dad muttered, fighting with his hood. 'It's getting wild. This has been such a blustery summer. One of the years we came with you three, we had wall-to-wall sunshine.'

Eleanor unthreaded hair from her lips. 'Yes. I remember walking through the village in bare feet and my soles sticking to the concrete. It was painful.'

'That was the year. You lived on ice creams, and I don't think any of you wore anything but swimsuits.'

'We always had fun here.'

'I sometimes wish we'd taken the opportunity to buy that cottage. Maybe we wouldn't have lived here full time, but we could have retired here. Country air might have been better for your mum.'

She shook her head sadly. 'I don't think it would have made any difference, Dad.'

The wind got so wild they wolfed their lunch. She battled to fold the picnic rug and shove it back into her bag. Lashings of rain hit her face as she flung the rucksack onto her back.

'Where has this come from?' Dad shielded his face. 'Was it forecast to be this bad?'

'I'm not sure.' She'd neglected to look at the weather forecast the night before.

'Let's get back to the car,' he said. 'I'm not keen on this.'

Heads down, they pushed along the path towards the car park. Trees waved wildly on either side. Eleanor wasn't looking forward to returning to the tent. It would be flapping all over the place and it would be a long afternoon entertaining Dad. Sneaking out to see Logan wasn't an option. He might still be out with Cha for one, but above all her dad would get suspicious.

She could hardly say she was going for a walk again when they'd just come back from one in this weather.

'Shall we get a hot drink?' she suggested. It didn't matter that they'd just had lunch. Her dad liked cafes, especially if he could get a cup of tea, a cake and somewhere out of the rain to sit.

'Good idea.'

She drove into Glenbriar and they spotted a café called the Drip Drop Coffee Shop on the main street with a space close by. She nipped the car into it and they sped towards the door. It slammed shut behind them.

'It's a windy one today.' A smiling waitress greeted them at the door with menus in her hand.

'It certainly is.' Dad flattened his wispy grey hair.

'It's going to get very stormy later. Marcus Bowman said so.' The waitress led them to a table.

'Who?' Dad shook his head.

'You know, "Scotland's favourite weatherman"?'

'Never heard of him.'

'I know who you mean,' Eleanor said. 'My friend hopes every year he'll appear on *Strictly*. Apparently, he'd be the hottest tango dancer ever.'

'Oh gosh, He would be. He's adorable,' the waitress said. 'I switch on *The Morning Show* just to see him, but anyway, he said there might be a hurricane, though that sounds a bit dramatic to me.'

'Don't say that,' Eleanor said. 'We're in a tent.'

'I'm sure it won't be that bad,' the waitress said. 'But then, Marcus Bowman is usually right. Though I don't think we really get hurricanes in Scotland.'

'Just as well,' Dad muttered, taking a seat at the table by the window.

'I have the lunch menus here.'

'Just drinks and cake, please.' Eleanor unzipped her wet jacket.

'Of course. All the drinks are on the menu and feel free to look at the cakes. They're on display on the shelf. We change them all the time, so they're not on the menu. I'll give you a few minutes.'

Eleanor took off her jacket and swung it over the back of the seat before scanning the hot drinks column on the menu. A gust rattled the striped canopy outside the window. 'I think they do get hurricanes up here,' she said, more to herself than her dad. 'I'm sure I heard about one before.'

'Hurricane-force winds, I expect.' Dad peered at the menu. 'Though I think they're rare. But if it's been on the forecast then maybe it's true.'

'Hopefully it's not for this area.' She sighed. Typical if one decided to strike the week they were in a tent. She shivered and clenched her shoulders, craving the warmth of a soft blanket... or Logan. Yes, Logan. Her outlook on spending a night in a tent in a storm might change considerably if she had him to cuddle up with. As it was, she wouldn't sleep a wink, panicking about the tent collapsing or trees falling on them. There was just as much danger of that happening even if he was there, but somehow, she'd feel braver with him beside her. The waitress took their order and she gazed out the window, trying not to notice the people getting blown along at top speed. Was this normal for June? *Four seasons in one day.* That was the joke her brothers used to make about Scotland. Maybe it was true.

'What shall we do this afternoon?' Dad turned his focus away from the window. 'It's not a day for birdwatching or outdoor activities but it's our last day. I feel we should use it.'

'How about a historic house? There are some not too far from here.'

'Might I suggest the Glenvorneth Estate,' the waitress said, laying two huge cakes in front of them. Eleanor's nose twitched and she tried not to screw up her face, but her stomach clenched with a wave of nausea. All year, she'd been off food when the stress of losing Mum caught up with her but now it wasn't that. All she could see was Logan.

'Where is that?' Dad asked.

'Not too far out of the village. Take the road on the north side of the loch, then the hill road. The house is having an open weekend starting today. My mum wants to go tomorrow. I just hope the weather improves. It's quite rare for the house to be open but apparently, they have a great collection of historic costumes and this is the first time they'll be on show.'

'Sounds like something you would like.' Dad smiled at Eleanor.

'Yes, it does sound interesting. We could try that.' She picked at her cake and checked out some photos of Glenvorneth House on her phone. 'Most of it is a private house but the older part is "well-preserved and beautifully furnished",' she read from the webpage.

'And how long will it take to get there?'

'Not too long. Twenty minutes maybe.'

'Let's go there then.'

After finishing their cakes and drinks, she drove them to the Glenvorneth Estate. Trees along the driveway swayed in the wind and she felt like she was pushing the car against an insurmountable force. The castle sat in a prominent hillside position, looking over a sweeping glen. Estate tracks sprawled in all directions through cultivated woodlands overridden with rhododendrons in full bloom; their huge flowers tossed and danced in the wind, barely hanging on.

Dad's eyes lit up and Eleanor was pleased she'd made the effort. He loved places like this. They hurried across the windy courtyard, holding onto their heads as the wind whipped their hair. As soon as they were inside, Dad latched onto a guide and listened intently to her stories about the costumes, putting on his glasses to examine them and asking questions. Eleanor wished she could match her dad's enthusiasm for the minutiae. She wandered around, browsing the collection but not really seeing anything, even though she normally loved old costumes and fancy houses. The windows drew her attention and the view over the rolling estate. What a vision. She could appreciate its beauty, but her heart had slipped out and been removed to a cold store, wrapped in cling film, forgotten and left behind. Tomorrow she'd be driving home. On Monday, she'd be back at work. All this would be left behind.

They stayed at Glenvorneth until almost five. When they left, the guide was outside the door, taking in the welcome sign. 'Safe travels,' she said.

The car buffeted down the track and the windscreen wipers hurtled from side to side. Eleanor squinted forward. 'This is getting worse. I hope the tent's still standing.' They stopped for a chippy tea in Glenbriar on the way home and ate it in the car, which eased the pressure to cook something in this weather.

The tension lifted from her shoulders as she drove into the campsite and saw the tent still up. The canvas shuddered and swayed with the trees surrounding it and great pools of water had gathered on top of it. She parked up and shook the water off the top before they ducked inside. The kettle still had some water in it and she set it to boil. A cosy hot water bottle and a blanket were called for. At some point, she was going to have to brave the elements for the shower block, but that could wait.

Her phone beeped with notifications, and she dismissed them all except one.

LOGAN: Hope you get back safe. Sorry if that was crazy this morning. I just miss you so much. Have a lovely time with your dad. XX

She sucked her lips and sighed. The end was upon them. This was it. Tomorrow morning, she and her dad would pack up and go. Hanging about would just prolong the agony. She hit reply.

ELEANOR: We had a great time, thank you. Back in the tent now. It's a bit scary in the wind. XX

Right on cue, the tent flapped and lurched. The canvas pulled tight over the table at the side. Dad raised his eyebrows. 'Wild.'

The violently crashing stream beyond sounded almost up to the door. Eleanor crawled to the flap and peered out. Water sped over the pebbles, racing in a tumble of foam and spray. Could it burst its banks and get this far? Dad had settled into his chair with a book. She filled her hot water bottle and sat, cuddling it. What a pathetic substitute when she really wanted to be cuddled up to Logan.

'Hello,' His voice spoke from outside and a hand slapped against the door of the tent.

'Hello?' she said, glancing at her dad. He took off his glasses and frowned.

'Can I talk to one of you, please?' Logan said.

She shuffled to the door flap, unzipped it from the bottom, and stood under the tiny awning, coming face to face with a drenched Logan. 'What's going on?'

'I'm going around all the tents close to the trees and the stream to check everyone's ok.'

'I think we're ok.' She gave a little shrug.

'I don't know if you've seen, but there's a severe weather warning for this area; high winds and rain all night. This stream doesn't usually flood, but there is a possibility.'

'What does that mean? Should we move the tent?'

'You can do, but you're quite far back and in a raised position, so I'm quietly confident you'll be ok. In fact, it's better than being too exposed. I hope the folks out in the middle have very strong pegs.'

'Oh dear. Is it the hurricane?'

'We're on the outer edge of the storm, so the winds won't be as bad as further north, but there will still be strong gusts.'

'Ok. That's something.' She gazed at him, wishing she could hug him, but aside from the fact he was soaked through, she didn't dare do anything with her dad so close by.

'I'll message you,' he whispered.

She nodded and ducked back into the tent.

'Dear, dear.' Dad rummaged about in his sleeping pod. 'I think I'll go to the shower now before it gets any worse. I'll wear my waterproofs over my pyjamas.'

'How about I drive us?' she said. 'I know it's not far, but this is an emergency.'

'Good plan.'

They collected all their stuff and ran for the car. Once she was alone in the shower block, she checked her messages.

LOGAN: If you want to move your tent, I'll help you later though I'm pretty sure you'll be fine. I'm helping some other people move but they are right on the bank. One of the grumpy women seems to think the weather is all my fault and is threatening me with god knows what. She wants me to pay for her to sleep in a hotel room tonight. Call me if you need anything. XX

Poor Logan.

Hot water revitalised her cold limbs. Pity she couldn't save some of this heat for when she returned to the cold tent. A memory of a previous visit swirled to the front of her mind. Inside the old shower block that had been run down and spidery, she'd seen a notice pinned to the inside of a door, advertising an opportunity for a couple looking for a lifestyle change. The previous owners had needed people to work with them, and that was how they'd presented it. Had Logan tried that? Advertising in the toilet block seemed like a long shot, but who knew? Perhaps a holidaymaker would see it and decide it was just what they wanted.

She closed her eyes and let the water hit her face. When she'd read that notice all those years ago, she'd fantasised all night about being the one to take on that job... with the boy from the campsite at her side. He'd gone on to do it, while her fantasy had blown off in the wind.

Dad was waiting in the car when she came out. She could hardly see for the rain as she drove back to the tent. They wasted no time getting inside. Cosying into her sleeping bag, she lay on her back, staring up at the flapping canvas. Her phone told her it was just past eight. So early. This was going to be a long night. She rolled onto her side and scrolled through social media, not really caring about any of it. Logan had accounts and she followed them or friended him. His pictures on Instagram were funny. She scrolled through, smiling at the selfies of him in different places, usually on the campsite, but a few from April showed him at a large country house with his family. She spotted Rowena and Iain. And there was Cha. She read the tags to guess who some other people were. Another cousin, Matthew, with his partner, Nina. Logan's sister, Sophie, with her husband, David, and a cute baby daughter. Some elderly grandparents and an aunt. This was the wonderful world of Logan. She nipped over to look at some of her friends. She'd neglected them this week. They wouldn't mind... Well, they might if they knew the real reason for her radio silence.

The wind battered the tent. Dad's snores from the opposite pod obviously meant he wasn't bothered by the weather. Eleanor rolled over. She'd never get to sleep. Her fingers strayed to messenger, and she opened it.

ELEANOR: I hope you got the other people moved. I don't want to move, but I can't sleep. Dad's flat out, but these winds are freaking me out completely. What's the caravan like? XX

She hit send and looked at a few more stories, willing a reply to come quickly, but the moments ticked on and nothing happened. Maybe he was still out and about moving tents and trying to appease grumpy campers. Should she go help? If she couldn't sleep, at least she could be useful. She sat up, keeping the sleeping bag around her. The thought of going out in this and leaving the relative warmth of the tent did not appeal, but for him, she'd do it.

Among the constant roar of the wind, the flapping tent and her dad's snoring, she discerned another noise. Something shuffling outside, then a whisper. Her hand leapt to her heart in shock.

'Eleanor, it's me.'

She smiled at the sound of Logan's voice. 'What are you doing here?' she whispered through the canvas.

'Can I come in?'

'Are you serious? That's crazy.'

'I know, but this is our last chance to see each other and your dad's clearly asleep. I can hear him snoring over the wind.'

'Ok,' she whispered. 'But for god's sake, be quiet.' She screwed up her eyes as she unzipped her sleeping pod, trying to make it as silent as possible but somehow making it louder. The same thing happened at the front door.

Logan pulled off his boots on the porch, then stepped inside in a gust of wind. He pressed his finger to his lips, took hold of the zip pull and attempted to zip up the tent without a sound – with the same level of success as she'd had when opening it. Her heart thudded. This could go so horribly wrong. Her dad was still snoring but even so... What if it was fake and he was just waiting to jump out and catch them? Logan pulled off his waterproof trousers, then sat down to take off his jacket. Eleanor had never noticed before just how noisy waterproof fabric was. Every movement caused a noise louder than the previous one. He folded them up, and she was surprised to see him in shorts and a t-shirt. He must be frozen.

Shuffling towards her, he lifted his bundle of wet clothes.

'Put them in here.' She held open a large carrier bag.

'You're very organised,' he whispered.

She smirked, pulled back the opening to her sleeping pod and shoved the bag into the far corner, out of sight, just in case her dad woke up.

'Budge up then,' Logan whispered with a grin.

She smiled and moved over as he zipped them into the pod. She opened the side of her sleeping bag and held it wide.

'Thanks.' He slid in beside her.

'Ooh,' she whispered. 'You're freezing.'

'Warm me up then.' He cosied in beside her and she relaxed into his arms. Now the sound of the wind was quite pleasant, nothing more than a dramatic backdrop. He kissed her brow. 'I missed you so much.'

'It's going to be torture tomorrow.' A lump rose in her throat.

He stroked the hair off her face, gently caressing her. 'I love you, Eleanor.'

Her heart stopped. Had she actually died? Then it started going again but at treble its usual speed. 'Did you just say…'

'Yes. I love you.' He leaned in and kissed her. 'I adore you with every particle of my heart and body. I'll do anything for you.'

Words failed. Her mind tossed, turned, and roved all over the place. This should be one of the most precious moments of her life. She needed to enjoy it, but her heart wept. He couldn't be hers. No matter how much she loved him in return, they really couldn't live on love alone.

'Logan... That's so lovely.' She swallowed. 'But you know I can't stay here. My life revolves around my dad, whether I like it or not. And I'm not saying I don't like it. It's important, but it means—'

'I know what it means. I also know what I feel. You're more important to me than anything. I'm not asking you to stay. I could—'

'Eleanor?' Her dad's voice spoke from the opposite pod and her blood froze.

'Yes?'

'Is everything ok? Are you talking to someone?'

'What? Oh... It must be people outside. You stay in bed; I'll check everything's ok.'

Logan crawled out of the sleeping bag and grabbed his stuff. She unzipped the pod. Thankfully, the tent was now dark, her dad still zipped into his side. Logan darted towards the exit, unzipped it, and ducked out. She followed, pretending to look about outside, before closing it back up.

She mouthed goodbye and Logan dipped in and gave her a quick peck on the cheek. 'No one's there,' she said to her dad. 'Must just be voices carrying in the wind.'

'Hmm,' Dad said. 'Well, you get back to sleep. We've got a long drive tomorrow.'

She crawled back into her sleeping bag, still warm and enriched by Logan's woody fragrance. She rested her head on the soft fleece and let silent tears fall. There was a man who loved her just metres away, but she couldn't have him. He might have been on the verge of suggesting he left all this and moved close to her or that a long-distance relationship might work, but she couldn't put him through that. He'd followed his childhood dreams and was doing everything he'd always wanted to. She wouldn't be the one to ruin it for him.

Chapter Twenty-Two

Logan

What even was sleep? Logan didn't bother getting undressed. He lay on top of his covers with only a light fleece blanket across him. The caravan nestled in a sheltered spot beside the shop building, but the wind still rattled the windows.

So, he'd done it. He'd told Eleanor exactly how he felt.

He'd never said those three words to anyone before – except his parents. Her reaction hadn't been quite the one he'd hoped for. He closed his eyes and listened to the rain falling on the roof. Maybe he'd shocked her. Of course he had. It was a bold statement and maybe he was crazy for saying it, but he had to let her know. And he hadn't lied. He would do anything for her. Did it matter if he gave up the campsite? What was it without Eleanor? What was anything? His mum would go through the roof – again. How often he proved her right. He really couldn't settle at anything. What a disappointment. Still, he was going ahead with the campsite valuation. If Eleanor was game for a relationship, he would bring it about as quickly as possible. They could give long distance a go in the interim. She was worth it. If only she could see that. Of course looking after her dad was admirable but she had her own life too. How could he get her to see that was just as important?

He must have dozed because he woke in an awkward position, his neck twisted. 'Ow.' He straightened it out and rubbed it. Grabbing his phone, he checked the time. Early yet, but he wanted to get up and make sure he was about when Eleanor left, perhaps catch her before she went. He thumbed out a text.

LOGAN: If you have a chance to chat, please call or come over. Really would love to see you and say goodbye. XX

The wind seemed to have died down; a few short gusts groaned around but nothing like the night before. The rain was still falling relentlessly but it was lighter and misty. Not the best weather for packing up. He would help in an instant, but he didn't want to muscle in. Eleanor hadn't told her dad about them – he didn't blame her – but it made things awkward. Once they were more settled, they could reveal everything to him. When they figured out how to work it so it wouldn't have a negative impact on his life. There must be a way to bring that about.

He opened the shop as normal while he gathered together some tools in case there was storm damage.

He hadn't had any complaints from grumpy campers about the shop being closed the day before but he'd paid for it later; he'd spent most of the evening getting soaked and helping move their tents back from the burn or into more sheltered spots. Mostly without much thanks. His treat to himself had been to spend those few moments with Eleanor.

He shoved the sign onto the door and strode out. As it was Saturday, a few people were leaving and already there were gaps where tents had been. They all looked like people had taken them down themselves and not been torn down by the wind. Nothing too alarming caught his eye. Some scattered branches here and there were the only evidence of the stormy night.

Eleanor's car boot was wide open, and bags were already sitting inside. He sighed, glancing over. She appeared around the side of the tent, loosening guy ropes.

'Hey,' he called. She looked around and his heart shrivelled. Her eyes were red and puffy. Had she cried all night? Why couldn't he just hold her and try to make things better, or if not better, at least easier?

She gave him a brief wave, then carried on loosening the ropes. Just beside a tree close by, he spotted Andy with a camping mug in his hand. Nope, even that couldn't deter him. He continued to the tent.

'How's it going?' he asked Andy. 'Did you sleep ok last night? That was some wind.'

'Thank you, yes. I slept like a log, though I'll be glad to get back into a proper bed tonight. A week camping is probably the limit at my age. The mind is more willing than the body. I've seized up completely. Poor Eleanor's trying to do the tent herself. Hopefully, I'll loosen up in a minute or two.'

'Can I help?' Logan said. 'I'm happy to do it.'

'Why yes. I'm sure she'd appreciate that. Eleanor!'

She appeared around the tent. 'Yes... Oh, hi.' She spotted Logan.

'Logan here very kindly says he'll help you take the tent down. That'll save my old bones.'

'Great, thanks.' She smiled but it was the sad smile from the beginning of the week that graced her face. The real joyful smiles were gone. Her eyes were glassy and far away again.

Logan prided himself on being an expert in tents these days and it didn't take him long to collapse this one. Eleanor took out the first pole, making no eye contact and seemingly trying to be as far from him as she could. Was this all because of her dad or was she trying to distance herself to protect her heart? Whatever it was, it hurt. His body ached to be close to her, yet here she was shying away.

As she folded the last pole, he dragged the edges of the tent together, piling each section neatly. He rolled the pole bag in the middle and started squashing it into its holdall.

'This is the bit I'm not good at,' she said. 'I can never get it back in the bag. I just don't have the strength.'

He shoved it in. 'Brute force.' Pulling his arm into a Popeye pose, he glanced up and gave her a tiny wink. It raised the smallest of grins at the corner of her lips. He sat on the bag to hold it down and dragged the zip shut. 'There we go. Where do you want it?'

'It needs to go in the boot.' She swept damp hair off her forehead. 'But I have to take the bags out first. I only put them in to keep them dry, but the tent has to go in first or nothing else fits.'

'No worries.' He lifted the tent and carried it to the car. He and Eleanor pulled the luggage bags out, then he packed the tent into the space. He tried to catch her eye, willing her to look at him so he could send her a nonverbal message explaining how he felt. How nothing would be the same without her and how he was going to do everything he could to keep them together. He could say it all by text or phone later, but it wasn't the same and he craved some assurance. Even if it came from her eyes, he needed to see it. But when she packed the last bag in, she waited until he backed off, closed the boot and walked over to her dad before looking at him.

'Thanks,' she said quietly. 'I appreciate your help this week. All of it. Everything.'

'Any time.'

'Yes, you've been a good host,' Andy said. 'And I wish you well for the future. I'm not sure if my body will hold up to another camping trip, so this might be my last visit here. I'm pleased we met you and I appreciate how you've taken care of us.'

Logan nodded. 'You're welcome.'

'Well.' Andy clapped his hands. 'That's pretty much that. We're ready to hit the road.'

Logan looked at Eleanor and motioned with his eyes to come and talk to him in private. She blinked but didn't speak.

'Safe travels,' he said. 'I hope I'll see you both again sometime.' He turned and walked away. *Please, please, let her follow me.* Was that her footsteps running behind him? He glanced back. She and her dad had their backs to him and were looking at the rushing stream. Was this it? The last he'd see of Eleanor for who knew how long.

Chapter Twenty-Three

Eleanor

Eleanor would never forget her mum's face just before she died. She was drugged up and calm, but she must have known she was leaving her family before her time. Eleanor had held her hand and told her through her tears they'd be ok. She'd look after Dad. Mum had given her the smallest of smiles through her misty eyes. Her eyelids had fallen shut and she'd passed. Eleanor wouldn't hear her voice again, experience her hugs or have her as a sounding board when she needed her. Like now.

Now, she had another face she'd never be able to forget. Logan's parting expression was burned to the insides of her eyelids. It cut her deep to think about it, but nothing would shift it. She tried to buzz herself up as she and her dad said goodbye to their pitch.

'Well, it's been a grand holiday,' Dad said. 'It's not easy revisiting places I came to in happier times but I'm glad we did.'

She nodded, not sure if she was glad or not. Maybe in the long term, it would have been better if she hadn't come. Her days with Logan had been too short and the parting was bitter. It felt like a dirty secret. Who could she tell without making it sound seedy and ridiculous? Even if her mum was here, she wasn't sure she would dare tell her.

'Let's go then,' Dad said. 'No point in hanging about. We got packed up so much quicker with help from that young man. He's very friendly, maybe a bit too friendly for his own good if the rumours are to be believed.'

'I'm sure they're not.' Her fingers froze on the car door handle. Dad was already in. 'I need to go to the loo and get something from the shop before we leave.' She pulled open the door. 'Can you wait a few minutes?'

'Yes, of course. Pick up a bag of sweets for the journey too; that would be nice.'

'Ok.' She shut the door and hotfooted it across the site, breaking into a run. This might not help, but she couldn't leave without saying something, not after everything Logan had done for them that week.

Her heart was full of love, deep-rooted and powerful, more than should be possible for someone she hardly knew. When she drove away, it would break again and how could she fix herself this time? She still wasn't healed from losing Mum. Why had she yielded to him when she'd known this day would come? But she hadn't expected him to express his love. Now, she couldn't pretend not to see it. He'd been quite plain. Why had she led him on? Not only satisfied with breaking her own heart, she was breaking his too. He had to follow his dreams as if he'd never met her. She shouldn't have got in the way.

She peered in the shop window and as far as she could see, it was empty. The door creaked as she opened it. Logan looked up from the counter.

'Eleanor.' He squeezed out from behind the desk and came straight to her.

'Stop.' She held up her hand. 'Please, Logan.'

He raised his finger. 'One second.' He stepped behind her and turned the sign to closed, then shut the door. 'Come away from the window. We can talk in the back.'

'I don't have long. My dad thinks I'm just buying a packet of sweets.' Every word that came out of her mouth, she hated, and he'd grow to hate it too. Mark had been a kind, considerate man in the beginning, but he'd grown bitter and sad when she'd chosen to spend time with her parents. When she couldn't devote time to him or dates, his anger grew, and he'd snapped at her for never thinking about 'their future' and always concerning herself with her parents. Nothing could stop it all from playing out again and she couldn't do it.

'Ok... So... Do you want a pack of sweets? Or is there something else?'

'Of course there is, Logan. I heard what you said last night.'

'And it's true. I love you.'

'I believe you but...'

'You don't feel the same.'

'It's not that. I just don't want you doing anything crazy. Not for me, not for something so unknown.'

'Eleanor, I don't care about that. I'll give up everything here if it gives me the chance to be with you.'

'No. No. You mustn't. Please don't. I couldn't bear it if you did that. It's asking for trouble. Please, Logan. Follow your dreams and run this place, make it everything you want it to be. I've learned the hard way that love doesn't last.' Her eyes misted over and she jabbed away tears.

'Ok, but listen, let's not close the doors on everything just yet. I'm still willing to work with you, and maybe we could try long distance. I'm happy to chat to you whenever and I could probably arrange for someone to look after here, so I could come and see you.'

A flicker of hope ignited in her chest but it didn't really alter the geography or the circumstances. 'I guess it's worth a try. What we had was good, but you deserve to be a success. You've given so much to this place. I shouldn't have been so stupid. I've dragged you away from everything important when I should have stopped myself and stayed away.'

He shook his head and a pained frown spread across his brow. 'Eleanor, this is just a job. You're—'

'I'm just a person. I'm sorry. Our lives aren't compatible.'

He held out his palms and mouthed silently, his eyes drilling into her as if trying to discover some hidden meaning or a change of heart. 'Why can't you see your own worth in all of this? You tell me I deserve to be a success but you deserve to be happy too.'

'But not like this.'

'Why not? You have a life too. You're not here just to serve your dad.'

'Logan—'

'No. Don't mistake me, I don't mean I think you should abandon him or do something drastic that would harm him. But at least talk to him. Sometimes you treat him like a child, but he's not. I think he'd be rightly upset if he knew you thought about him like that. Why not tell him about us? About *your* dreams. See what he says. Don't just assume you know how he'll react. Find out.'

She stared at him, her veins filling with ice. Never had she thought she'd hear him say anything like that. It was Mark all over again.

'You know, I can't do that. I've told you.'

'No, that's not what you told me, and all I'm saying is that you should consider a different outlook. I don't want you to give up on your dad for me. Just make sure when you make a decision, it's based on fact and not what you imagine to be the truth.'

An intense weight pounded on her brain, making it impossible to make sense of these words. Everything she'd dreaded happening from the minute she embarked on this fling was unfolding.

How had she ever thought it would be different? He had a kinder way of putting it than Mark but it didn't change the substance of his words.

'I'm sorry, Logan, I have to go. Goodbye.'

He stood stock still, staring.

She turned to leave but the key jammed in the lock. He came up behind her, reached around, and unlocked it. He was right there, so close with his woody scent and body heat filling the air. She could easily fall into those arms, but she'd travelled that road too often already this week.

'Do you still want sweets?' he said, his voice hoarse.

'Oh god, yes.'

He grabbed a packet from a nearby display. 'Take them on the house. My parting gift, for what it's worth.'

She took the packet and held her fingers to her lips. 'Thank you, and I'm sorry, Logan. We were doomed from the start. Not because I don't trust you but because I know myself and my circumstances.'

'Please, Eleanor, don't hate me for this. Talk to your dad. I'm not the bad guy here, neither is he, and neither are you. Your misplaced beliefs are the problem. You're allowed a life, you're allowed to be happy. Why on earth would you think your dad wouldn't want that?' He put his hand on her shoulder.

'You don't get it, do you?'

'I think I do. I think I get it a lot more than you do.'

'No, you don't. No one does. No one ever does.' She pulled open the door and ran. At the back of the car, she stopped, breathed slowly, and wiped her eyes. *Compose yourself, Eleanor, now. Don't let Dad see what a state you're in.*

When she jumped into the driving seat, she smiled and dropped the sweets into the central compartment.

'Is everything ok?' Dad asked. 'You were quite a while.'

'There was a queue.' She started the engine. Her hand shook as she put the car into gear.

'Are you sure you're all right? You look a bit upset.'

'Just sad to be leaving.'

'Yes, I understand.' He placed his hand over hers and patted it. 'You're a wonderful daughter. You always do the right things.'

She nodded, holding back another raft of tears. 'If you say so.'

'I do. I don't know what I'd do without you. After your Mum, and now the boys going off, you're all I've got.'

Thank goodness someone appreciated her because her self-esteem was at rock bottom. In the bright morning light back in Chapel Brampton, she'd be sure she'd made the sensible decision, but right now, she may as well have stabbed herself through the heart with a serrated knife.

Chapter Twenty-Four

Logan

Logan picked up a file on the desk and threw it back down, letting paper fly everywhere. So what? Just so what? Did anything matter right now? Eleanor had driven through the gates and left. She was gone. Gone without any hope of anything. He'd well and truly thrust his size twelves in it.

'Just a frigging mess,' he muttered, grabbing papers and shoving them into the folder. Maybe he was being childish. His mum would certainly think so, but he couldn't bear the weight of loss. Sure, Eleanor was alive and well, but she was gone from his life. Had he contributed to it? Maybe. But why couldn't she see her own importance in this? There was being selfless and there was being a martyr. She had a life to live, and he was convinced her dad wouldn't want her running around after him if she wanted to do something for herself. More than likely, he'd be horrified at the thought, but clearly there was no telling her. Now Logan had ruined everything by doing exactly what her ex had done. So much for good intentions.

'Right, stop.' He ruffled his hair and took a deep, calming breath. Now was the time to follow his own advice. Eleanor had a life to live and so did he. She'd given clear reasons why she didn't want him to give up his dream. He didn't want to give it up either. Proving to his parents he was a failure once again wasn't on his priority list. But if he took off the coloured glasses and looked at his role objectively, it was a total nightmare. Maybe cutting his losses wasn't a bad move after all. He'd shunned office work all his life, but if he had to, he could do it again. It would be better than cleaning toilets anyway. He'd lived near Northamptonshire in his Cambridge days and hadn't disliked it. It maybe wasn't as wild and rugged as up here, but did that matter? Northamptonshire had Eleanor and Scotland didn't. The problem now was, would she want him? Had he messed this up good and proper to the point where she'd never want to see him again? If he could just focus on something, anything... Except he never could.

The rattly door burst open.

'Bloody door,' he said, forgetting himself. Worst luck. Mrs Grumpy Camper came in, her husband hiding behind her as best he could. She narrowed her eyes and pursed her lips. Logan summoned his smile but, hell, he knew it would look fake. It was painful moving his lips and straightening his brow. He probably looked deranged. 'Good morning.'

'Is it?' she muttered. 'You might not be saying that if you'd been trying to pack your tent in the wind and rain for the last hour.'

He turned away so he could roll his eyes. When he looked back, he said, 'Yes, it's not the best weather for packing up.'

The woman huffed and the man shuffled around behind her as she scanned the shelf for something.

'You know what's lacking here?' she said, presumably to her husband, but in a voice too loud for Logan to miss. 'There's no fresh food. I mean, there should be sandwiches made every day, warmed croissants for breakfast.'

'Or bacon rolls,' the husband said.

'Yes, like that place on the Mull of Kintyre. That was a great campsite.'

Logan breathed deeply and made a silent wish they'd go back to that one next year. If he could magic staff out of nowhere to make said croissants and rolls, he'd be one hundred per cent in.

'Lovely couple that ran it too,' the husband said. 'Always happy to help.'

I'm happy to help! He balled his fists on the counter. *If I know people want help.* Only last night, he'd helped move tents in the storm and warned people of the bad weather. He was always on hand. What more could he do?

With a disgruntled expression, the woman banged a loaf of bread on the counter.

'I hope you've enjoyed your stay.' He scanned the bread. Why did he bother speaking? He knew he wouldn't like what she had to say.

The woman's sour expression looked like she was trying to eke out the juice from a slice of bitter lemon. 'It's not really been what we expected if I'm honest. It's all a bit jaded, which is a pity. The countryside is so beautiful here but the facilities all need updating. The toilets were acceptable but this shop.' She screwed up her nose. 'And the unpredictable hours. It just doesn't work.'

He handed her back the bread. 'I'm sorry it's not up to your standards. I've been let down by staff, then I lost a really good worker and unfortunately, I've had no more interest.

'That's the state of the world,' the man said.

They left with their bread and Logan's shoulders sagged, partly with relief and partly with the knowledge that they were right. This had the potential to be a bustling little hub with a well-stocked shop, possibly a small café, or at least somewhere with a coffee machine. Around the back, instead of his ancient static, would be the meeting point for the outdoor centre. He could store a range of hillwalking and climbing equipment. There could be bikes to hire and a place to service them and those belonging to guests. He could devote his time to that while he had trained staff working the admin, overseeing the shop and café, and a proper cleaner. Down by the loch would be a fit-for-purpose boat shed with paddleboards and wetsuits and a dedicated changing area.

Once it was all up and running, then he could build his own house and actually enjoy things. So the dream went. Or it was meant to. Was he going to shove it over the cliff and into the sea? Or should he follow Eleanor's parting wish and try and make a success of it? Neither course was appealing. Going into hiding and hibernating for a year was what he wanted to do right now.

With most of the campers packed away, Logan closed the shop to do his rounds while it was quiet and before the rush of newcomers that afternoon. His phone buzzed in his pocket and he scrambled to drag it out, hoping it was Eleanor but at the same time hoping it wasn't, in case she'd had an accident or something horrible had happened.

The name *DOUGHNUT* flashed boldly on the screen.

'Hi,' Logan said.

'Hey, Berry Boy. How's it hanging?'

'Pretty shit, if you must know.'

'Seriously, man? What's wrong?'

He scanned around the site to the hills beyond. Mist covered the pine trees on the lower slopes, leaving the view hazy and blurred, but higher up, a golden glow told him the sun was trying to get through. 'Just stuff.' He puffed and filled up the cart, with one hand still pressing the phone to his ear.

'Is it that girl?' Duncan said. 'Are you pining over her?'

'None of your business.'

'I'll take that as a yes then. Has she left?'

'This morning.'

'Well, don't sweat it. There are plenty more fish in the sea, especially if you're hitting on the campers these days.'

'Look, shut up. That's not what happened. I like her, ok. But I don't normally do anything like that. This only happened because...' He screwed up his face and let out a sigh. There was no way of saying it without sounding like an idiot.

'What?'

'You know... Or you probably don't. We connected.'

Duncan roared with laughter. 'That's one way of putting it.'

'I mean, on a spiritual level, you bloody caveman.' Though he half grinned.

'So, what's happening? Are you keeping in touch?'

'I don't know. I want to but she's got a lot of responsibilities and if I want to make something happen, we either have to try long distance or I up sticks.'

'After knowing her for a week? I think you should forget it, mate. It sounds more trouble than it's worth.'

'How would you know? Maybe it's trouble I want to make, but I might have put my big foot in it anyway.'

'How so?'

'Ah, you know me. I never know when to keep my mouth shut.'

'Listen, mate. I can tell this isn't a great time, but I've got some good news for you. Well, it could be.'

'What?'

'You know I work at Harrington Energy Solutions, right? Well, my boss, Geoff Harrington, is working on some deals specifically for this area that include projects that'll not only boost the local economy but give cash injections to struggling small businesses if they can prove they're working on sustainable projects. I thought of you, straight away. Would you like me to talk to him about what you're doing here? I'm not directly involved in the negotiations, but I'd be happy to put you forward. You could get your hook-ups working on a turbine and solar, plus you've got native woodland all around that you already preserve. I'm pretty sure with a solid application, you could get a shedload of cash.'

Logan sighed and rubbed his forehead. The euphoria he knew he should feel just wasn't there. Instead, his blood felt sluggish, weighing him down and thumping against his brain. 'It's a great idea in theory,' he said. 'But I'm not sure.'

'Why the hell not? What do you have to lose?'

'I'm just not sure if I'm going to be here much longer.'

'What kind of talk is that?'

'I'm thinking about selling up. I don't think I'm the right person to do this job anymore. It's beyond me.'

'Bullshit,' Duncan said. 'This is what you came back to do. You've always wanted this kind of thing and here's your chance. What's got into you?'

Logan didn't reply.

'Please tell me it's not because of Eleanor.'

'It's everything to do with her,' he snapped. 'And maybe it seems like I've lost the plot and gone crazy, but I'd rather lose the plot than her. I'll go even more insane if I don't at least try to make something happen. I know what you're thinking and what my family will think. I fully expect my mum to march down here with committal papers when she finds out, but I have to do it.'

'Wow. Ok. You've really got it bad.'

'Yup. I do, but I'm not leaving her. I'd rather leave this place. I can get a job anywhere, but there'll never be another Eleanor.'

Duncan let out a long low whistle. 'Ok, so you won't thank me for saying this right now, but I have to because when your brain fog clears, you might need to hear it. I know you think you're in love or you've clicked, or whatever, but it's only been a week. You know nothing about how she lives normally or what her daily life is like. I thought she seemed a nice person but it's not exactly a solid base for a relationship. And, really, Berry Boy, she doesn't know that much about you either. What happens when the thrill dies away? What if you give up everything only for your relationship to fail? I'm not saying this because I think it will, but because you can't just ignore it.'

'Yeah. I know all that.' How could he not? He also knew Eleanor had explicitly stated she didn't want him to leave. If he sold up, the pressure to make the relationship work would be immense, especially for her. Not to mention the guilt she'd feel if they split after he'd given up his dreams for her. How could he put her through that? Was it kinder to walk away, even if it broke his heart?

Chapter Twenty-Five

Eleanor

Eleanor put her head down and slung her bag over her shoulder. Her heels clicked across the car park towards the glass-fronted building of Nexus Solutions. The reflected early morning sun dazzled her. Going back to work after a holiday was never much fun but her insides were in turmoil; it was almost as bad as the day she'd returned to work after they lost Mum, only this time nobody else would know. If she just acted normally, there was no reason for anyone to ever know. Having her colleagues tiptoeing around her on eggshells again was not something she wanted.

'Morning,' a bright and overly cheery voice called. Eleanor cringed. Worst luck, of all the people she had to meet first, it was Amanda, the office gossip. Though why should she care? No way could Amanda have got wind of what Eleanor did on her holiday.

'Morning.' Eleanor sped up as Amanda waited at the door.

'Nice to see you back. How was the holiday?'

'Great, thanks.'

Amanda nodded and looked forward with sad eyes. 'How was your dad?' Her tone was hushed, and she rested her veiny and heavily ringed fingers on Eleanor's arm. 'I hope it wasn't too distressing for him. Sometimes visiting the old places can be heartbreaking. I know it was like that for me when my dad passed.'

'He was ok, thanks.'

'Good. So glad to hear it.' Amanda tucked a platinum lock behind her ear. When Eleanor had started here six years before, Amanda had been dark haired, moaning every few weeks that her grey stripe was back and she'd need to visit her stylist. Since turning fifty, she'd gone for the platinum look and no one was sure if the regrowth was white from a bottle or her natural shade. 'Did you get my messages when you were away?'

'Er...' Eleanor bit her lip as she waited for Amanda to sign in. She'd completely ignored the messages from everyone at work and when she'd got home, she couldn't face reading them all.

'Hello.'

Eleanor turned around to see another colleague, Molly, bursting through the door.

'You're back.' Molly flung out her arms and ran to her, engulfing her in a huge hug.

'Hi, Molly.'

'I'm glad you're back. I hope you had an epic time.' Molly patted her back. 'Has Amanda told you the shocking news?'

Eleanor frowned at her. She and Molly were about the same age, but while she was happy to get on quietly with her work, Molly liked to be a sensationalist about every little thing. Her idea of shocking news could be something as trivial as the boss telling them they weren't allowed to eat at their desks anymore.

'Not yet.' Eleanor broke away to sign herself in.

'Wait until you hear. I sent you loads of messages, but I don't think you were getting them.' Molly took the pen and scrawled her name on the sheet.

'Scotland's terrible for reception from what I've heard,' Amanda said.

'Well, some parts are,' Eleanor said. 'I was in a very rural place, you know.'

Amanda hit the *call lift* button and they waited.

'Well...' Molly lowered her voice as two men came in the front door.

'Get in here first.' Amanda ushered them into the lift and hit the number three. 'I didn't recognise those two guys, so best not say anything in front of them.'

'What's going on?' A fresh build-up of butterflies was breeding in her chest. What was with the conspiratorial voices? This had the air of something much bigger than she'd initially expected.

'Well, I don't know if you remember when the finance report came in Mr Ross-The-Boss wasn't happy because we hadn't made as much profit as he hoped.'

'I remember,' she said. How could she forget? He'd sent them a newsletter saying cuts would need to be made, starting with their Christmas bonus, which was "an archaic and unnecessary payment". Not a man noted for his charity. 'It's nowhere near December though,' she mused. 'So, what's he planning? Surely he can't legally cut wages... can he?'

Molly shrugged. 'He's not going to do that. He's cutting some positions.'

'Redundancies?' The heat drained from her cheeks.

Amanda nodded. 'He's asking for voluntary but if no one wants to, he's going to make them compulsory.'

'But who?' Her heart was racing. Surely not her. She'd never put a toe out of line. She'd always worked hard.

'He hasn't said yet,' Amanda said as the lift stopped. 'But I'm panicking because I'm fifty-two and he might want me to take early retirement, but I can't afford not to work.'

'Or it could be me,' Molly said. 'I was last in, so I might be first out.'

'There are loads of others though.' Eleanor swallowed hard, trying to think of ways she could justify her job if she had to. Ron and Lillian, who worked in her section, were both older and more experienced than her, but she had the most up-to-date knowledge. But she didn't want either of them to go. They both had kids and mortgages. What was she going to do? She'd had this job since she qualified and, good or bad, it was all she knew. She wasn't sure how she'd cope if she had to go somewhere else. What if she didn't fit in? No one would know her or her circumstances. She'd have to explain it all over again, hope people understood and were kind. There would be new colleagues to meet, new systems, new everything. Perhaps a longer commute. How would that work with Dad? Bosses were notoriously unsympathetic to people with kids and even worse when it was aged parents. Nobody got that.

Once out of the lift, they couldn't talk freely as several other colleagues were milling about the open-plan space. Eleanor waved goodbye and made her way to her little desk, squashed in the corner beside Lillian's. Neither Lillian nor Ron were in yet. She dropped her bag on the desk and sighed. She was getting ahead of herself; redundancies on the cards didn't automatically mean her, though it did no harm to be prepared. She sat down and leaned on the desk, running her hand along her forehead. A headache was gunning for her and she was pretty sure she had no paracetamols.

'Morning,' Ron's slow voice drawled from behind.

'Oh, morning.' She straightened herself out and switched on her computer.

'You got a holiday hangover?'

'No, just a headache.' Didn't he know by now she wasn't exactly the hangover type? She'd never come in with a hangover or had a day off for anything like that. If he took a report like that to Mr Ross, she'd become an instant redundancy candidate.

'You read your emails?' Ron said.

'Not yet.'

'I daresay you'll have heard on the grapevine about the redundancies though.'

'Yes. Has anything else been said about who it might be?' She spun around to stare at him, wishing she hadn't as her head throbbed. She winced.

'Nothing much. He's looking to streamline departments though, so I don't see all three of us being allowed to stay. Lillian's part-time but I suspect he'll want one of the full-timers out.'

Eleanor raised her eyebrows and shook her head. 'I don't know what to say. I don't want to go and I doubt you do either.'

'Not really,' he said. 'I'm not at a good age for finding new jobs. I'm heading for fifty and no matter what employers say, they never look favourably on applicants over forty.'

'I guess.' She bit her lip as Ron sat in his cubicle, his back facing her. So what did that mean? They'd be fighting it out between each other. She hated fighting. Letting out a sigh, she waited for her computer to load. Her phone vibrated and she tilted the screen to check it.

LOGAN: Hope you have a good day back at work. I miss you and I haven't forgotten about you. I hope we can still do some work together at the very least. Please don't be angry about what I said. Just think about it. XX

She raised her hand to her mouth and stayed the rising emotions. Think about it? Like she could stop herself thinking about it – and him. But he may as well be on another planet. She couldn't bear to imagine how it would be to have him nearby, to talk to and explain her predicament. Just the comfort of his arms would help, but no. She mustn't allow herself to think about it. They were finished. Logan didn't understand her life, just as Mark hadn't, and as none of her friends did either.

Between the frostiness in the office and an atmosphere you could cut with a knife, she decided she would have to leave the building come lunchtime. She couldn't face the staff room. Usually, she didn't dare leave the office during the day. She had a fear of something happening and not getting back on time, but the rebellious spirit that meeting Logan had kindled was still simmering. Her best friend, Hattie, was forever asking to meet for a working lunch and Eleanor had never once said yes. On the off-chance, she messaged her to ask if she could do it today.

At eleven thirty, a reply pinged in.

HATTIE: Are you pulling my leg? You go AWOL for a week, don't answer any messages, then boom, you want to meet for lunch when you NEVER meet for lunch. WTAF has got into you?? Of course I'll bloody meet you. One o'clock at Franco's.

Eleanor swallowed the panic that she might not fit everything she wanted to tell Hattie into an hour and took a calming breath. She just needed to make sure she was back in time.

Hattie dragged Eleanor into a hug the second she saw her. 'What has been going on?' She stepped back, looked her up and down, and frowned. 'What have you been up to?'

'Why?' Eleanor blinked, wanting to find a mirror to see what was wrong with her. Did her guilt show on her face? Guilt at leaving work at lunchtime... At abandoning Logan... At being with Logan in the first place... Having considered leaving her dad even for a second... For not replying to messages... For wanting Ron to be given the redundancy over her, even though she liked him. Her whole system was riddled with guilt like a slug-infested drain.

'You just look odd. Let's go inside and you can tell me.'

They ordered quickly, as neither had long to hang about. It didn't leave her much time to spit out everything she wanted to say, but if she didn't get some of it out, her head would explode. She started with the redundancies. That seemed the most neutral problem. The one that, while it bothered her, affected her brain more than her heart, and talking about matters of the heart was never as easy.

'That's a bummer,' Hattie said. 'So, it's just a waiting game, I guess. I know you won't like this suggestion, but what about Mark?'

'Mark?' The name of her ex slipped into her chest like ice. 'What about him?'

'Couldn't he give you a job? He's still in the sector and I remember he used to talk about the two of you working together someday.'

'Why would I put myself through that? I don't really want to see him again, especially not every day at work.'

'Hey.' Hattie leaned over the table and took Eleanor's hand. 'I get it. I know you split up and I know what you think his reasons were.'

'I don't *think;* I *know* what they were.' This conversation had taken an unwelcome detour. 'He was angry because I wanted to spend more time with my dying mum than him.'

'I know that's what it seemed like. But, Eleanor, you were in a terrible place in your life. Understandably. What you didn't see was how he tried to get you to value yourself. He wasn't stopping you from seeing your mum. He was trying to remind you that you had your own life too. Your mum wouldn't want that to stop. Life goes on for the living.'

'Look, I know that.' Her cheeks felt too warm. This was exactly what Logan had tried to say about her dad and she'd shut him down. 'But that's not how it happened.' Was it? As soon as she said it, she started to doubt herself. Maybe she'd been so absorbed in the pain she hadn't been able to see rationally and she'd repeated the process with Logan. 'I don't want to see Mark again.'

'I wish you'd think about it. I know he'd have you back.'

'Do you still see him?'

'Sometimes. He asks about you all the time and hopes you're getting on ok.'

Eleanor frowned and shook her head. How things had been for a year or more with Mark had never been as good as a few days with Logan. He'd supported her with her dad. Why had she taken it upon herself to believe he was trying to hurt her when maybe he'd seen things clearer than she did? Maybe Mark had too. Had she misjudged everyone because her brain was so addled with grief? How many more people would she hurt when she just wanted to help her dad? Why did helping the people she loved have to hurt other people... Including herself? Because Logan was right. She was hurting herself. Helping her dad like this meant she had no life of her own, even though she wanted one. 'I don't... I couldn't... like him like that again. I don't think I really loved him.'

'Oh, come on. I'm sure you did.'

Eleanor shook her head. *Nope.* She was pretty sure he'd never elicited the feelings Logan had. 'I met someone when I was on holiday.' The words tumbled out.

Hattie's eyes opened so wide they almost popped out. 'What kind of someone? A man?'

'Yup.'

'And... What did you do with him?'

'Everything.'

'Oh my good god.' Hattie's mouth dropped open. 'Is that why you didn't reply to my messages?'

Eleanor sipped her water, then nodded.

'But you never do anything like that.'

'I know.'

'So... When you say everything...'

'I mean everything. We walked, we talked, we kissed, we did the business.'

'Bloody hell. Who are you and what have you done with Eleanor Kendrick?'

'I knew that's what you'd say.' She allowed herself a tiny grin, then swiped her phone awake and found a photo. 'That's him. Logan.'

'Wow. He's a hottie.'

'Isn't he?'

'So, what's happening with him?'

'Nothing. What can happen? He lives on the site, I live here. His responsibilities are there, mine are here. I can't leave Dad and sail off to the highlands to live with him and he can't give up his job and his dream to come down here.' She tapped the table with her fingertip. 'Though he said he would.'

'Did he?'

She pressed her lips together. 'Yes. But I told him not to. My life is stuck the way it is.' Though maybe that was her own doing. She needed to talk to her dad. That was what Logan said and he was right. Nothing could be settled until she understood her dad's feelings more clearly. 'And now that Jamie is moving away, there's no one else who can help with dad. I can't devote time to a relationship. Who wants to be with someone who has to be home by five-thirty to make their dad a meal? Someone who has to be about to entertain him in the evenings and weekends?'

Hattie looked at her plate and Eleanor remembered Logan's words. *Your dad's not a child.* That was true but she couldn't help wincing at the thought of him being lonely and left to his own devices. Did that mean she had to be always around? Maybe he didn't mind some time alone. She hadn't asked.

'Oh, Eleanor.' Hattie sighed. 'This is exactly what Mark meant. You don't have to give up your life for your dad.'

'I know that.' She almost shouted, but only now could she see it clearly. Back in the campsite shop, she'd thought Logan was having a go at her, but he hadn't been. He'd pointed out home truths she didn't want to hear. Maybe Mark had done the same. And now Hattie. The knowledge of her misbeliefs didn't wholly solve the practicalities though. 'I know you and everyone else think his life is his own problem and he should learn to do all this stuff by himself, but it isn't that simple. Not in real life. Sure, in the airy world of fantasy, he'll just suddenly learn to cook, clean and take care of himself, but that's not how it works. He's already had a massive upheaval in his life. It would be like taking a beaten animal and forcing it to pull a cart fifty times its weight in the baking sun. He can't do it and I can't abandon him to that fate.'

'Hey, I get that.' Hattie held up her hands. 'But there must be ways. What about Meals on Wheels or home helps?'

'It's not the same. How would you feel if you were in his shoes? Your wife's gone, your two sons have left for other countries and your only other child suddenly decides she's off to Scotland and you're left with a home help coming in every day with your food on a tray? Hardly fair, is it?'

'Maybe not, but things like that do happen.'

'But I can't let it. I need to find a better way.' Eleanor checked the time on her phone as she swallowed a mouthful of ciabatta. 'I have to get back.'

'Yes. And keep talking. Don't crawl back into your shell and bottle it all up. Let me know if anything changes – with the job or Logan.'

'Yeah. Nothing's going to change there,' Eleanor assured her. 'But I'll let you know when I find out what's happening at work. And I forbid you to tell Mark. I don't need his charity.'

Hattie smirked. 'Ah, Eleanor. You might be the quiet and well-behaved one, but you're also bloody stubborn!'

Chapter Twenty-Six

Logan

The woody smoke from the fire pit filled the evening air and Logan looked through the haze. Plumes rose above the licking flames and he rested back in his chair. Cha flipped the pull on a can of coke with her heavily ringed fingers and toasted him with it.

'Spit it out,' she said.

He crossed his legs in front of him; a week of baking sun had bronzed his skin.

'What do you want to talk about?' Cha said, taking a sip of her coke.

'Just thought you'd like to spend a balmy evening with your favourite cousin.'

'What, Sophie's here, is she?'

'Haha, very funny.'

She shook her hair free from its ponytail. He never bothered to ask why she dyed it blue. She was a law unto herself, and she suited it.

'How's the tree cutting going?'

'Finished it. I'm heading back to the office and my favourite boss.' She tipped him a wink and raised her can at him.

'Is he awful to work for?'

She pulled a noncommittal face. 'We have an interesting relationship. Let's put it that way.'

'Does that mean he disapproves of your hair?'

'Probably.'

He rested his shoulders back. 'What would you say if I told you I was thinking about selling this place?' He stared into the flames, watching them leap and dance. The evening was warm and the fire pit not entirely necessary, but he liked a tattie roasted straight out of the flame and toasted marshmallows were calling.

'What are you talking about?'

'The estate agents are coming to value the place tomorrow.'

'Why?'

He sighed and rocked back in his chair. 'A few reasons.'

'Then do tell.'

'I just can't do it.'

'Can't do what?'

'I don't know how to make this place work.' His head reeled back to Duncan's call the previous weekend. But even if he jumped through all the hoops, there was no guarantee Duncan's boss would choose him as a deserving local project. Like every other scheme, it was pie in the sky. 'I had big plans, big ideas, but they're not happening.'

Cha tilted her head and fixed him with a stare. 'Logan, you only took over this year. We're in June. You haven't even hit the high season yet. I know you've always been an impatient twat, but this is pretty spectacular even for you.'

He couldn't help but grin. 'Yeah. I know that. And I guess it looks like I'm bailing before I've even tried. I guess I don't have the staying power. Isn't that what my mum's always saying? That I never stick at anything. But it's mentally and physically draining. I need more staff but I can't get anyone. It's a losing battle.'

'Well, I'm shocked.' She thrust her can into the holder on the arm of the chair, leaned back in the seat and pursed her lips. 'I can't believe you'd give up like that. I always thought I was the flake in the family.'

'That's an unfair reputation though, considering you've always had a steady job.'

'Exactly.' She pointed her finger at him. 'So, come on. Don't quit. Give it a year at least.'

'A year?' That seemed unimaginable when he considered it without Eleanor. 'Maybe, but it's not just that.'

'Well, what then? Are you ill or something?'

'I want to move to Northamptonshire.'

Cha shook her head like she was trying to de-fog it. 'Northamptonshire? Why? Have you even been there before?'

'No. Well, yes, when I was at Cambridge, I passed through it, but that's not the reason. It's because that's where Eleanor lives.'

'Eleanor? The woman who was camping here last week?'

'The very same.'

'Logan.' Her expression turned sympathetic. 'I knew she was important to you, but is she worth giving up your dreams for?'

'Yes. She's worth everything to me.'

Cha let out a breathy laugh. 'Wow. Ok. Who'd have known you could be this romantic?'

'I know, huh?' He sipped his drink, nodding at the flames.

'And she's cool with you moving down there?'

'She told me not to.'

'So why are you even contemplating it?'

'Because her reasoning is messed up.'

Cha shook her head. 'That doesn't matter, Logan. If she's not cool about this, then stop. Don't go all out just for a Hollywood moment when all you're doing is going against her wishes.'

He let out a long sigh. 'Yeah. I kind of thought that earlier. I don't want to put any more pressure on her. She's already got her dad to look after and she thinks that'll drive us apart. But how can I just sit here and do nothing?'

'Following your dreams isn't nothing. Make this a success, stay in touch with her, have patience...' She grinned at him. 'Yeah, I know. It's the one thing you really can't do. But just this once, don't do something so impulsive you regret it the rest of your life.'

He raised an eyebrow. 'Speaking from experience, are you?'

'Not exactly. I just don't want you throwing away a good thing. If Eleanor is relationship averse because of her family situation then it's not like she's going to be throwing herself at anyone else, so sit tight, and see what happens.'

'I cannot believe that's what you expect me to do.'

She leaned over and grabbed the bag of marshmallows from under his seat. 'I think we need a sugar hit.'

Rowena Ramsay really should come with a public health warning. Logan was never sure which version of her he was going to get. Sometimes she was as docile as an old labrador, other times as fierce as a rottweiler, and then there were those days when she was as hilarious as a poodle with a rainbow rinse – though they were usually wine induced. Why she'd chosen today for a visit, he wasn't quite sure. She'd only been recently for the Segways.

Had she heard he'd had the campsite valued? Even if he wasn't going to sell up, it didn't do any harm having a valuation, especially if he was going to apply for Duncan's grant. Having accurate information was always good.

Rowena all but crashed the car into the front of the shop in her haste to get to Logan. He cringed as he served a customer, watching the scene unfold in horrified fascination. Had she even put on the handbrake before she darted around to the boot? And what was she bringing in? His dad had only just got out as Rowena bustled back round carrying a large box. The sound of her voice carried through the window.

'Open the door, will you? I don't want to drop this.'

'I'm just about to,' Iain said in his long-suffering tone. *Poor Dad.* He pushed open the door and it thumped off the wall. The customer Logan was serving jumped.

'Sorry,' he said. 'That door needs replaced.'

'Gave me quite a start,' the customer said, taking her purchases.

'Logan, can I take this round to the caravan, or do you want to see it first?' Rowena called across the shop.

He smiled at the customer, who looked like she wanted to leg it. He felt the same, that or jump into a gaping chasm in the floor. 'Just whatever you think best, Mum. I'm not sure what it is, so I can't make that decision.'

'It's a pineapple upside-down cake, of course.'

He half-opened his mouth and glanced at the customer who edged past Rowena and left.

'Of course it is. And why do I want one of them?'

'Because it's your favourite.' She beamed at him.

'Is it?'

'You used to eat nothing but. Now, I think I should take it round to the caravan. There's nowhere here I can leave it. Is it open?'

'Yes, go right in.' He frowned and scratched the top of his head, trying to recall a time when he'd eaten nothing but pineapple cakes. Maybe when he was about six? 'Hi, Dad.'

'Hello.' Iain sighed as Rowena nudged the door fully open with her foot and made a scene manoeuvring her way out.

'I'll just close up in here and then I'll come around.'

'Need any help with anything?' Iain shuffled about with his hands in his pockets, looking very much like he could do with an excuse to keep away from his wife.

'Yeah. Can you check the shelves in the fridge and see if anything's on its use-by date? If it is, take it out and we'll eat it for dinner.'

'Certainly, I can.' Iain bustled straight over.

Logan put up the closed sign and cashed up. Ten minutes later, they headed out of the back door to the caravan with a block of cheese, two cartons of milk and six yoghurts. Rowena was inside with her pineapple cake on a stand on the worktop and several shopping bags worth of food taking up the tiny floor space.

'Er... Where did all that food come from?' Logan gaped at it.

'It was in the box with the cake. That's why I didn't want to drop it.'

'How many people are you planning to feed?' He pulled open one of the bags and frowned. 'I was going to cook for you.'

'Oh, nonsense. I know how busy you are. Now, you and Dad can go and sit somewhere out of my way and I'll fix us some food.'

Logan grabbed two beers from the fridge and handed one to his dad. A strange, awkward sensation fluttered in the air as they sat at the outdoor picnic table. Had they come to give him bad news?

'Caught any salmon this year?' he asked.

'No,' Iain said.

He sipped his beer as his dad talked about his fishing episodes. It passed the time and Logan nodded and smiled when required, remaining calm on the outside, but his insides had started to churn. *What is going on?* Mum was usually far too busy to come and see him, especially when she'd been here so recently, and now she'd appeared with bags of food and a cake she was convinced was his favourite thing.

When she emerged carrying plates laden with pasta, cheeses, olives, tomatoes and a green salad, Logan jumped up to help her. Normally he'd have loved every bit of this platter, but his stomach lurched.

'Listen, Mum, Dad.' He took a gulp of beer. 'What's going on? Why are you here?'

'To see you.' Rowena poured herself a large glass of wine.

'Obviously.' He swigged more beer.

Rowena banged her glass on the table and peered at him with searching eyes. 'I just wanted to check you were ok. I had a message from Cha, saying you were feeling a bit down,'

'Seriously?'

'Yes. She's a funny one sometimes, but I think she's onto something. You didn't seem quite yourself last time either.'

Logan rubbed a niggling pain on his forehead. 'Things aren't going too well here. You might have noticed. So, I had an estate agent value the site.'

Both his parents frowned, glancing at each other.

'Are you planning on selling it?' A succession of expressions played across Rowena's face: shock, surprise, acceptance, then pity. 'I thought you were struggling a bit, but I'm not sure you need to sell up. Give it time.'

'I'm trying, but you know that's not the easiest thing for me to do. And it's not like you wanted me to do this in the first place, is it?'

'That's not strictly true. I didn't think you'd be happy here, as it didn't match up with what you'd trained to do. That was my prime concern. You have to admit cleaning toilets and keeping the shop stocked hardly equate to a degree in sports science. But, let me tell you something, I called up the local rag after our last visit and gave them a piece of my mind regarding their dealings with Malcolm McManus.'

Logan restrained his eye roll. Mum just couldn't help herself meddling, could she? 'And what did they say?'

'Well, I got right through to the reporter. She was very apologetic. Said she'd been lured here with promises of a story, but none of it had transpired. Which, of course, it wouldn't. Malcolm is full of shit.'

Iain pinched the bridge of his nose and sighed.

'She was all up for writing a highly favourable article,' Rowena continued. 'Said everyone she'd spoken to seemed to be having a great time on the Segways.'

'Well, that's something.' Logan lounged back with a sigh.

Rowena frowned. 'So, are you actually selling up? If so, I assume you have something lined up? It would be crazy to walk away if you didn't.'

He looked away, almost grinning despite himself. That was his mum in a nutshell, career obsessed and always with a bombproof plan – unlike him. He remembered countless lectures as a boy about never having a gap in his CV. Employers would apparently notice, even if only a few days were unaccounted for. He wondered how many people Rowena had turned away over the years because they had a day missing on theirs.

'I don't really know what I'm doing. I was considering a move to Northamptonshire but I don't think that's going to work out.'

'Oh.' Rowena sipped her wine, looking moderately impressed. 'What's down that way to intrigue you? Is there some big sports facility? Or is it a connection from Cambridge?'

'No.' He shook his head. 'Just Eleanor.'

Rowena glanced at Iain with an unexpected look of triumph on her face. 'Aha, I see.' She snapped her gazed back to Logan and held it.

He shook his head. 'Do you?'

'Yes. I said as much. Didn't I?'

'You did,' Iain said.

'Ok. So, what do you think I should do?'

'It's your life, son,' Rowena said. 'I could see by the way the two of you were looking at each other that something was brewing. And I'm glad. You looked right together, if that makes sense. But what you do next is your decision. Just make sure whatever you decide, it's not too rash. I know how impetuous you can be, but step back, and think hard about everything.'

Logan ate a mouthful of pasta. 'So, everyone's advice is for me to be patient.' It was almost funny. How could the world's most impatient man wait? Especially when he didn't know what he was waiting for.

'Exactly.'

He wolfed down more food. 'You realise I have no idea how to do that?'

'Of course we do. And that's why we're here. We can help out around here for a while if you want. You can spend some time filling out the applications and we'll see to the cleaning.'

'You?' He raised an eyebrow.

'I've been cleaning toilets since before you were born. I think I'll manage.'

He shared a smile with his dad. At least he knew she'd do it thoroughly. His mum never did anything by halves.

Now he just had to hope this new resolve to be patient and follow his dreams reaped the results everyone seemed so certain it would. And how long would he have to wait to find out?

Chapter Twenty-Seven

Eleanor

An email notification pinged, and Eleanor leapt for her phone. She wouldn't put it past Mr Ross-The-Boss to serve her notice, even on a Sunday. Nothing had been said during the week but the staff at the office were like people strapped to a ticking time bomb waiting for it to blow up at any second. Mr Ross seemed to be out on the floor more than usual, pacing and watching. Eleanor's nerves were shredded. Ron, who'd always seemed so nice, had started casting her evil looks and barely spoke to her, even when they had to collaborate. It was horrible.

When she leapt for her phone at the breakfast table, Dad jumped. 'Goodness, Eleanor, you gave me a start. Surely, your boss will wait until Monday before giving out any news, good or bad.'

'Who knows?' she muttered, opening her phone.

'Maybe it's time to move on anyway. You've been there almost seven years and that's when they always say you get itchy feet.'

She didn't reply, her eyes locked on the new email. Occasionally she got them from The Heather Glen Campsite but the subject line was familiar. She'd written it back in Logan's office.

Love the outdoors? Don't miss this exciting new opportunity.

She opened the email. 'Oh god.' Seeing the ad brought back so many memories.

'Oh no. What?' Dad said. 'Have you been let go?'

'What? No. It's Logan from Heather Glen.'

'Is he in trouble?'

She glanced up at the shake in her dad's voice. 'Nothing like that. He's advertising for staff.' He was going ahead with living his dream just as she'd told him to. That was what she wanted, wasn't it? But the thought of life going on at Heather Glen without her was almost unbearable. Sometimes in the dead of night, she could almost hear the stream rushing over the rocks and the wind in the trees.

'Why is he sending that to you? You don't want to work there, do you?'

'No. I get the emails because I'm on the mailing list.' She rubbed her forehead. 'I just wish—'

'Wish what?' Dad poured himself some tea and looked back at his fishing magazine.

'I just miss it, I suppose.'

She thumbed out a message.

ELEANOR: Just saw the ad. It brought back memories. So happy you're going through with the dream xx

She must have checked her phone about twenty times in the two minutes before a message pinged back.

LOGAN: I'm trying, but you know it'll never be the same for me without you. How's things with you? Hope your dad's ok. xx

ELEANOR: Dad's ok, and so am I. Lots of unpleasant stuff going on at work. I won't bore you with details. xx

She barely waited a minute for the next reply.

LOGAN: Nothing you say would bore me. Your company was one of the most special things in my life. I miss you all the time. I never meant to hurt you with what I said. You truly deserve to live your own life. It doesn't have to be with me but you aren't bound to be your dad's carer forever. He'll understand. If anyone knows your worth, it's him. Give yourself some credit and cut yourself some slack. You've been through a hellish time and you need to heal, that's a given, but make sure you don't use your dad's situation as a substitute for getting help if you need it. I'm always here and I'll listen to anything you want to tell me. I care so much about you and I'm ready to give up everything for you, if you want me. Right now, I'm doing what you asked me to. I'm living my dream but it feels like only half a dream without you. XX

The words made her heart skip a beat. Half a dream? Could she be the other half and make it her dream too? Her heart filled so full, she almost burst, but the stronger she loved, the worse it was to part. Could she bear to love so strongly? Did she have the nerve to risk it?

But it didn't change the Dad equation. Would he go and live in Scotland? He was happily back home and settled into the old routines. His dream of buying a cottage there to retire in was forgotten the minute they crossed the border and he hadn't mentioned it since.

'Mrs Crawford down the road had a fall,' he said later that day, pouring gravy over his Sunday roast. 'Poor woman. She's on her own and she was stuck upstairs. It's very worrying.'

'Can't she get an emergency button or something?'

'Possibly. I'm not sure how it works. I'm just very grateful I don't have to worry about things like that.'

Eleanor forced a smile as she cut her chicken. She'd never resented looking after Dad and she didn't dare regret it. Maybe one day she would, but she couldn't afford to let that idea take over at this stage. Every now and then, wayward thoughts crept in, questions that wanted answering, like how long would she have to do it? What if he died when she was past child-bearing age? And she hoped that was the case – she didn't wish him an early death for her selfish reasons. Far from it. But would she regret never having kids?

'You said earlier you missed Heather Glen,' Dad said. 'Why not book another holiday for next year?'

'Ok.'

The thought brought tears swimming to the surface. She wanted to drop everything and run there right now. If she was free, she would fly to Scotland, do something wholly new and crazy. Even if it didn't last, she wanted the chance. She would take it and accept the consequences. She didn't want to be bound to this life forever.

'Dad, do you think...?'

He smiled at her, then worry lines crossed his forehead. She couldn't bring herself to say the words.

'Eleanor? Are you quite all right? You look a bit tearful.'

'Sorry.' She wiped her eyes on her napkin. 'Just all the work stress, you know. It's so difficult. I hate the not knowing.'

Come the late afternoon, Dad was full of food and exhausted. All part of the Sunday routine. It was too late to start anything or do much else. She dropped him off at the house and changed into her walking boots. She rarely had time for a good brisk walk these days, so it was almost like a treat, though also a necessity after the giant lunch she'd just packed away.

Dad was happily ensconced in his armchair, looking at his book when she left. She doubted he'd last five minutes before his head drooped and he started snoring. She took the path through Chapel Brampton towards a field, walking at a steady pace, building it up as she went. The sun was high in the sky and baking hot as she walked the exposed path by the field.

Everything was familiar. The sights and sounds she'd grown up with. Rambling fields, hedgerows and birds twittering all around. In the distance, the pretty little church steeple poked skyward. Visitors probably found it even more beautiful than she did. Other people's scenery was always more interesting than your own. She flicked her hair off her neck, rubbing a tender patch of skin, the work of the glaring sun. No matter how much sun cream she threw at herself, it didn't wholly protect her very pale skin and she always missed a bit. Best to head back to the village and get into the shade.

Two cyclists were powering along the path towards her, and she stepped into the verge to let them pass, her eyes roaming over the wheat fields.

'Hi, Eleanor.'

She started and turned her gaze back to the cyclists. One of them had stopped and was holding his bike steady, watching her with cool dark blue eyes. Mark.

'Hi.' Her focus flickered to the other cyclist. Curiosity more than anything made her want to know if his companion was male or female, though she didn't really care if he was with someone else. It was a man. Someone she vaguely recognised from their days together.

'I heard there are problems at Nexus Solutions.'

'Did you?' She didn't want to know how. It could be common knowledge, but she suspected a bit of Hattie meddling.

'I've got a couple of options if you're after something. You wouldn't have to work in the same department as me. I kind of get the feeling that's putting you off.'

Definitely Hattie.

'I was going to call you tomorrow,' he said. 'But this is serendipity.'

Eleanor held on to her eye roll. Mark loved OTT words. She'd frequently heard him using discombobulated or juxtaposition in sentences, then look around to check everyone's reaction. She'd even heard him use antidisestablishmentarianism, which brought more groans than appreciation.

'I'm not sure what's happening yet. I might not be the one made redundant.'

'Well, if you're the lucky one, then I can give you two options, one at the Cambridge branch or one in London, which I might add is a very exciting position. It comes with accommodation, a splendid apartment near Hyde Park.'

Was he serious? He knew her circumstances. Even Cambridge was an hour's drive away, which would double her commute. She couldn't bring herself to reply, certainly not to justify herself or remind him. If he was that forgetful or deliberately provoking, then she was thrilled she'd let him go, and she didn't need to feel any guilt about turning down the offers. She was done justifying herself to others. Sometimes it was hard enough doing it to herself.

'Thanks,' she said. 'But no thanks. I'll find something for myself if I need to.' She turned and walked on, half expecting him to call her back or say something else, but he didn't. She was almost back at the village before she dared turn around. Mark and his friend were nowhere to be seen.

She made her way back to the house, muttering to herself. The conservatory doors were wide open and her dad was sitting at the little bistro table on the patio, sipping water from a beer glass.

'It's so hot,' he said. 'I'm not sure if it's better outside or in.'

'I've got a burnt neck. I need to put something on it.' Eleanor nipped into her bedroom for some cooling moisturiser. She caught her reflection in the mirror and stared at her pale face shining back. *Am I doing the right thing?* What if putting her dad's needs before hers did ruin her future? How would she square it with herself in ten or twenty-years' time if she hadn't even tried to do something for herself?

When she came out, Dad was closing the patio doors. 'The flies are terrible.'

'Dad. Can we talk about something?'

'What kind of thing?'

'Come and sit.'

'Oh, right. Sounds ominous.' He sat in his armchair and peered at her.

She flumped onto the sofa but didn't lean back, sitting bolt upright, hands in her lap like she was about to be scolded.

'Eleanor?' Frown lines creased his face. 'What's wrong?'

'I've been thinking a lot recently about the future and how things will work.'

'Ah, yes. Of course. The job thing is very unsettling and sometimes I feel like I don't help your situation. I'm a great burden to you.'

'What?' She gaped at him. 'No, you're not. That's not what I meant, I just—'

'Listen, I appreciate everything you do but you're young and I'm not your keeper.' He glanced at the picture of him and Mum on the mantelpiece and his shoulders sagged. 'Goodness knows I couldn't have coped without you after she died. I would have gone to pieces. But I know you can't stay here forever.'

She frowned. 'Really? You don't want me to stay here?'

Dad chuckled and his eyes gleamed. 'You're welcome here as long as you like, and I'll not deny it makes my life easier and much more pleasant. But if this job thing happens and you have to move somewhere else, don't think you're bound to me.'

A tear trickled down her cheek. 'I can't. I'd feel so guilty.'

'You mustn't,' Dad said. 'You have a life to live yourself. Think of the guilt I feel keeping you here. You're not responsible for me. I'm your father. I'm responsible for you, and I want you to do what's right for you. If you staying here is a comfort, then that's fine, but recently you don't seem quite yourself. I wonder if this job thing has made you think somehow you're tied to this house or me.'

She wiped her tears away. 'I wish I could do what's right for both of us.'

'And you can. Whatever you choose for yourself will be right for me. I'll manage somehow.'

But nothing could stop her from worrying. If she did what she really wanted and went straight back to Scotland, what would he make of that? She'd seen how upset he got when he'd heard Jamie's news. Perhaps he would be ok with Cambridge, possibly even London, but Scotland?

'What if I were to move somewhere far away?'

He let out a sigh. 'I would miss you but I would be happy to know you were doing what you wanted. I wonder if the time has come for a change for me too.'

'How do you mean?'

'I bought this house as a retirement property for your mother and me, but it became little more than a nursing home for her last few months. I don't feel tied to it. With the boys off here and there, I was thinking you might want to do the same thing. And maybe I could downsize.'

'I don't want to emigrate,' she said. 'That's not what I meant.'

'I realise that. I just thought if job opportunities were too thin, maybe you'd have to move elsewhere. I'm not against the idea. I would need my own place, though I can't deny I would like it if you were within easy commuting distance, but it's your life.'

'I met Mark today. He offered me a job in Cambridge or London.'

Dad pulled a face. 'Well, Cambridge is nice but very pricey and London... Well, I think I'm too old for London, but if that's what you want, then you go. I could look into getting a little bungalow somewhere, perhaps Kent. There are some nice places there.'

She shook her head and swallowed. 'What I really want is to go to Scotland and work at Heather Glen with Logan.'

Dad frowned and blinked. 'You would? Whatever for?'

'Because... He and I... Well, we kind of fell for each other.'

Eleanor was sure she'd never seen Dad's eyes that wide. He gaped and his mouth dropped open. 'Well, I most definitely didn't expect that, but if that's the case, then what are you waiting for?'

'Really?'

'I assume that's why he was so friendly with you on our trip. He lost his mind with love over my daughter or something equally romantic.'

'So... If I write my resignation, take the voluntary redundancy and go to Scotland, you'll be ok with that? I mean... What will you do?'

'I'll do my best to muddle along, but if you find somewhere suitable for me to live, I'll happily take it.'

'You'd move to Scotland?'

'Of course. I've always loved it up there. Your mother and I talked countless times about moving, retiring there, or getting a second home. I think she'd be over the moon if I did it. I might even get the little cottage we always dreamed of, or at least a similar one.'

'I don't know what to say.'

'Then don't say anything. Get on that computer of yours and write to your boss.'

Her eyes misted over again, but this time, she couldn't stop smiling. She bounded over to her dad and hugged him.

Chapter Twenty-Eight

Logan

July

Logan straightened out the collar of his white shirt. It was going to chafe. He hated dressing up like this, but business was business. Turning side on in the mirror, with only a tiny gap between it and the bed, he weighed up his reflection. Not bad. He'd pass as a respectable business owner anyway. If he was going to get this grant, he had to at least look the part. What had started as a couple of innocuous forms to fill in had suddenly become full on.

Curse his impatience, but really, in this instance, he'd have welcomed more time to prepare. The owner of Harrington Energy Solutions, Geoff Harrington, was on his way to Heather Glen at that precise moment with a delegation of 'interested parties', all ready to scrutinise everything on the site to see if it warranted their investment. Duncan couldn't help now. This was above his paygrade. Logan had to do this himself.

His stomach churned as he hopped down the caravan steps. Having his parents around the previous week had given him time to go all out on the application and now was his moment to make it happen. He fidgeted and paced around the shop, sorting shelves that didn't need sorting and constantly checking the time.

This place had been his dream as a teenager, and he'd committed to it, just as he'd been willing to commit to Eleanor. He adjusted his cuffs. If only she were here. Together, he was sure they could do this. But she had her own life to live and she'd chosen to devote it to caring for Andy. What did he make of his daughter's insistence? Had she asked him yet? Logan had said his piece and didn't think he could say anything else without upsetting her even more. She'd made her choice and he had to accept that it didn't include him.

All through his life, he'd jumped ship at the first sign of trouble; this was his big chance to prove himself. 'Can they just hurry up and get here?'

Just after two, a black Mercedes pulled up. A man sidled around from the passenger side. He had salt and pepper hair and a very slick suit. Although clearly well into his fifties at least, he was suave with a debonair look. From the driver's seat, a young woman with long, very glossy blonde hair emerged. She pushed a large pair of sunglasses onto the top of her head and looked around with a screwed-up nose. Definitely not the camping type then. Her slick black suit and heels said no. Hopefully, she had a pair of wellies stowed in the boot. Logan stepped out of the shop to greet them, but as he did so, the back door of the vehicle opened.

'What the hell?' The words came out loud and he raised his hand to his lips. *Her!* From the other side, a man got out and Logan shook his head. Should he pinch himself? Never in a million years had he expected that grumpy duo to come back. It was Mrs Grumpy Camper and her husband. What the blazes were they doing here now? His heart sank. If they were involved in the process, no way was he getting this grant.

Biting the bullet and making a final adjustment to his collar, he fixed his smile in place.

'Good afternoon,' he said.

'Good afternoon,' the older man said. 'I'm Geoff Harrington. Very pleased to meet you.'

'Logan Ramsay.' He extended his hand.

Geoff shook it. 'Let me introduce everyone. This is my daughter, Genevieve. She's a business studies student. She's just here to observe. I hope you don't mind.'

The young woman smiled, though it looked a little forced. She shook Logan's hand with fingers covered in pretty rings and tipped with immaculate nails.

'And these are my friends, Alice and Paul Langford.'

'I recognise you. Lovely to have you back.' Logan's smile grew; he'd said that without an ounce of sarcasm. *Hand over the Oscar!* 'But I'm a bit in the dark as to why you're here.'

Mrs Langford looked him up and down, her expression screwed up like she was still juicing that bitter lemon for every last drop.

'A stroke of luck really,' Geoff said. 'We were having a chat and I discovered Paul and Alice had just been here which is excellent. Paul works in the same sector as me so he'll be able to lend his expertise.'

'Right.' Logan doubted that. 'Haven't you travelled some way?' He thought he recalled from their booking that they were from the borders.

'We're from Dumfries but we're staying with Geoff tonight,' Alice replied. 'This is one of our favourite areas and we'd love to move up here. I wondered if perhaps you were thinking on selling up.'

'Um...' Had he given her that impression during her stay? Did she fancy taking it on, so she could move to her favourite area? 'I'm not selling up, no.'

'Pity,' Paul Langford said. 'We're in a position to make you a fair offer.'

Geoff Harrington cleared his throat. 'That's a secondary piece of business, but first, I'd like you to talk me through your vision for how renewables would work here and why it would benefit the community and the local area.'

'Yeah, sure,' Logan said, his eyes darting back to Alice and Paul. This felt like an ambush. Was there any chance of him getting the grant now? Should he consider their offer? Would it be fair? Somehow, he doubted it.

'Well, Mr and Miss Harrington...' Logan said.

'Geoff, please. I don't stand on ceremony. First, can we look at the field where you could locate the solar panels?'

'Sure.' Logan led them across the site, painfully aware very little had changed since the Langfords were here and knowing their low opinion of everything.

'I'm not sure a grant for renewables is what's needed here,' Alice said. 'There are a high proportion of things needing upgrading and I really don't think renewables is a priority.'

'It's always a priority,' Logan said, unable to keep the snap from his voice. Just who did she think she was? 'My business is to encourage people to enjoy the outdoors. How can I do that if I'm indirectly destroying the environment? Making this site greener is a top priority for me and everything that comes after is built with sustainability at the heart.'

'A very good way to look at it,' Geoff said.

'Can I wait back at the building?' Genevieve asked. 'My shoes are going to get ruined.'

Geoff gave her a hard stare, then nodded. She picked her way back to the shop.

'You realise,' Paul said, 'your application may be for several thousand pounds to install solar or wind power but that doesn't mean you'll qualify for the full amount. You may end up with a few hundred pounds. Do you think you'll be able to use that wisely enough to create a sustainable foundation?'

'That'll be for me to decide,' Geoff said.

'Any little help is a start,' Logan said. 'I'm not running my business by spending thousands of pounds I don't have. Everything I'm doing is budgeted and every improvement I have on my list has a link to sustainability. This grant would help me make changes on a far grander scale than I can currently afford, but I won't be skimping on my current projects even if I don't get it.'

Paul moved closer to his wife, muttering something to her.

Geoff shielded his eyes and scanned over the site. 'I thought your current plans looked very well thought out.'

That was something at least, and it gave Logan a bubble of hope. If he had the time to do something properly, he could do it, and last week he'd got his plans wrestled into shape.

'They are,' Paul agreed. 'I just think it's a pity you're struggling on with this. It's a hard job for one person.'

Logan ran his hand through his hair. Couldn't he get rid of these two and talk to Geoff privately? The Langfords' desire to buy him out was surely a conflict of interest. But as Geoff Harrington was a private investor, he could do whatever he wanted with his money. *And he probably won't want to give it to me if I'm not willing to sell up to his friends.*

'And you don't seem to enjoy it,' Alice said.

'Actually, I do. Now, if you'll follow me,' he said to Geoff. 'I can show you the proposed area for the Eco Pods.' As they walked around the site, Logan imagined his dreams coming to fruition and his heart swelled, but the idea of the Langfords taking over made his blood boil. When he'd worked here as a teenager, Shirley and Eck had run the place like a big family. As it expanded, the site got less and less personal, but in time, he could bring that back. With upgrades, new facilities and better staffing.

'The owners' accommodation is hardly viable,' she added to her husband.

'But there's planning permission granted on the grounds for a two-storey dwelling house, isn't there?' Paul looked at Logan.

'There is, but I'm not selling.'

Alice huffed. 'Don't you even want to hear our offer?'

'I like what I see,' Geoff said. 'And I think Logan's made it clear he doesn't want to sell up.'

What would Geoff decide? Logan flexed his fingers, wishing he had Eleanor beside him, so he could take her hand and not feel so alone and out on a limb. If he didn't get the grant, it wasn't the end of the world, but if he did, there was so much he could do. He almost didn't want to think about it. It was like spending money he didn't have.

'The layout here would have to change completely,' Alice said to her husband, making sure she was out of Geoff's earshot, but Logan could still hear her. She pointed across the site. 'There's too much grass and not enough hardstanding. Caravans are a lot more lucrative than tents.'

'It was always part of the vision,' Logan said and she narrowed her eyes at him like she hadn't realised he was listening to her. 'That we'd be primarily a campsite. Again, it's part of the eco drive. Caravan waste is always an issue.'

'Always stay true to your values,' Geoff said. 'The vision can evolve with the times but don't lose the core values.'

'Hmm,' Alice muttered. 'We tried a tent this year and you saw the disaster. It's the noise. I have no desire to hear people getting up to all sorts with only a thin layer of canvas between me and them, and I'm sure there are many who feel the same. And don't say that's all part of the ecosystem or whatever.'

'Well, it is kind of natural.' Logan ran his fingers through his hair, trying not to smirk.

Geoff let out a half laugh. 'We seem to have strayed into unforeseen territory. Paul and Alice may wish to talk about buying and selling, but that's not why I'm here.'

'Logan!' A woman's voice on the path behind made him spin around so fast he cricked his neck.

His eyes almost burst out. 'Eleanor... What are you doing here?'

She ran to him and flung her arms around his neck. He hadn't forgotten who was with him, but he didn't care. He wrapped his arms around her waist and swung her above the ground.

'Why are you here?' he said into her ear.

'Don't sell Heather Glen.'

'I'm not.' He lowered her to the ground and let her go.

She stepped back and her cheeks bloomed as she looked at the others. 'A girl in the shop said these two' – Eleanor indicated the Langfords with her eyes – 'were here to buy you out.'

'They want to,' he whispered, 'but I'm not selling. This is my dream, remember? You told me to make it work and I'm trying.' Everyone had said to be patient and he'd done his best. Was this his reward? Even if he didn't get the grant, he'd much rather have Eleanor.

Alice Langford arched an eyebrow.

'We're in the middle of a business meeting,' Geoff said.

'Oh.' Eleanor looked at him. 'I... er... can wait.'

'This looks important however.'

'I'm not going to deny that Eleanor is the most important thing in my life,' Logan said. 'But if—'

'I can wait,' she said.

'No need,' Geoff said. 'I've made my decision.'

'Please.' Eleanor swallowed. 'I shouldn't have butted in like that. Please, don't judge Logan badly because of me.'

'It's not exactly surprising,' Alice said. 'I knew the two of you were at it this summer.'

Geoff shook his head, then smiled first at Eleanor, then at Logan. 'My decision hasn't been influenced by this.' He gestured at the two of them. 'Whatever this is. You're free to conduct your personal life however you please and you look like you're very happy together, far be it from me to interfere. Hopefully, I can add to your good cheer by letting you know I accept your grant application and am going to award you the full amount.'

'Oh my god.' Logan burst out laughing and almost hugged Geoff. 'Thank you so much.'

'Not at all,' Geoff said. 'I'll be in touch with the details. I'm very impressed with your commitment to renewables.' He shook Logan's hand, smiled at Eleanor and began walking down the path, engaging Paul and Alice in conversation as if nothing very remarkable had happened. Both of them looked back, throwing Logan and Eleanor disgusted looks.

Eventually, Logan turned to Eleanor and took her hand. 'What are you doing here? It's midweek, aren't you working? Where's Andy?'

'He's at home.'

'On his own?'

'Yes. I just called him and he says he's fine.'

'That's great. And you're just passing by?' He raised an eyebrow.

'Kind of.'

'From Northampton?'

'Well, I've taken a redundancy package, so I don't have a job. If Dad doesn't need me, I don't have a house... I wonder if you know anywhere round here where I could get a job with live in accommodation?' A smile played at the corner of her lips.

'Are you saying what I think you're saying?' He shook his head.

'I'm saying that I love you,' she said, her eyes watery. 'And I want to live this dream with you.'

He laughed and ran the pad of his thumb down the side of her face, catching the tears. 'I love you too and I'm delighted to have you here as long as you want. But what about your dad? How have you settled things with him?'

'Well, Dad wants to come too.'

'He does?'

'Yes. But I don't mean to live with us. He wants to get his own place nearby. It's a new start, a clean page. We both needed it more than we realised.'

'It's amazing.' He looked around and didn't see problems any more, just solutions and projects he and Eleanor could do together. Some of them would be funded by the grant, others they'd budget for and make happen as and when they could. Patience was the key. This was a long-term project and wasn't going to happen overnight. With Eleanor at his side, he was sure he could be content enough to not stress if things didn't happen immediately.

'It feels like it was always meant to be,' she said. 'Otherwise, why did my parents bring me here for my holidays in the first place? I think my mum's been looking out for me and she wanted me to come back. For you.'

'For us.' He dipped in and kissed her. 'We found each other again, so you must be right. We were always destined to be together.'

Chapter Twenty-Nine

Eleanor

August

Dad closed the door on the house in Chapel Brampton for the last time. He gave the door handle a little pat and a smile. Eleanor took his arm, biting back tears. 'Someone else will be happy here.'

'Yes, they will.' Dad patted her hand.

A little robin flew down and landed on the path in front of them, then quickly flittered away and sat on the car roof.

Dad chuckled. 'Daft little bird. I think she wants to come with us.'

It was the end of an era, but with the excitement of driving to Scotland and seeing Logan again, Eleanor soon forgot to be upset. The house had sold quickly and her dad had got good money for it. Now, they had a new adventure to pursue.

'Couldn't have gone any smoother,' Dad said as she drove towards the motorway. The removal van was on its way to a storage unit in Perth and Logan would meet it there. Eleanor and Dad were going to take it slowly, knowing it would be late before they arrived. They first had to hand in the key to the estate agent in Northampton.

'Yes. Those removal guys were very good.'

Eleanor stopped outside the estate agent and Dad nipped in. With the money from the sale of his house, he would part fund the building of the new house on the campsite, with his own 'dad annexe', though he was ever hopeful his favourite little cottage would come on the market. Logan and Doughnut – she'd almost got used to the name – had drawn up plans for starting on solar and wind power installations over the winter. Hopefully, they'd have an exciting off-season with no guests but lots of building work. Eleanor crossed her fingers on the wheel.

Dad hadn't been in such a happy mood for ages, and it brightened her heart. Years had lifted from his shoulders. He smiled and hummed a funny little Scottish ditty as he looked out the window.

'I honestly didn't think you'd be this happy about moving.'

'The time was right,' Dad said. 'I'm sorry to be so far from my grandchildren but in a couple of months they'll be in New Zealand and that'll be that anyway. I'll have to train myself up on using the Face screen thing.'

'FaceTime.' Eleanor smirked.

'Yes, that. And what about you?' He peered at her. 'Are you sure you won't miss your friends?'

'I will, but I'm sure I'll meet other people.'

'Yes. It's one thing I've learned in life. You go on making friends. I used to laugh when you children set so much store by your friends at school. They're the ones you're most likely to leave behind and the ones you meet later are the important ones.'

Perhaps it was true, even if only in part. Hattie was one of those friends she'd had forever. And yes, she'd miss her chats with her. But as she'd discovered Hattie was now dating Mark's cycling buddy, having an excuse not to attend any parties where she might run the risk of meeting him again was ideal.

It was pushing nine o'clock in the evening when they finally reached the campsite, green and splendid amidst the rolling hills in the glen. The glory of Scottish summers meant the natural light was only beginning to fade. Eleanor was ready to drop. Exhaustion washed through her limbs and she couldn't wait to close her eyes.

'I hope the caravan is ok for you,' she said. Logan had organised a temporary one for Dad close to his static.

'I'm sure it'll be fine,' he said. 'I feel like I'm arriving for a permanent holiday.'

Logan greeted them with open arms and a smile splitting his face. 'You made it.'

'I know. We're actually here to live.' She clutched her cheeks.

'It hasn't quite sunk in.' Dad clapped his hands. 'I'm not sure it will for a good while yet. Not tonight anyway. I hope you don't mind me being anti-social, but I don't think I can stay awake much longer.'

'I'll show you to the caravan.' Logan took his arm.

'You know.' Dad gazed around with a fond smile, clasping his hands together. 'I wouldn't want to get a reputation as an old eccentric or anything, but while I'm here, I'd like to help out. Maybe you'd let me welcome the campers and check around the site for anything that needs sorting.'

'Of course I would. You go right ahead.' Logan clapped him on the back.

Eleanor grinned and kissed her dad goodnight. She ascended the stairs into the static she was going to share with Logan. The cosy space welcomed her and she slumped into the sofa area. Logan returned a few moments later, grinning.

'Your dad's so funny. I can imagine him becoming quite a well-known character here.'

'Very probably.' She yawned. 'I'm so tired.'

'Get to bed then,' he said. 'Come on, I'll keep you company.' He winked and she giggled.

As August entered September, Eleanor contacted different tradespeople and she and Logan drew up the plans for the sustainable site, working with Doughnut and his colleagues. Dad filled his days fishing, birdwatching, chatting with visitors and even attending the social club, which surprisingly enough, he seemed to enjoy.

'I'm going to strim the area around the fence this afternoon,' Logan said. 'While it's dry.'

'Ok.' Eleanor kissed him goodbye, her lips lingering a bit longer than was necessary on his stubbly cheek, then went back to the desk. They'd decided not to take on any extra staff this season but to hold off until the upgrades were done the following year, then hopefully business would boom and they could afford to pay a bit more, maybe entice people into the different roles. Once the new house was built, they could offer the static as seasonal staff accommodation if necessary.

She looked out the window and sighed. Everything was coming together nicely. She was sure her mum would approve of her choice – perhaps she'd even ordained it from above.

The distant drone of the strimmer carried across the site and Eleanor stood up. Outside, the balmy sun had made an appearance and the happy sounds of children laughing and shouting echoed around. Not far off, she spotted her dad showing a map to some visitors and gesticulating, probably telling them the best places to capercaillie watch.

Not entirely sure why, she flipped the sign to 'Closed' and stepped outside. She needed to stretch her legs. As she walked towards the fence where Logan was strimming, the sun caught one of the posts and something glinted like a star, reflecting beams in an almost impossible way. It was in the exact place where she'd sat waiting for him as a teenager, pretending to have caught her foot. She made her way across and put her hand on the object reflecting the light. It was a five pence piece. Frowning, she picked it up and turned it over in her hand. There was nothing unusual about it, but it felt significant somehow and it reminded her of the one she'd tossed into the waterfall, wishing for her dad to be happy. Biting her lip, she scanned around. With a gentle tweet, a little robin hopped onto the fence just a few feet away.

'Oh, hello,' she said. Another of these bold little birds. She remembered again her mum's belief that they were the messengers of people who'd died. Silly really, but maybe there was something to be said for it. 'And if there is, who sent you?' Eleanor whispered. 'Mum?' Tears welled at the words. 'I know it's crazy to think you've come from Mum, but I'd like it if it was true.'

The robin hopped closer.

'I hope this is a message that you're happy with what we've done. Just take a look at Dad. He's like a new man.'

Twittering, the robin hopped onto the ground and pecked about.

She smiled and wiped her eyes, then pulled herself onto the fence.

'Oh, it's you,' Logan said, and she jumped.

'I didn't hear you coming.'

'I was finishing that section down there. Were you talking to someone?'

'Just a robin.' She flicked her hair out of her eyes. 'It was so close.'

'They do that.' His eyes seemed to x-ray her as he moved closer. 'Why are you sitting there? Have you hurt your foot again?'

She chuckled. 'Maybe. You might have to rescue me and carry me back to the sofa.' She rested the back of her hand on her forehead in a melodramatic move.

'I very nearly had to do that for your dad just a few months ago.'

'Without that, we'd never have met, not officially.'

'So true. What's that?' He peered into the grass not far from her feet. With a frown, he knelt down and pushed some blades away. Eleanor jumped down to see.

When he looked up, he was holding another shiny five-pence piece. Someone must have dropped some coins out of their pocket, trying to climb the fence. Their eyes met and her heart quickened. She suddenly realised what this looked like. Logan perched with one knee on the ground, holding up the coin. The coin, not a ring. He wasn't...

'Eleanor, I think fate pulled me here for a reason.'

'What are you talking about?' She swallowed her uncertainty.

'Well, I don't want to waste the opportunity... So, I wonder... Will you marry me?'

She clasped her face and stared at him. Laugh or cry? Or both? She was completely flummoxed. He was right. Fate had lured her to this spot with glinting coins and chirpy robins.

'Yes,' she said. 'I'd love that more than anything.'

'Phew.' He jumped to his feet and she lifted the coin from the top of the post. She held it out and he pressed his against hers, frowning.

'I'm not sure what's going on, but I know we're doing the right thing.'

'Me too.' He leaned in and kissed her. She melted into him, savouring every precious moment. This time, she wasn't going anywhere. She was staying right here. Her heart was light and her insides sighed with contentment.

They broke apart at a loud tweeting and turned to see the robin sitting on the fence.

'I think she approves,' Eleanor said, 'though she probably wants us to take it somewhere more private.'

Logan laughed and took her hand. 'Come on then, let's oblige, and take those coins. I think we should save them.'

'Definitely.'

She looked into his eyes and smiled. For over a year, she'd been lost, but she'd finally found the way and the path ahead was full of excitement. She gripped Logan's hand. As long as they had each other's love, they could do anything, and Heather Glen was waiting for them both.

The End

More Books by Margaret Amatt

Scottish Island Escapes

A Winter Haven

A Spring Retreat

A Summer Sanctuary

An Autumn Hideaway

A Christmas Bluff

A Flight of Fancy

A Hidden Gem

A Striking Result

A Perfect Discovery

A Festive Surprise

The Glenbriar Series

New Beginnings in Glenbriar

(A free short story to introduce the series)

Stolen Kisses at the Loch View Hotel

Just Friends at Thistle Lodge

Pitching up at Heather Glen

Two's Company at the Forest Light Show

Highland Fling on the Whisky Trail

Snowdown at the Old Schoolhouse

Free Hugs & Old-Fashioned Kisses

A short story only available to Newsletter Subscribers

Acknowledgments

Thanks goes to my adorable husband for supporting my dreams and putting up with my writing talk 24/7. Also to my son, whose interest in my writing always makes me smile. It's precious to know I've passed the bug to him – he's currently writing his own fantasy novel and instruction books on how to build Lego!

Throughout the writing process, I have gleaned help from many sources and met some fabulous people. I'd like to give a special mention to Stéphanie Ronckier, my beta reader extraordinaire. Stéphanie's continued support with my writing is invaluable and I love the fact that I need someone French to correct my grammar! Stéphanie, you rock. To my lovely friend, Lyn Williamson, thank you for your continued support and encouragement with all my projects. And to my fellow authors, Evie Alexander and Lyndsey Gallagher – you girls are the best! I love it that you always have my back and are there to help when I need you.

Also, a huge thanks to my editors, Meg and Ani, at Leannan Press!

About the Author

Margaret Amatt

Margaret has told and written stories for as long as she can remember. During her formative years, she spent time on long walks inventing characters and stories to pass the time.

Writing books is Margaret's passion and when she's not doing that, she's often found eating chocolate, walking and taking photographs in the hills around Highland Perthshire. Those long walks still frequently bring inspiration!

It's Margaret's pleasure to bring you the Scottish Island Escapes series and The Glenbriar Series. These books are linked (even the two series have crossovers!) for those who enjoy inhabiting Margaret's world of stories but each can be read as a standalone if you'd rather dip in and out with individual books.

You can find more information about Margaret on her website or by signing up for her newsletter.

www.margaretamatt.com

Printed in Great Britain
by Amazon